SHADOWBLADE

Book 1 – The Beginning

By Conor Newman

CONTENTS

Mount Barendar
Twin Cities
Deep Crag
Tarrathan
Oakenvale
Oakun Wood
Dead Mire
Glanmyrdwyrr

Dedicated to the wonderful women in my life who inspired me. My wonderful wife and soul mate Gillian, my warrior priestess, my eldest daughter Freya, stronger than she knows, who inspired the main character in this book. My darling daughter Ériu, a gentle soul, my little druid, and my youngest and craziest, my little ginger Cali, may your axe always be sharp. I love you all dearly. Thank you for being my inspiration, my muses.

Of Taverns and Traders
Chapter 1

Nuthionel dragged the first body slowly from the roadside, deeper into the undergrowth. They'd have to be buried. Wolves or less pleasant scavengers would be attracted. Worried, he knew he needed to speak to Athress, Goblins shouldn't be this far south. As far as he knew what was left of them in this part of the world were all under the Northern Mountains. To find them only ten miles out of the village of Farrowfields was troubling.

Stopping to fix his hood, he adjusted his bow across his back and continued dragging the body until he found a quiet spot, well away from the road. He retrieved his arrows from the dead Goblin. It was unlikely anyone would see the bodies here, no point in scaring the villagers. He headed back to drag the other three. It took several hours to dig a hole large enough to bury them where they wouldn't be dug up by wolves.

By the time he was finished the evening sun was just a memory; a gentle half-light crept across the trade road from Deep Crag. It was too late to continue to the tavern in Farrowfields tonight. He would have to aim for tomorrow evening instead. If there was local trouble like this, best he keep his hood up and not draw attention. Some towns had lost many sons in the war and despite the peace, were none too fond of ears like his. He smiled at the irony. Here he was, killing Goblins on their borders, yet he was the undesirable in many of their minds.

<><><>

Ysabell swept the dried mud and waste from the floor, cursing the farmers and their damn fields. The place was filthy. As the only tavern in town the Dirty

Duck was always busy, and always needed cleaning. It was like mud grew from the floor.

The tavern's door swung open, the afternoon sun blinding Ysabell for a second before a dark silhouette appeared. A man in a long travelling cloak, expensive looking but well worn, stood framed in the light, his hood up. She knew who he was straight away. No one visited Farrowfields just for the sake of it. They were expecting a trader to spend the night, though he should have arrived yesterday. He had reserved a room in a note delivered some weeks previous. The note was a novelty to Ysabell, reserving a room in a tavern with three bedrooms and no visitors. She couldn't imagine it ever being booked out.

"Hello, welcome to the Dirty Duck," she said. "I'd ask you to wipe your boots, but they are probably cleaner than the floor."

The trader smiled at her sarcastic greeting. His mouth was the only part of his face she could see. "I have reserved a room," he replied in a soft, but confident voice.

"Aye, you did. In writing too. Poor Bernard had to get someone to read it and then have a lie down at the thought of someone reserving a room. For future reference, the only time you'll find no rooms available here is if it burns down. I'll give Bernard a shout and he'll show you upstairs."

Ysabell's lithe frame loped off into the back kitchen behind the bar and shouted out the back door to where Bernard was emptying the slops from the night before. The portly, red-faced tavern owner dropped what he was doing and rushed in to greet his guest. The trader was worth a fortune to Bernard. They were the only news source towns like this had. By the night, everyone in Farrowfields would be in to get a drink and find out if there was any news from the world outside the muddy little cocoon they lived in.

Ysabell stalked up the stairs leading to the bedrooms in the attic. She needed to make sure the room was clean before Bernard brought the trader up. Slim and wisp like, Ysabell walked a lot and looked it. Her dark, curly, shoulder-length hair bounced when she walked, giving the false impression of a bubbly personality. She didn't have much time for the small minds of most of the town. Her green eyes, often filled with sarcasm, didn't hide it too well.

As the evening approached, the crowds arrived as predicted, settling themselves into the hard, uncomfortable chairs around rickety, old tables. Her father among them. She sighed, he would be drunk in an hour. He had lived in a tankard since the day her mother had been killed. She had only been four and had very little memory of a time when he wasn't a sad quiet man, drowning his memories. The villagers said that day broke him, he found his wife dead. Bodies of raiders she had killed all around her, she had given her last defending their daughter and only child.

Ysabell took orders, cleaned up glasses and made sure no one was getting drunk enough to cause any trouble. She found herself lost in thought like usual, standing at the bar waiting on a drink order when one of the usual drunkards knocked two empty glasses off the end of the well-worn wooden bar, stained almost black from decades of spilled ale. She caught one glass in her right hand and the other on the instep of her left foot. She placed them back up on the bar, out of the reach of flailing arms.

Two less glasses shattered on the floor for me to clean up later, she thought, as she almost unconsciously side-stepped the groping hand of one of the regulars. Her mind was elsewhere, all night she had an odd feeling, like someone was watching her. She had a suspicion it was the trader, seated by the large stone hearth protruding from the wall opposite the bar. It was stacked with burning logs.

Traders always got the best seat as they were plied with free beer, mead, ale or whatever they drank courtesy of the townsfolk. It was all in exchange for stories and gossip from whichever city he had most recently come from. Sometimes for a small fee they would carry letters intended for sons and daughters who'd packed up and left; either by marrying someone from another town, or, like Ysabell, had enough of mud and farming and moved to one of the cities in hope of a better, or at least less dismal, life.

With a loud slam, the door burst open. Sean Mackay, a farmer from a few miles down the Deep Crag road, staggered in. All heads turned to look. It was a bit early in the evening for someone to be as drunk as he looked. He was deathly pale, and lurching more than staggering. One step in, and he toppled forward, two black shafted arrows protruding from his back, blood stains around them. As the tavern filled with screams and shouts, the town guard, Barlon Fletcher, ran to check if Sean was breathing. He was dead.

"Goblin arrows," Barlon said. "They must be raiding his farm; he only finished getting the harvest in this afternoon. I need volunteers, with weapons. Assemble out front in ten minutes. If you have armour, wear it. We'll head straight out the Deep Crag road to the farm." He glanced down at Sean's body. "I only hope Mary and the kids are ok."

Ysabell thoughts went dark. Sean wouldn't have left his wife and children alone to Goblins. They had to be dead, or else they were holed up good and tight hoping he made it to get help.

The tavern emptied fast. The trader was gone from his seat, probably up to his room. This wasn't his issue. Ysabell took her chance to duck out the back and sprint home. She crept in the back door, in case her father was home before her, Ysabell didn't want him hearing her. Best if he thought she was safe and sound back at the tavern. She dressed in a long cloak and hood, that would hide who she was, and once she was sure her father wasn't there, she quickly went to his room, to the loose floorboards he thought she didn't know about.

She pulled them up and withdrew a hunting knife, a short sword and a leather belt with loops for holding them. They had been her mothers. Ysabell could still see them dancing in the evening twilight, weaving a tale of death. She had hid behind her mother on that last day. Raiders dead all around her, until the arrow came whistling through the battle. She could still hear the sound it made as it had sank into her mother's breast. Still see her mother falling slowly. She remembered the raider reaching for her, and the arrows that peppered him, the dagger that followed and then the soft, slender, pale hands of the archer that saved her, picked her up and took her to the safety of the inn.

Swinging the belt on as she ran, Ysabell made her way back to the side of the inn and listened in as the crowd assembled. As a girl, she would never have been allowed join the group to go and fight, but she couldn't just sit and do nothing. She had to help.

"If everyone's ready, we'll move out now," Barlon Fletcher's voice rang out over the crowd assembled. "Don't get separated, don't try to be a hero, pick a buddy and keep them at your back and you at theirs once the fighting starts. Let go."

Setting a fast pace, the group started off towards MacKay's farmstead. Ysabell followed along, sticking to the shadows to try and remain unseen.

As they approached the farmstead, Ysabell saw fires in the barns, dead cattle in the fields, some already carved up by the Goblins. Worst of all, the farmhouse was on fire. If Mary and the kids were alive, they would be in there.

The townsfolk's rag-tag militia headed straight up the main driveway and engaged the goblins head on. 'Fools' Ysabell's thought. Their first concern should have been finding if anyone was still alive. She slipped off the roadway and into the wheat fields. Keeping her head down, and trying to disturb the stalks as little as possible, she crept around to the side of the farmhouse. At the edge of the field she was only two road widths from the house. Four goblins however were between her and the side door.

"Help, oh gods help us. Sean, Please!" The terrified cries from inside the house tore at Ysabell's heart. Mary was alive, still trying to keep the children safe from the raiders. She made up her mind in a heartbeat. Sprinting from the wheat, she vaulted the fence and rammed her mother's dagger into the back of the closest goblin. The other three turned to her as she let it go and drew the short sword. Her bravado faded fast when she realised she was no swordsman. She swung wildly at the raiders, praying for a miracle from Asetha.

The goblin on her right charged suddenly. She swung to meet him, realising too late it was a trick. He stopped short, grinning as one of his fellows grabbed her from behind and disarmed her. Her arms pinned behind her, she knew what would come next. The goblin in front of her sheathed his blade, chortling, his green hued skin wrinkling as his misshapen face twisted into a grin, he began to undo his belt.

A burning rage blazed in Ysabell's eyes, she swept her foot forward, burying it as hard as she could in the groin of the approaching goblin, then leaning forward suddenly she whipped her head backwards shattering the nose of the one holding her, she'd seen enough bar fights to know how to fight dirty. She saw stars as her arms broke free and she stumbled towards the house. It would have worked, if there hadn't been a third goblin, a filthy fist slammed into the side of her head and sent her reeling into the dirt.

Her vision blurry she looked up at the creature standing over her. Her head swam as she struggled to try and fight off the raiders, gasping as she strained against them. She couldn't even raise her voice to a scream, her cries for help coming out as sobs instead. The goblins laughed as they pinned her arms. She finally found her voice as she felt her leggings torn open and rough clawed hands wrenched her legs apart.

Above her the goblins scarred and deformed face was inches from her own, his stinking breath swamping her, she turned her face to side to avoid him, the raiders rough tongue slathered saliva up the side of her face. Through her blurred vision Ysabell saw feet approaching. Running. '*Oh gods, no, please, no more*'. But the feet didn't slow as they approached; she winced expecting an impact as one of the light leather travelling boots swung towards her face at speed. Missing her by inches it took the goblin raider full force in the left cheekbone. She closed her eyes in horror as she heard it crack the bones.

The raider rolled to the side screaming unintelligibly, Ysabell rolled the opposite way, struggled to her knees and crawled towards the field. She heard screams and clashing of weapons behind her, she didn't look back until she reached the cover of the wheat. Tears streaming down her face, trembling still, she stood, grasping her leggings trying to hold them together to cover herself. Four Goblins now lay dead, very dead, she had killed one. The other three weren't just killed, they were slaughtered. One was almost beheaded, another's entrails spilled from his gut to the dirt and the last was pinned with his own sword through his throat into the boards of the house behind.

A cloaked stranger stood at the back door, removing the barricade placed by the Goblins to prevent the inhabitants escaping the fire. Mary fell out the door into his arms, her two sons clutching at her apron. Ysabell recognised him now; it was the trader from the inn. It took a moment to register; it seemed such an unlikely scenario. The trader helped the trio across the wheat field where Ysabell now stood. He removed his cloak and placed it around her. Putting his bow and quiver over his shoulder again, he motioned for them to follow. Without raising her eyes, Ysabell clutched the cloak and wrapped it tight to cover herself. Her mind racked with guilt,

Ysabell fell in behind her rescuer, with Mary and the children in tow, as he led them back, quietly through the field towards the village. *'It's my fault; I should have kept out of it. None of this would have happened if I stayed in the inn.'*

She berated herself the whole way back to the village. As they reached her house, Mary stopped their escort and thanked him. It was the first time Ysabell looked at him properly. He was an elf, blonde hair, shining emerald green, almond eyes. His voice low and calm he said;

"Mention me to no one, until I am gone from town. I need no attention drawn to me. I wasn't here." He glanced at them both to ensure they understood, then hurried off into the shadows towards the inn.

Mary escorted Ysabell into her house to get her cleaned up. The kids waited in the main room, while she helped Ysabell strip, clean herself and get dressed in similar but not torn and muddied, clothing. "Ysabell, you came to save me and my boys, I'll not forget that. Whatever happened, you tried to save us." Mary smiled, tears in her eyes, "Now, you've a bad bruise on your face, lie and say you fell out back of the inn. Better no one knows what happened. Time will heal. But your father, and the other men, it ain't none of their business. Ok?"

Ysabell nodded. She couldn't speak yet. Even after cleaning up and washing herself, she felt dirty and unclean. Like he had polluted her somehow. He hadn't managed to rape her, but it felt like he had. She was bruised, sore, but none of that mattered, she felt used, sullied, unclean. Like his stench and foulness still clung to her. Mostly what clung to her was fear. Her confidence was gone, her self-belief, she was terrified. Slowly she pulled herself together. *'I can't let them find out, put on a face, and act normal, get back before I'm missed.'*

"Thank you Mary, for everything. You and the kids come back with me, Bernard will give you somewhere safe to stay as long as you need." The four of them walked around the corner up to tavern. Inside the elven trader was back at the hearth nursing a drink. Bernard immediately came over to fluster over Mary and the boys. Ysabell looked around, but there was no sign of Sean's body. Thankfully it had been taken away before Mary came. She had taken the news surprisingly well on the walk back here. The elf had told her quietly, out of earshot of her boys. Ysabell figured her composure was for the boy's sake.

"Ysabell, where have you been?" Bernard questioned, "Quickly get a room ready for Mary, they'll be staying here." He looked back at Mary and down at the two boys, "For as long as they want."

Ysabell nodded and headed upstairs to prepare a room. Her mind raced as she made up extra beds and lit candles, unable to take in everything that had happened in the last hour. She had killed a man, a goblin, but still. A mysterious elf had saved her from being raped... *Who is he? He is no trader.*

She finished up in the room and headed downstairs to get back to work. The militia had returned. Only two men were injured, not seriously and none dead. All of them were talking of the mystery archer. It seemed Ysabell's guardian angel had been busy. She listened to talk of arrows peppering the goblin's seemingly from all side, perfect shots, not an arrow missed. Her eyes wandered constantly to the trader, quietly seated by the fire. He seemed to be watching someone intently, it was her father. It made no sense, it looked like the stranger knew her father. She got the feeling there was more going on than she knew.

Trading Dishcloths for Daggers
Chapter 2

As the night dragged on, slowly the crowd began to thin as patrons wandered home, still regaling each other with tales of their bravery. The inn became emptier and quieter until only Clare the cook, Bernard, Ysabell and trader were left. Mary and the boys were up their room. He still sat in the same seat, had barely spoken to anyone all night, and oddly still had his cloak and hood on, it was only a slightly different shade to the one he had worn earlier, that now lay on the floor of Ysabell's room at home. His face hidden in its shadows. He raised his head to catch her eye and beckoned her over.

Ysabell looked around, Bernard was heading into the Kitchen to start washing up the tankards, Clare was finishing her clean-up of the stove. They were alone in the tavern. Nervous, but comforted by the fact that he had saved her, and Mary, she approached and sat down opposite him by the fire side.

"You are no trader, who are you really?" Ysabell asked bluntly, staring into the mysterious almond eyes.

"You are small, petite, you are quick, I watched you catch those glasses earlier, very good reflexes and you move well." He countered. "You've been dodging the wandering hands of many drunken men in here tonight. But you walked into a situation where you were outnumbered, and outmatched, carrying weapons you didn't know how to use." His face darkened, "Do you feel safe here anymore? Feel confident to walk the streets of your village alone?"

His hand disappeared into his cloak and withdrew a dagger. Ysabell recognised it at once, it was her mother's dagger, she had forgotten it, left embedded in the raider back at Mackay's farm. He handed it to her. As he rose from his seat, he looked at her again, intently. "What will you do if attacked again?"

"I'll gut anyone who touches me ever again!" Ysabell rising to her feet as she spoke, clutching the dagger, her anger boiling over at what she perceived as condescension from the strange elf. Her anger replaced by confusion as the elf's mouth seemed to smile slightly as he looked at her.

"Not if you don't know how to." He turned and walked away, up the stairs to his room. Leaving her alone with her anger and uncertainty.

She finished clearing off the last of the tables and swept the floor. Seething at how he had spoken to her, especially at the doubts in her mind that told her he was right. Shouting her farewell into Bernard and Clare, Ysabell headed out the door to make her way home. Her dagger hidden in the folds of her cloak, but its handle gripped tightly in her hand all the same. '*Just in case*'.

As Ysabell approached the small house she shared with her father, something seemed off. It was fear that someone was watching her. '*It's just silliness, I have a knife. Relax*' She told herself. Her hand slipped out from her cloak to make the dagger visible, if anyone was watching they would see she was armed. A slight movement across the road to her right made her jump, she turned to face the threat holding her dagger out in front of her like a talisman of protection. Then with a meow and disdainful look the cat turned its back and stalked off into the night. Relaxing, her hands falling down to her sides, Ysabell shook her head at how jumpy she was, '*Will this fear ever just go? How long will I be like this?*'

As she turned back to her house something grabbed her, her left arm was twisted up behind her back, the right hand still holding dagger was forced up to her own throat. The blade was cold, cold as the grave. Ysabell froze, her mind blank, shock, terror, anger, everything just melded together. A sibilant voice came from next to her ear;

"Scream and you will never make another sound. Walk slowly to that quiet alley over there. Any sudden movements and..."

She started to shake, the elf was right. A knife was utterly useless if you didn't know how to fight. She was helpless again. Only hours later. '*How could this happen, how? What did I do?*' Her attacker stumbled, without any conscious thought she took her chance, she threw herself to the ground, her attacker falling over her, then as she scrambled to her feet she plunged the dagger for his back. But he was already gone. Rolled to his feet and standing before her, drawing his own dagger. Ysabell stood up, steadied herself and tried to think what to do, if she screamed people would come but no doubt he'd kill her before fleeing. She should have listened to the damn elf. She had no idea what to do with a knife in a fight. The man before her was dressed in mismatched armour like the Goblin raiders, but he was too tall for a goblin. His face was covered, the leather skull cap he wore bore a mesh cloth draped over to cover his face.

He lunged at her suddenly, Ysabell reacted without time to think, she swung wildly with her knife, miraculously blocking his to the side, her left hand swung as hard as she could to try and punch him. As her hand came close he moved like lightning, all clumsiness he had shown in his stumbling before gone. He leaned back out of range, his dagger dropped, his right hand swept up and caught her shoulder continuing her punch, causing her to spin and stumble. As she did, a nimble foot kicked the blade from her hand. She hit the ground hard, knocking the wind from her. Looking up, she him pick up both daggers and approach. She was no match for him. He leaned over and spoke.

"Never carry a weapon you don't know how to use. Your mother knew how to use this blade. You need to learn. She didn't die defending you to see you throw your life away." The voice was angry. He offered a hand and pulled her to her feet. His hands were soft, slender and pale. Then he handed her the dagger. The elf slipped the cap from his head and spoke again. "I leave here at first light, you can come and learn how to use that weapon or stay and live in fear. Your choice. If you are outside your house at dawn I will take that as a yes. Else I leave alone." He strode off without another word, back into the darkness towards the inn. Ysabell stood shaking in the street. Half raging at his assault, the other half wondering what would she do? She gazed at the dagger in her hand. It felt right there. Her mother's blade. *I can't live with this fear for the rest of my life, and I always wanted to leave. But with a strange elf? A warrior of some kind, I know nothing about him...'* Another voice in her head answered unbidden. *'Except that he saved your life, Mary MacKay's, and her sons. Whatever else he is, he is a good man...And he knew my mother. His hands. Asetha... It's him. Those hands...He saved me and took me to the inn that day.'*

The sun rose behind a screen of mist and fog the next morning. Ysabell awoke early, with nervous butterflies in her stomach. Last night seemed so long ago now. The cold light of dawn was beginning to glow in her window.

Ysabell had lain awake all night, getting more and more anxious as the dawn approached. Without consciously having decided on anything, she rose and started packing a bag. She figured she'd need to travel light, so packed a few clothes (A few was all she owned) and some food, a spare pair of sandals and a second heavier cloak. Once packed she ate a small breakfast of bread and cheese, and picked up a quill and paper. Her father could read a little, reading and writing was seen as a soft option in the village. Suited to women, men had more important things to learn about, like lifting bales of hay and drinking ale. She wrote in large letters and small words, so her father would understand. Promised to send a letter back as soon as she reached the city. She left the letter on the table pinned by a loaf of bread, so a breeze wouldn't blow it away.

Ysabell picked up her small bag of belongings. Leaving her father was the hardest thing. They were all each other had. She hoped he would be alright, once she felt she had some control of her life again, she would return. She would make sure he was looked after into his old age. She had to go. This elf knew her mother or knew of her. He had saved her as a child and now again. She had to know more.

She took one last look around the house. The house she'd lived all her life in, and then walked out the door, into the pre-dawn light, filtering through the morning mist. She closed the door gently behind her and stood, alone in the grey swirling fog. Refusing to even think about her decision, there'd be time for that later. She wanted to leave this life for years, she'd let no fear of failure, or second guessing herself ruin her chance. It seemed she had made up her mind without even realising it.

A shadow detached itself from the wall of her cottage, Ysabell turned, startled, to see the trader standing there. What had been a shadow on the side of the building was now the slender elf. Dressed in a long grey travelling cloak, drawn close around him, and below, grey wrapped boots. His steps were silent as he approached and nodded to her then taking the reins of his horse, he turned away, led the horse and cart towards the road out of town. Ysabell fell in beside him, not a word between them. Their silhouettes faded slowly from view into the morning mist.

Travelling light on the road less travelled

Chapter 3

After about an hour walking in silence, Nuthionel came to a stop and turned to Ysabell.

"We can ride the cart for a while. It's slow going with Seren pulling the cart and us, but we need to keep moving so won't be stopping to rest until he needs to." Seren was a beautiful, tall, dusk-coloured stallion. His coat shimmered, almost like silk as the muscles rippled beneath.

Nuthionel didn't say it, but it was obvious to her that Seren was not a cart horse. That must have been why he had a dirty old blanket thrown over him while in the village. Had he ridden in to any small village on such a stallion he would immediately be spotted for something other than a merchant.

The road was quiet. Nuthionel had taken them off the main way to Carraigbán and they were on a smaller trail now. It didn't look well worn, which left Ysabell a little concerned. There were no Guard patrols on the smaller roads. Everyone knew you avoided them if possible. Perhaps he was trying to avoid the Guards and was more than an adventurer... or worse. She decided to let it go for the moment. They spoke little, though one question burned at her. She didn't want to push him until she was sure he would answer. She wanted to know about her mother, about what had happened that day, and how he was involved.

When they did talk, over the camp fires at night, she'd ask Nuthionel of the world. The Elven cites, the Dwarven races who lived beneath the Western mountains. The swift and light footed halfling race that lived in the forested states far beyond the borders of even the elves. He told her of far off places, races, creatures that lived in the deep and darkened places of the world. Of Mages that could summon creatures at their command, how all the worlds were linked through the planes. Stories claim that some of the most powerful Mages had once opened these portals and that's how Man, Elf and Dwarf races came to be in this world in far distant past.

She loved the tales, the stories of adventurers who made legends of themselves, of great treasures found and lost. Of wars fought, it all seemed so exciting and different, so different from all she'd known. But he avoided any discussion of where he came from, what he did for a living, or where they were going. He never mentioned her mother again. When she raised the subject he looked at her in silence for a few minutes before answering.

"I knew of her. Your father too." He looked away into the distance. "That's a conversation for another time." His voice made it clear she shouldn't push the issue. Yet..

A little after noon, as the road took them through a small copse of conifer trees reaching out of the forest like a finger, a small swarthy man stepped out on the road in front of them. Dressed in old cloth, but with not so old looking leather armour strapped on across one shoulder and down the left side of his chest. His boots were home made by the look, animal skins knotted together, he carried a heavy looking short sword by his side and a bow in his hand. Ysabell felt a tightness in her stomach as she realised he was a bandit. They would be robbed or killed or both.

As they approached the bandit drew the bow and shouted at them to surrender their cart. Beside her, Nuthionel face tightened. He glanced sideways at Ysabell, cursed softly and pulled the cart to a halt. Nodding to Ysabell to follow he slowly dismounted, taking a small bag from under his seat.

"You can leave the bag," The Bandit called. "Then be on your way if you want to live." Nuthionel reached back into the cart and drew his bow and daggers from it.

"I leave with my bag of food and my weapons," Nuthionel's voice was calm, but cold. "Or we can see who's aim is better. Walking from here without weapons or food is as good as a death sentence, I may as well make my stand here and take as many of you as I can with me."

The bandit weighed his options, keeping his bow aimed at the companions. Nodding eventually, he agreed. Ysabell and Nuthionel, stepped away from the cart and walked towards the Bandit, he stepped clear to one side as they passed. Behind them they could hear more bandits running from the trees to take the cart. Glancing at the elf's angry countenance, Ysabell wondered why he had choose to walk away rather than fight. But her companion never spoke a word, he looked straight ahead without so much as a backward glance as they walked clear of the trees back out onto the open road.

They walked for more than thirty minutes before he called a halt and stepped off the road. Asking Ysabell to gather some brush and wood for a fire, Nuthionel began to rumMage through the small food bag he had taken. Ysabell returned with a small bundle of twigs, dry moss and leaves and a few larger branches. To her surprise there was no food in Nuthionel's bag. It contained clothes and daggers. The light was fading fast; soft shadows began to deepen and stretch across the landscape as the day sank into night.

"What are we going to do?" She asked as he began to slip off his travel clothes and change into a sleek leather armour. It was dark grey and non-descript, the buckles dulled. But it was clearly kept in good condition, the leather was soft and supple, and silent as it stretched on over him.

"We are going to find their camp and retrieve our belongings. You may stay here or come with me, the choice is yours. But if you come you must do everything I say without question. If they catch us, they will kill us... Eventually." His voice was still soft and calm, but she could feel the strain, he was struggling to keep his temper.

Ysabell didn't need to think the offer over. If she stayed she would be on her own on the side of a quiet, dark backroad. Her presence advertised to the world by her campfire which would be seen for miles. She was going with him. Rummaging again in his bag, he produced a dark grey travel cloak, with hood.

"Put this on, keep it covering you." He instructed her. "Grey is harder to see in the dark than black. Don't be seen and don't be heard." With that, he placed his bow across his back with his quiver, strapped his daggers on across his chest. Ysabell had her dagger by her side, concealed now by the cloak. They set off quietly, off the road, keeping to the shadows of the undergrowth. Far in the distance a tiny light flickered and danced between the trees.

As they reached the trees, Nuthionel paused, waving Ysabell down behind him.

"No speaking or noise from now on. They may have sentries anywhere. Follow behind me, stay as low and quiet as you can. Stick close." Nuthionel's face was tense, his elvish features appearing sharp in the leaf filtered moon light.

The flickering light dancing between the trees in the distance gave an eerie, eldritch feeling to the forest. Shafts of silver moonlight piercing the canopy lit up clearings and breaks in the tree cover, bathing them in a haunting silver glow. Two shadows crept through the undergrowth of ferns quietly, making their way towards the bandit's camp. Nuthionel leading them to avoid all light,

Once they were close, they scanned the bandit camp, it was in a ruined courtyard of some kind. Small ruined walls were all that remained of the buildings, large flagstones, now crooked and cracked lay across the ground. Amongst the fallen walls and mounds of moss and lichen covered rubble, tents and camp fires were scattered here and there. Nuthionel frowned. This was far bigger than he had expected. There must be at least thirty of them if not more. His eyes with perfect night vision scanned the tree lines around the camp, seeking those glowing red shapes that would indicate heat, body heat of the sentries. He could find none. *'They are confident in their safety here. That will help.'*

"Listen carefully." He spoke to her in a whisper, barely audible. "You will stay here, come no closer, if anyone approaches, move further back into the forest, do not be seen. Hopefully I won't be long."

Once she had nodded her understanding and he saw the agreement in her face, he crept away to the right. Circling the camp towards the rear of the largest camp there. *'If they have a leader, he will be there.'* Once he had reached the rear of the tent, he slipped through the ruins and came to stop at the canvass listening. Someone was in there, the breathing deep and rhythmical, a man, a large man by the sound of his breath, fast asleep.

He dropped down and raising the tent canvass and he quietly slid underneath and in to the tent. On one wall was a bed, a large man passed out asleep on it, an empty flagon of mead lay on the ground beside him. The flagon was from Nuthionel's cart. His eyes scanned the tent, a central pole to hold it, a table sat against it, gems, gold artefacts etc sat upon it with an eyeglass. He must have been appraising valuables. On the opposite side were several chests. They lay open. Some contained clothes, silks, others books and trade goods. Nothing of interest to Nuthionel. He took his bow from his back and drew an arrow, then picked up a gold goblet from the table he lobbed it across to hit the sleeping bandit.

He woke instantly, he turned his head and saw Nuthionel, bow drawn, standing in the middle of his tent. The bandit's leader sat up slowly and quietly. Nuthionel could see his eyes darting around to look for an escape or weapon.

"So," The bandit spoke gruffly but quietly. "I am to be robbed? Or killed? I knew I shouldn't have left you your weapons today."

"But you did." Nuthionel's voice was low and cold. "Whether you live or die depends on you. I want my cart, my horse and my belongings. I will trade them for your life." He drew the bow back farther, ready to fire as the bandit stood.

"But I also have something to bargain" The man responded, an ugly threatening smile breaking out on his face. He nodded towards the tent flap. Nuthionel glanced over his shoulder. Ysabell stood in the doorway, her face bloody, one eye swollen and a sword against her throat.

'Shit' Nuthionel looked at Ysabell, she looked shaken and scared, but as their eyes met he could see she wasn't broken, she was furious. *'Good, she'll need that anger'*

Looking beaten and dejected, Nuthionel released the tension on his bow string and dropped the bow and the arrow to the floor and slowly reached to his daggers.

"Ha," Roared the bandits leader, "No one gets the best of me elf." He laughed loudly at them, stopping in a gasp as Nuthionel's hands instead of dropping his daggers flipped them, he hurled one from right hand towards Ysabell first. It flew in a blur and with a sickening sound embedded itself in the right eye socket of the Guard holding Ysabell. Turning on his heel Nuthionel loosed the second.

Diving towards his sword the bandit's leader was hit in the side of the throat, his jugular sliced open. He collapsed to the ground gurgling, trying to hold in his blood with hands. It spurted from the wound and pooled around him on the floor.

The Guard had fallen backwards out of the tent when hit, a shout went up outside. They had no time. *'And no chance. What the hell have I gotten her into?'*

Nuthionel ran to retrieve his daggers, he grabbed the leader's sword as he did, turned back and saw Ysabell, pale, and wincing at the sound as she drew the other dagger from the Guards eye socket. Past her out of the tent, forms were gathering, fast approaching.

"Here, take this too" He handed his second dagger to Ysabell. "Don't try to fight, defend as you must, get to Seren and try to get the hell out of here, I'll follow." Not waiting for an argument, he dashed straight out of the tent, sword already in motion, the first bandit collapsed as the sword slashed across his waist, Nuthionel spun on his heel following through, the sword rising as it did. It swung down from above at the second bandit easily slicing through the leather armour on his shoulder, carving down through the collarbone. The elf kicked the bandit's body off his sword.

Ysabell was to his right, she was unskilled but vicious. He watched her drop to her knees as a bandit ran at her, then drive Nuthionel's dagger into the bandit's groin. The force of the bandit's charge knocked her over, a second bandit reached her and kicked hard into her ribs, she screamed in pain. *'No way her ribs aren't broken'.*

In front of Nuthionel the bandits knew if they charged more would die, instead they had stopped, and several had stepped forward with small clay globes in their hands, a flickering flame on top of them. *'Alchemical bombs, shit!'* He turned and sprinted to Ysabell, a shoulder charge sent her attacker flying, stumbling, Nuthionel reached down hauled Ysabell to her feet and shouted at her; "RUN!" They fled to the side of the tent, but too late, the explosives landed near them, a deafening roar and blast of heat struck them from behind throwing them forward.

Bracing himself for the fall, Nuthionel's expression turned to horror as the ground below them fell away. The explosives had collapsed part of the courtyard, exposing a dark yawning chasm. The pair fell straight into it. Rocks and broken flagstones around them. They hit hard on the collapsing floor, and tumbled and slid down amongst the rubble, eventually coming to rest on the cavern floor. Bruised broken and battered. Silence descended as the last rocks rolled to the ground.

Tempering the steel
Chapter 4

Pain. Everywhere. Ysabell struggled to move, it felt like there was a knife in her side, her left-hand side along her ribs was throbbing with pain. Breathing hurt, moving hurt so much. She tried to breathe slower to ease the pain. Groans and movements to her right told her Nuthionel was alive and moving. She twisted her head around to see him, he was up on his knees trying to rise.

"Ysabell?" His sharp whisper carried across the silence, the sound almost eerie in the dust and stillness after the collapse. "Can you move?"

'What happens if I tell him no?' She wondered as she tried again to push herself up, the pain was excruciating. She tensed up and forced herself to her knees, groaning in pain. She could see Nuthionel to her right, he was on his feet now, rummaging in the wreckage of the Bandits' leader's tent and its contents that had collapsed down into this cavern with them. He had several items in his hands already when shouts from above drew both their attention.

At the edge of the opening far above them stood several of the bandits, the glowing spheres in their hands were unmistakable. They planned to finish the job with more bombs. Ysabell froze. *'This is it, I am going to die in a pit in the ground.'*

Even as the thought passed through her mind a strong hand gripped her right arm and yanked her to her feet. She screamed in pain. Her right arm was unceremoniously draped across the elf's shoulders, and he ran, literally dragging her with him. The sound of clay shattering rung in her ears barely seconds before a blast of heat hit them from behind and threw them forward. As much as it hurt, Ysabell was thankful for Nuthionel's manhandling of her, he kept his feet and continued forward, her legs trying to keep up. They clambered through a gap in the mounds of collapsed rubble and found themselves inside a building, cut stone lined the walls and floors. '*Passage back there must've looked like this before the collapse.*' She thought as her eyes scanned the darkness ahead.

"Ok, we can rest a moment." The elf's words were like wine to Ysabell. She felt close to passing out from the pain. "Sounds like more stone is collapsing back there, doubt they'll try and climb down after us.

"I have to look at your injuries Ysabell" He helped her slowly to the ground, dropping the items he was carrying in his other arm. He picked up some leather armour and placed it under her head. She nodded her consent and he began to undo her tunic, slowly peeling it back from her left side. She could only imagine how bad it looked. She glanced down and groaned at the sight of the blackened and purple colours of her side. Nuthionel's face was creased with concern.

"It's not good" His voice was worried. "You have several broken ribs Ysabell. This is going to take a few weeks to heal unless we can find a healer somewhere. Even then." He paused and shrugged, "It's going to be sore for a while and limit your range of movement.".

Exhausted, Ysabell drifted off as Nuthionel applied a numbing ointment to her side and covered her again. Even through the fog coming over her consciousness she could hear him muttering. The Elf was clearly very worried. Then she heard no more.

<></><>

Several hours later, Ysabell awoke in the darkness. Nuthionel was sitting cross legged at a small fire a few feet away. Carefully running an oil stone along his blades. The crackling of wood the only sound. He looked up hearing her stir.

"How are you feeling?" His voice mirrored the concern in his face. "You took quite a beating."

"Not too bad," She lied. "Pain's easing off. I can move on when we are ready."

The elf nodded, almost to himself. '*Can't let him think I'm too soft for this.*' She thought. He rose, sheathed his blades and approached offering a hand to get her on her feet. Ysabell grasped it gratefully. Grunting as she slowly came to her feet. Her ribs throbbed, every time she breathed in the pain hit again. She looked around to distract herself from it.

They were standing in a small antechamber; the only path was a turn to their right leading off into the darkness. The stone had cracks and chips in it, it was rough looking, it had been centuries at least since it was last cared for.

Nuthionel handed her the armour he had collected from the fallen chests earlier. Soft oiled leather, dark brown, a jerkin, leggings and moccasins. She fumbled trying to strip down, her injuries reduced her range of movement. Nuthionel helped her without a word. Before long she had the leather leggings on, they were slightly too long, and a little too loose. But they'd do. The Jerkin was uncomfortable and chaffed, but it was armour. Lastly, he helped her into a harness, like his own, sheathed in it, under each arm, were two long bladed daggers. Split to come to a twin point.

The elf gave her a silent nod to signal they were ready. He crouched down and kept close to the wall as he began to creep down the corridor. From what Ysabell could make out there were two exits from the corridor. Both on the right-hand side, one after the other, the second right at the end of the corridor. They both looked pitch black. It occurred to Ysabell that without the Elvish ability to see at night, she was at a serious disadvantage. Seeming to read her mind, Nuthionel drew what looked like a miniature lantern from his pack of loot he collected from the rubble earlier and lit it with a few clicks of his flint. It was just enough to illuminate the path without creating a bright light that could be seen by curious eyes.

He reached forward and clasped a metal ring at the back of the lantern to one of the buckles on Ysabell armour. It hung just below her breast, where it could shine light ahead of her without her having to hold it. Without another word, Nuthionel turned and crept on down the corridor. He took the first right turn. Ysabell, feeling a little more confident with her light, followed him as quietly as she could. She was painfully aware that she could hear no sound from his soft footfall, but despite the oiled leather she wore and her soft soled shoes, she could still hear each footstep she took. She found it frustrating and somehow unnerving in this silence, the air thick and heavy with age, her feet making perhaps the only sound heard there in centuries.

This new corridor immediately turned right again, and left and right and left again, and on it continued. They were in a maze, but Ysabell trusted Nuthionel's lead. He seemed completely unfazed and confidence oozed from his every pore.

She counted the turns they took, hoping if they did get separated she could find her way back. After ten turns, (six right, four left, she was careful to note) they turned left into a large room. The walls within looked somehow different. Too hard to make out at this distance, but there were markings or grooves, maybe a pattern cut into them.

They stuck close to the wall on the right, and followed it till they reached the side of the room, where they continued to follow the wall ahead. Ysabell realised markings she thought she could see were alcoves cut into the wall for bodies and sealed over with stone slabs. Each one had strange writing engraved on it; she had no idea what language it was. She had no time to examine them either, Nuthionel reached over and dropped the blackout flap over her lantern, plunging them into darkness.

Ahead, on the right, a doorway was visible. Ysabell wondered how she could see it, then realised this was why he darkened the lantern. There was a light coming through the opening, faint, but growing stronger. Guttural screeching sounds echoed as the light approached. Her palms grew sweaty

Two short, humanoid forms appeared in the doorway. *Goblins!* Ysabell realised.

Ysabell didn't know much about them beyond her first encounter back at Farrowfields, but she knew they tended to stay in large hordes numbering into the hundreds. These two would not be alone and if they got away, Ysabell and Nuthionel would almost certainly be overrun.

She barely breathed, praying that they'd go unseen. The goblins seemed oblivious to them as they crouched in the shadows by the wall. The light from the Goblins torch was harsh and bright, Ysabell was smart enough not to look directly at it, as it would blind her. Down here that would put her at a major disadvantage. Goblins could see in the dark, not as well as Elves, but certainly a lot better than humans. Once the Goblins were a little past them, away from the door, Nuthionel began to move. Not through the door as Ysabell hoped, however. Instead, he moved after the goblins, his daggers sliding silently from their sheaths.

He crept up behind the goblins and glanced back at Ysabell to see if she was following. She wasn't. She remained crouched in the shadows at the wall. Killing someone in a fight was one thing, but to creep up and murder someone from behind, even a Goblin, was shocking to Ysabell, it seemed wrong.

Nuthionel sprang forward, his right hand plunging its dagger through the neck of the first Goblin. The second didn't last much longer. It took less than two seconds, but both Goblins lay on the floor, blood pooling from their throats. The light fading from their eyes. Ysabell was shocked at how unaffected Nuthionel seemed, He wiped his blades, oblivious to the twitch of the creatures dying at his feet. He seemed so brutal and callous in that moment.

He returned to Ysabell like nothing had happened and nodded his head towards the next door. He approached it, paused looking through it, his face setting in an expression of resignation, then he let out a roar that shook the air. It tore through the silence, shattering the atmosphere and letting everything in these damned Catacombs know he was here.

Ysabell froze. *What the Hell is he doing?* Then she heard it, the feet and shouting. Goblins, lots of them, coming from the door beside her, no lights though, they had extinguished their torches to give them advantage over their prey. They had no way of knowing he was an elf with perfect sight in any darkness. Nuthionel, sure that he had their undivided attention bolted away, through another door.

She remained perfectly still, not even breathing as Goblins poured through the doorway right next to her. Their bare feet and ragged, looted boots pounded on the flagstones as they sprinted after Nuthionel. Ysabell reasoned he was trying to lead them away from her so she could escape. Logically that's what she should do, it's what he wanted. But there was no bloody way she was leaving him there to fight off the fifteen or twenty Goblins who'd poured through that door.

Her sympathy for the two lying dead with slit throats burnt away in a wave of anger. Ysabell rose and hurried after them. The fear of losing her guide, without him she was stuck in here. But not just that, she had grown close to him, he cared what happened to her. He took risks to protect her. Like a father should, and now there was the chance of losing that just like she'd lost a mother and, through drink and sorrow, a father.

Her fear fed a deep pool of seething anger in her she never knew existed before. Keeping a safe distance back to remain unseen and unheard, she headed after Nuthionel. Through the shroud of darkness, she could hear the clash of weapons and screams as Nuthionel fought the Goblins. It didn't sound like only fifteen or twenty of them; he must have run straight into another group. With no time to think, Ysabell just reacted. She screamed to Nuthionel as she ran towards them, "Shield your eyes!" then she reached down and removed both flaps of cloth from her lantern. The light dazzled the goblins who had turned to face this new threat.

She didn't hesitate and cost herself the advantage. She spun to her left, into the midst of the blinded Goblins, daggers cleaving from their sheaths in two arcs on either side of her. Blood sprayed through the air as the first two Goblins fell. She followed through with her spin, turning her blades so both sliced with her movement. As she came to face her next opponent, both daggers slashed down, one across his face, the second slicing the artery at the side of his neck.

A large Goblin swung a heavy, two-handed mace at her. Instinct kicked in and she dropped to her knees, stabbing the femoral artery in his groin. The mace slammed harmlessly to the floor inches away from her and she continued towards Nuthionel.

He was a few feet away, blood dripping from a slash on his face and a deep jagged cut on his left collar bone, right through his leather armour. It didn't slow him.. He moved with his blades like a dancer, barely a shadow as he dodged and weaved and spun. Goblins cowered from him. Some dead, others wounded, all realising they had met a foe far superior. Several of those that fell back unexpectedly found themselves in reach of Ysabell's blades.

A blur of movement to Ysabell's left caught her off guard, she couldn't move fast enough. She barely had time to register the flash of steel, her eyes winced expecting the blow that never came. Spinning to look she saw a large, swarthy

Goblin lying dead on the ground, a cleaver near his hand and the hilt of one of Nuthionel's blades jutting from his temple.

A shout of dismay rang out from the Goblins and, almost as one, they turned tail and fled. Nuthionel, checked his cuts quickly and turned to Ysabell.

"Are you injured?" he asked. "Some of their blades are dipped in poison. Even a small cut can be lethal."

Ysabell looked up, she had been briefly lost in thought, staring at the bloodied knives in her hands and the blood on her armour. She checked her body.

A small slice across her chest, above the left breast, and a slightly deeper one on her hip, and lots of bruises seemed to be her only injuries. She noticed none of them during the fight and was surprised to see them. Her ribs were in agony, but she wasn't going to raise that. She figured it would take a few days for that pain to subside.

"They look clean," he said. "We need to move now. They got a fright, but they'll be back. By the way, brilliant use of the lantern. You even took me by surprise with that." He flashed her a smile. It wasn't often she'd been praised for anything.

Though her gut was churning and she felt anything but utter terror at what had just happened, what she had just done, Ysabell put on a brave face, returned a grin and said, "Let's move."

Mary had a little lamb, who's fleece was drenched in blood

Chapter 5

The Goblins had fled by the arch to the east, but they came in from the south so that was probably the best way back to the path out of the catacombs. Ysabell and Nuthionel ran back into the room where the first two goblins he killed lay dead. It was too dark to see the way out, but they ran in the right direction.

Ysabell placed a lighter mesh over her lantern so it only provided a dull faint light for her to see by. As they got closer, she noticed the arched door ahead of them was being lit from lights in the corridor beyond. "Damn it!" swore Ysabell in a soft whisper. They stopped, crouching down as she covered her lantern completely.

Glancing around as she did so, she saw another exit to their left. With any luck it would lead towards an exit. She tapped Nuthionel's shoulder and pointed to the door in the distance, he nodded immediately, rose and ran as quietly as possible towards it. Ysabell followed close behind him.

The room they entered was yet another large, empty, stone chamber, the walls lined with crypts of the long dead and forgotten. Bundles of something were piled in the corners, but they had no time to investigate. The Goblins were only one room behind. Glancing behind her, she could see the flickering light of torches in the room behind. The goblins were close.

Nuthionel waved at Ysabell to slow down and they crept up the length of the room staying close to the wall. As they reached the next doorway, they were met with the rank and overpowering odour of rotting meat. Nuthionel glanced through the arch. It opened into a large space, lit with torches. Small animals shuffled around in a pen against the far wall, a pile of scrapped skins drying near them. It was a slaughter house.

The gentle lowing of lambs and sheep stood in stark contrast to their surroundings. No goblins were visible. They took a moment to look around. Ysabell thought to herself, *Goblins don't breed livestock, certainly not underground. What would they eat?*

Then it hit her.

The floors of the catacombs had no animal droppings on them. A herd of sheep would have left a considerable mess being marched in here. The animals looked healthy, like they were only recently brought down. That meant there must be another way out nearby. *One that doesn't require fighting through a bandit camp,* thought Ysabell with satisfaction.

Nuthionel pointed to a second exit, further along the western side of the room, about 15 feet up from where they had entered. He smiled at Ysabell, clearly thinking the same as her.

They exited into a small ante-chamber, with stairs at the far end; stairs that only went down. They were wrong, the animals didn't come this way. The noise of their pursuers grew louder There was no time to turn around and try find another way. They were penned in with two choices. Take a stand in this ante chamber where the narrow walls would prevent more than a few goblins from reaching them at a time or continue the chase and flee down below toward who knows what.

Nuthionel looked at Ysabell, concern in his eyes. Then swiftly turned away and headed down the stairs with Ysabell in tow.

They reached the bottom of the cracked and crumbling stairs, where the darkness was almost physical it felt so heavy. But the air wasn't as dead or stagnant as Ysabell expected, she could tell from the expression on Nuthionel's face he was thinking the same. They were in a small narrow corridor that headed off to their left. The walls were of older stone here, the flagstones uneven in shape and size. The sounds of pursuit grew louder and almost gleeful, yet no Goblins followed them down the stairs. Nuthionel and Ysabell exchanged a concerned look. If the Goblins wanted them down the stairs, that wasn't good.

They started along the narrow passage in front of them. Ysabell's lantern providing enough light for her to see by. Ahead were a group of small mounds in the middle of the corridor, lots of them, scattered randomly. At a signal from Nuthionel, Ysabell darkened her light and they crept silently toward the piles. Without the lantern, Ysabell had to trust Nuthionel completely. The oppressive darkness essentially had her blind. She heard an exasperated sigh from Nuthionel.

"Uncover the lantern," he whispered.

Ysabell lifted the veil from her lantern and allowed light seep back into her world. In the dimly lit passage ahead of her lay the scattered bodies of dead Goblins.

Dried blood stains painted the walls and floor, but all their weapons remained in their sheaths. *What could have killed them so quickly that not one of then managed to draw their blade?* No answer came.

Nuthionel's gaze swept over the scene, but he had not moved any closer to the bodies. Ysabell decided to see if there were any marks that could identify their killer and stepped forward. Like lightning Nuthionel's arm caught her and swept her back.

"Traps," he said. "This is why the goblins did not follow us down here. They believe they need only to guard the stairs and our choices will be death by traps or return to face them. They are wrong."

Ysabell scanned the passage in front of them. Nuthionel smiled and shook his head.

"Don't look for signs of traps," he explained. "The whole point of traps is that they are hard to see. Look for stonework where the blemishes, cracks, placement of stones, is too perfect. If the traps were built well enough to still work, the places they are hidden will likely be in better shape than everything else down here. "

Nuthionel grasped the closest Goblin by the ankle and dragged him towards them. They heard a loud creak. Nuthionel leapt at Ysabell and the two of them tumbled back away from the bodies. Both their heads spun to look at what was making the noise.

Ysabell could see nothing with her lantern extinguished by the fall, but Nuthionel could see clearly. .

Ysabell sat up, took off her back pack and found a flint. She relit the lantern and hung it back on her breast.

"What did you see?" She asked. Nuthionel told her swiftly.

"A large metal arm slowly wound back up into the ceiling, it had smaller attached arms horizontal to it. They were wide enough to nearly touch both sides of the passage. A range of sharp, pointed and hollow spikes protruded from each appendage." He stared back down at the bodies. "I'd guess there's a pressure plate trigger." He smiled again; "These traps are easy to get by if you know they are there, without disarming them. If we disarm it, the Goblins could follow us from behind. If we leave it intact and working, anyone following will have a very short journey."

He stood up and beckoned Ysabell to follow him, when he was close to the trap; he reached down and dragged the dead Goblin again towards him. Nothing happened this time. Once the goblin was clear of where he believed the trap to be. He picked it up and threw it forward towards the other bodies on the floor. The metal spiked arm shot down from the ceiling with frightening speed. Ysabell jumped back in spite of herself, though it came nowhere near them. Once it started to retract,

Nuthionel quickly stepped forward towards it and, with Ysabell at his heels, moved quickly past it. She felt several of the stones beneath her shift slightly as they walked on but didn't look back.

They cleared the dead bodies quickly and followed the passage until they reached a split. The path to their left continued straight for another fifteen feet then turned right. There wasn't a breeze exactly, but it had a fresher feel to it than the passage straight ahead. Ysabell hoped it meant a nearby exit. She'd endured enough of this labyrinth.

They followed the cleaner air and turned right at the end of the passage into a long corridor. Ysabell's light wasn't bright enough to see the end of it. Nuthionel stood in front of her for a moment to let his eyes see without the interference of the lantern.

"About seventy feet long, a passage heading to the right halfway down, it turns right again at the end." He turned to her. "We must be near a way outside; the air is lighter and getting cleaner with every step."

They crept on, the darkness between them was almost palpable, Nuthionel was as apprehensive as her. Neither of them wanted to take a risk of being found, by anything, now that they seemed so close to the end. They reached the mid-point where a passage wound off to the right. It was hard to tell which one the fresh air was coming from, but it was definitely fresh air now. Ysabell could smell the spring night air, grass and a faint coconut scent from wild gorse.

She lifted the mesh off her lantern and held it to the passage to the right. The flame didn't waver. She turned and held the open side to the passage ahead. The tiny flame flickered and leaned towards her. She replaced the mesh and smiled to herself. Nuthionel looked pleased as well.

They continued straight ahead, no longer hiding. They were close. Sounds of the outside world greeted their ears.

They reached the end of the passage, turned right, and nearly crashed headlong into something large and bulky. Ysabell quickly became aware it was something alive. They stepped back, looking on in horror as the creature turned its huge bulk around to face them. A Ciaróg Fuil, or Blood Beetle, darted forward with an agility and speed that belied it massive size. A shiny hard carapace shell protecting its curved back, which hung down below its body to shield the upper sections of its legs as well. It was a deep, murky, red colour, with a black head and legs. If the stories Ysabell heard were correct, neither Nuthionel nor her were wielding blades capable of killing the creature.

Nuthionel shoved Ysabell clear of the charging creature, then with incredible speed he leapt toward the wall. On contact he shoved off to launch himself over the ciaróg fuil. He landed right behind it and he plunged one of his daggers into a seam that ran up the length of the creature's shell. The creature released an inhuman shriek. It swung around, its pincers sweeping Nuthionel's legs from under him.

Ysabell didn't think twice. She roared in rage and joined the fight. The dagger was still protruding from the blood beetle's back where Nuthionel had stabbed it. She knew she didn't have the strength to drive it any deeper than he could have. So instead she jumped and slammed her right foot onto the blade, driving it all the way to the pommel guard. The shell cracked around it. A white, thick and disgusting sludge leaked from the wound. She used her momentum to propel herself to Nuthionel's aid. When the beetle swung at her, it found an empty passage and both enemies behind it.

Nuthionel rose swiftly, drawing his second blade as he did. His right hand shot out and slid one of Ysabell's daggers from its sheath. As he did, the Ciaróg Fuil spun again. Ysabell stepped back and stumbled on rubble in the corridor. The creature charged shoving her to the ground, its pincers opening to clamp her. She screamed as the pincers snapped closed on her leg, its long trunk like mouth approaching her to feed.

A flash to her right caught the creature's attention, too late. Nuthionel's blade sliced its feeding trunk clear off. The pinchers opened as it shrieked again. Ysabell clawed her way backwards away from it. Watching in shock as Nuthionel unleashed his fury on the creature. He threw himself towards it, diving to one side at the last second, as he rolled he slashed out under the creature's carapace. His blade finding its mark, the soft underbelly. White sludge erupted from its gut.

The elf rose to his feet, spinning on his right heel, his left foot rose and slammed into the hilt of the dagger in the Beetles back. The dagger was kicked out of the creature, splintering the rear of the carapace as it did. Nuthionel rammed his borrowed dagger into the exposed soft interior. The Ciaróg Fuil collapsed. Bleeding from several wounds, it had lost too much blood. Gasping for breath it struggled to rise again but gave in with a last sigh. Dead.

Just past where they fought the Ciaróg Fuil were the skeletal remains of a previous visitor to the creature's lair. Shriveled and sucked dry by the beetle, the corpse looked almost like it was made from stretched leather. Heavy armour plating covered most of the body, the leather at his neck perforated where the creatures feeding tube had entered.

Nuthionel knelt by the body and took a small leather pack from around its waist. He opened it and spilled the contents out onto the floor.

Ysabell gasped at what she saw and Nuthionel smiled. Several bright gem stones rolled out onto the floor, she didn't know what they were, but she figured they looked pretty expensive. With them was a pair of leather wrist bracers with strange black gem stones set in them. Last was a head band affixed with several gems of red and green.

Ysabell didn't find it to be the most attractive piece of jewellery, but Nuthionel grasped it excitedly and held it up to her. "This alone is worth more than your entire Village."

Flames in the Night
Chapter 6

Ysabell and Nuthionel made their way out of the cave and up a steep hill, back towards their camp. It was slow going. They were both exhausted. Ysabell realised they had been running and fighting all night without rest. She could hardly lift her legs.

An hour later or so, and after a climb much higher than she remembered going down, they were back at the woods. The remains of the bandit camp visible ahead. From this side, they could see Seren, the cart was fully loaded and hitched to the horse. Nuthionel looked in disbelief. He waved Ysabell down.

"Head back towards the camp on the road, swiftly." His eyes still watching the bandit camp, there was only one bandit visible. "Get ready to hop on the moving cart when I reach you. I may have company."

With that he silently crept off towards the camp, Ysabell watched him for a moment, then turned away and headed back towards the road using the bandit camp as marker to set her direction from. Twenty minutes later, as she sat by the side of the road, watching the sun creep over the horizon pouring light across the landscape. Her eyes turning to watch the tree line every few seconds.

At last she saw a horse and cart emerged from the trees. She rose and waited as Nuthionel approached. He brought the car to a stop beside her.

"Only one guard. It seems the others followed us down the hole." He offered her a hand up. "They haven't returned." They rode on for an hour or two before pulling off the road to set up camp. After throwing Ysabell the bracers they had found underground, Nuthionel started a fire. Ysabell examined her new bracers. They looked soft and were comfortable, flexible. Yet hard, she doubted a blade would easily pierce them.

They were expensive looking. They had intricate designs carved into the leather, swirling patterns like wandering vines. On the top side was an elongated, diamond-shaped layer of soft black cloth, inlaid carefully. It felt like silk, and in the centre of this was a jet-black gem. If she stared at for too long, she could see shadows seeming to move within the stone.

"What kind of gem is this?" she asked Nuthionel.

He finished tending to their fire and stood over her shoulder to marvel at it. "I'm not sure. Never seen anything like it."

She lifted the second bracer. It was identical. She tied them both around her wrists and stood up to make sure they didn't get in the way when she swung her weapons. She stepped clear of the fire, then crouched and drew her blades in one fluid motion. Nuthionel watched.

"Crouching isn't much good in the open." He commented. "Try and use the shadows to make yourself harder to see"

Ysabell moved into the shade of a tree and tried to blend in with the shadows. A gasp made her look up. Nuthionel stood open mouthed watching her.

She looked at him. He was standing in front of her, his mouth and eyes wide open in shock. She spun to see what was behind her but found nothing. What is it?" She asked, worried by his expression.

Nuthionel looked at her in disbelief. "You didn't notice anything there?"

Ysabell was even more confused now. Of course, she didn't notice anything; she was focused on her blades like he'd taught her to be.

He started to chuckle and explained, "The bracers are enchanted. When you hid under the tree, a dark swirling darkness seemed to seep from all over your body, making you seem more shadow than girl. What did you do different?"

She glanced down at the bracers, eyes wide in wonder. "Really? Nothing just concentrated on staying hidden."

"Well, then that's probably the trigger. You'll be a hard target to find in the gloom of ruins with those bracers on. May I?" He reached out a hand indicated one of the bracers. Ysabell removed her left hand one and handed it to him. Nuthionel examined it slowly, tracing the gem with his finger, looking into its swirling depths.

"Truly incredible." He handed it back to her. "We'll get Athress to take a look at them in Carraigbán. He's a Mage, I was on the way to see him about the Goblins in Farrowfields anyway. He should be able to figure out what they are and how they work."

He shook his head in wonder again looking at them. Then turned back to the fire to prepare some food.

They spent the rest of the afternoon and evening examining everything they had found loaded on the cart, courtesy of the bandits. Along with what they had found on the dead adventurer in the Ciaróg Fuil's lair. Nothing else seemed to have magical enchantments, though, Nuthionel told her only a Mage would really know. Once they reached the city, they could go to the Mage district and have their spoils checked by Athress. They would be on the city outskirts by tomorrow afternoon. Ysabell spent some time practicing with her new bracers. She could control the swirling mists a bit better now. While she couldn't see them herself, she could feel a slight chill in the air when she used them.

Ysabell could barely sleep that night from the ache in her side. It was much improved. The ointment Nuthionel kept applying to it was incredible. But it still hurt like hell. She also kept thinking about the City she would see for the first time tomorrow. What it was like, what the people were like, would she see other races? Eventually she drifted off, dreaming about creeping through goblin infested caves. Cloaked in mist like shadows.

<><><>

They broke camp early, anxious to get under way. Bright lights had been visible in the eastern sky since before dawn and now in the day, smoke plumes were visible. They were still three or four hours from Carraigbán but Nuthionel reckoned the smoke was coming from the same direction as the City.

The sight made Ysabell nervous. If Nuthionel was, he didn't show it. But he set a hard pace. As the sun rose towards midday, buildings started to appear on the horizon. Sporadic at first, fast becoming more densely arranged. The track they followed became harder and firmer, its edges more defined as they got closer to the city. Seren pulled them and the loaded cart with ease, cantering along as though he pulled nothing.

When they reached the outskirts, it had become a road, bigger and wider than any Ysabell had ever seen. Carts were busy trundling in and out of the city. People were scurrying everywhere. No Guards could be seen. This was what Ysabell found strangest. Even in her village they had a village guard. It was also strange that there were no walls. She had imagined the city to be a giant, walled-in fortress, but this was just lots and lots of houses and warehouses all squashed together on either side of the road.

Nuthionel dismounted. Ysabell followed suit and they set a fast pace with Seren and the cart in tow. He clearly had a destination in mind, but as he seemed lost in thought, Ysabell thought it better to leave him be. The people here, aside from looking panicked about something, looked poor, their clothes ragged. The streets were filthy and stank of human excrement. She started to wonder how long she would want to stay in the city if it was all like this.

The road up ahead forked, the larger split headed off to the right. Nuthionel took the smaller street branching left. Ysabell could see the white towers and domes of a multitude of Temples as they neared the end of it. Before they reached these,

Nuthionel led them over a bridge to the left, water rushed beneath them, the run off channels from the streets emptying into it. She realised then the stink was from sewage running through these drains to spill into the water. It was disgusting. In her village you dug a pit behind your house, a wooden outhouse over it. Bed pans etc were emptied into it, once it was filling up, it was buried and a new one dug, the outhouse moved to cover it.

Nuthionel told her they were headed towards the Mage district. She couldn't help but notice it was also towards the plumes of smoke and flickering flames they'd noticed, still burning since last night.

After crossing the bridge, Ysabell found herself hopelessly lost in the labyrinth of streets and lanes and taverns and inns. She'd never seen anything so extensive. They'd walked a few miles already, but there seemed to be no end to the streets or the people. People everywhere! The closer they got to the Mage district the more of them were fleeing in the other direction, shoving passed each other.

Nuthionel stopped in front of a tavern called the Goblin's Head. Outside, a wooden placard shaped like a head hung from a noose.

He tied Seren and the cart up outside then they headed in. Ysabell immediately felt back at home. The tavern was mostly old wood, stank of old beer and spilled ale. It was dark and poorly lit, with a crackling, roaring fire in a four-sided hearth in the centre of the room. Tables and chairs were scattered around, some full, many more empty.

Ysabell followed Nuthionel to the back of the tavern, past the wary glares of patrons. A few muttered comments about knife ears were barely audible. '*Seems city folk are as small minded as the villagers.*' She looked around in disgust. They sat at a snug booth deep in shadow and waited. Without ordering anything, two mugs of ale arrived from one of the serving girls. She bent over to place the drinks down, Ysabell turned her face away, not sure where to look. The girl was hiding very little with her choice of clothes.

Nuthionel smiled and thanked the barmaid, tipped her and once she left turned to Ysabell. "Something wrong?"

She retorted. "Is this a tavern or a brothel?"

Nuthionel merely shrugged. He was clearly worried about bigger things than the appearance of the bar maid. She let her eyes wander around the tavern. Worry and fear were on most of the faces, just like those they had seen fleeing the streets outside.

"Why are they just sitting here drinking if they are so afraid?" she asked. "Why not leave like those outside?"

Nuthionel turned to her, genuinely surprised. "And go where? If your village were to burn, where would the villagers go? Would they just walk away and leave?" She had to think about that for a moment. Then realised that no, they wouldn't leave, it was their home, they would stay, wait for the flames to wither, and then rebuild. While she was contemplating the thought, a short cloaked and hooded figure approached the table. A very short figure, almost like a child.

The stranger drew back the hood. A mop of ginger hair shook loose and a Halfling woman eyed Ysabell for a moment before addressing Nuthionel. "No word yet as to what caused it. About four in the morning, explosions and flames shook the Mage district. The Mage tower is under assault, but from the inside of the compound. Drudir and Lasairlaoch have been spotted around the grounds of the tower; a few have made into the streets. No word from Athress, but it'll take more than a few demons to finish him."

Nuthionel remained silent for a moment in thought. Then indicating the Halfling. "My apologies Ysabell, this is a colleague and friend of mine, Cali. Cali, this is my, well... I suppose apprentice would be the right word. Ysabell, I told you already of Athress? It seems he is caught inside the Mage district where all this chaos is centreed."

Ysabell looked with curiosity at the Halfling woman now seated at their table. "What are Drudir and Lasairlaoch?" she asked.

This time Cali responded. "Drudir are a type of demon, often summoned by powerful Mages to fight for them. They're hard to kill, but their bodies are filled with some kind of demonic smoke. Make enough holes and they drain out." She smiled grimly. "As for Lasairlaoch, they are a type of six-armed fire elemental."

"Six arms?" Ysabell exclaimed.

"Yup. They don't belong in this plane so need a magical skin to hold their flames in form,. You batter their skin enough, the flames burst out and they fall back to their own plane. If you can use those blades half as well as Nuthionel here, you shouldn't have too much trouble with them." She grinned again, her eyes glinting at the mention of fighting.

Nuthionel's forehead creased as he scrutinized Ysabell. She guessed he was wondering if she was ready for this, or if he should leave her in the tavern.

Cali glanced at Nuthionel with a mischievous look in her eye. "I hear a human priestess was seen in Yrniv's tavern last night. Drunk and fighting half-a-dozen patrons at once."

Nuthionel's face lit up. "Perfect. Cali, get to Yrniv's tavern to find out where she is now, fill her in and tell her we are going in after Athress. I need you both back here ten minutes ago. No stopping to fight. We'll meet at the end of this road where it crosses the avenue of trees. Athress may need us."

"What about you?" Cali asked.

Ysabell watched the exchange with interest. She'd never seen a halfling before, but didn't want to stare, as it may seem rude.

"We have a cart full of spoils from our journey here." Nuthionel answered. "We will trade them for better equipment for Ysabell. Do you have all you need?"

Cali nodded, put her hood back up and disappeared out into the street again.

Dressing For The Shadows

Chapter 7

"Why does she keep her hood up?" Ysabell asked once she was out of sight. Nuthionel paused a moment watching, then responded. "A drunk, off-duty guard was harassing a tavern girl one night. She said no over and over but that didn't deter him. Cali has strong views about that. She taught him a lesson he won't ever forget. She broke no law acting in defence of another, but the City Guard would look for any excuse to try and get even. It's just less hassle for her to remain inconspicuous while in Carraigbán."

Ysabell's face darkened. She had fairly strong views on that herself. Her opinion of Cali rose massively. After Nuthionel was done talking he threw some coins on the table and they headed out the door, back into the chaotic streets.

It was quieter than when they had come in. Ysabell's eyes took a moment to adjust to the light before they set off through the maze of streets which left her feeling hopelessly lost again. They were heading away from the smoke-filled skies of the Mage district, northeast through the city.

Nuthionel decided it was time to ride their cart. Seren made better progress than they would on foot with pedestrians moving out of the way of a large horse far more quickly.

"Who is the priest Cali mentioned and how do you know this Mage, Athress?" Ysabell asked as they rode.

Nuthionel frowned. "Athress is a human Mage. A good one. He saved my life when I was very young, and it was he who first taught me to use and sell my blade across the southern Kingdoms. I owe him a great deal, more than I want to explain right now. Guinevere is a human priestess. Not some mealy-mouthed preacher like most of them, she worships the Goddess of life, death and battle, Asetha."

Nuthionel drew Seren to a halt to let some panicked looking people cross in front of them. He continued, "She sees value in all three as her goddess does. Life is important, but without Death it can't exist, and without battle, the balance of all things, Life, Death, Good, and Evil could not be maintained. Without that balance there could be no life. I think you'll like her."

Ysabell had realised weeks ago that Nuthionel was probably an experienced mercenary or similar. He had admitted he was no trader, but that was all. She had never broached the subject further, but now she knew. Was she to be part of this mercenary band? Or once she was trained would he send her off to find her own way?

<><><>

Finally, they arrived in a market square. It was easily ten times the size of Farrowfields. Stalls and tents and carts were everywhere, traders hawking their wares. They rode the cart to a large warehouse on the south west of the square, where there was a fenced off area for horses and carts to unload.

A dwarf with a large black beard stood on a loading dock at the back of the building. He shouted at several human men unloading a series of carts. "Come on! I don't have all day, get that gear in here; more carts are due in later from the West. I want this dock cleared and ready for then. Bartleby, BARTLEBY!! Oh, there you are, get everything catalogued and priced. There'll be mercenaries queuing for gear if this Mage district business isn't resolved soon. I don't want to lose their money on account of not having things priced yet!"

As he was shouting his gaze paused on their cart. Hands on hips, he smiled broadly. "HA! My Favourite Elf! Well, tree-hugger, what do you have for me? Leaves and moss and sissy herbish crap as usual is it?"

Nuthionel called back, "Ho Dragar. Some good gear we relieved a bandit camp of and a few pieces we found in old ruins beneath the camp. I'll fill you in another time."

The dwarf kicked several empty crates and sacks off one side of the loading dock for them to line their cart up to it.

Nuthionel backed the cart up and tied Seren's nose bag on. "We didn't have time to get these checked for enchantments. With the Mage district as it is, I doubt I could have found anyone to do it."

The dwarf shot a concerned glance at Nuthionel "Athress?"

The elf shook his head. "We don't know yet. We're about to go in to find him."

"You're a fool if you do. City Guard already lost two squads in there. Now it's all they can do to keep the damn demons from spreading out of the district. You go in; you'll be in as bad need of rescue as the damn Mage!" The dwarf's lips twisted. "But you won't listen to me, will you? Humph. Alright, I'll get Bartleby to get this lot unloaded and he'll give you a fair price. I assume you want credit for supplies?"

Nuthionel nodded. "I'll also need young Ysabell here kitted out. Good quality leather armour only, soft and quiet. It'll need to have some protection on it if you have any enchantments. Daggers too." He signaled Ysabell to give hers to the Dwarf. "She's been using these, so something with a similar weight and style, but they have to be able to cut demons. If the cart doesn't cover it all, do me a favour Dragar, give me credit. You know I'm good for it."

"If you don't come back I'll need to square it with Alir. Leave the horse here, I'll stable him for free." He looked directly at the Elf. "You get that old fool back alive, and I'll owe you. I mean that." He rubbed a gnarled hand over his forehead. "If anything's happened to him, I'm coming with you to find whoever did this, that clear?" Dragar rested a hand on the elf's shoulder, then with a nod turned and walked into the warehouse behind. Ysabell and Nuthionel followed.

The interior was far more impressive than the outside. Old, dark, wooden shelves, counters, stands were everywhere. All the way up to the cavernous roof in places. They were filled with just about everything imaginable, from weapons to potions, armour to books.

A huge spiral staircase wound its way up to the second story, where Mages in different coloured robes could be seen perusing the shelves. They wandered between shelves of scrolls and magic books, and rows of robes, staffs, and wands. Dragar led them to the front of the building and then left through an aisle to a section seemly devoted to sinister exploits. Black, grey and green, softened, leather armours, weapons racks filled with all manners of small and discreet blades. Wicked looking stiletto blades, hollow blades for injecting poison, you name it, they had it. Nuthionel had seen it all before. He needed to get Ysabell geared and move on fast. He didn't know how things were looking in the Mage district and it worried him.

Dragar walked past all these to a steel cage at the back. He unlocked the door and led them inside. On a stand near the back was a full outfit of black tight leather, buckled and straps keeping it in place. When Dragar lifted it off the stand and presented it to Ysabell, it made no more noise than silk would.

"That'll never fit me," she said.

Dragar smiled. "Just try it."

The two men turned away and began to discuss the daggers on the wall. Behind them Ysabell changed. The black leather leggings pulled on with ease, they were huge as was the chest piece. Nuthionel turned to see how she was getting on. The armour looked ridiculously big on her lithe frame.

"Tighten the buckles" Dragar instructed.

Nuthionel watched as Ysabell tightened the buckles at the waist of the leggings and went to roll or pull up the bottoms as they were too long, except, they weren't any longer. The loose folds and creases in the leather after she had pulled them were tightening all on their own, the waist shrinking. Within seconds they were a perfect fit. Nuthionel stared in surprise. Like the leggings the jerkin was huge but within seconds of her tightening the buckles, the whole thing had adjusted to her lithe frame. It was tight all over, like a second skin. It also looked incredibly light and supple.

Ysabell stretched and moved around to test its range of motion.

"It's like being naked it feels so light, there's no tightness or pull against me from the material in any position." She looked up at Nuthionel in shock "Well, it fits," she said

"I'm impressed Dragar. Any other enchantments on it?"

The Dwarf bent down and picked up the black-gemmed bracers Ysabell had left on the floor with her clothes. "Nothing as potent as the enchantments on these. Mind if I ask where you acquired them?"

The elf told him of the fight with the Ciaróg Fuil, and the discovery of a desiccated adventurer.

Dragar nodded. "He was a good man, Sven. Tough ye know? Wouldn't have figured a single Ciaróg Fuil would take him down. Must have gotten him by surprise. He told me he was going after these. I offered him a king's ransom if he'd sell them to me, if, of course, they were actually there. Don't suppose you'd sell them?" he asked turning to Ysabell.

"No!" she replied, almost defensively. She blushed. "I mean, they're more useful keeping me alive, than as gold.".

Dragar smiled, nodded, and handed the bracers back to Ysabell. "You ever change your mind, you be sure and give me first refusal on them. They'd set a dwarf up for life. The Shadow Bracers of Cloch Dubh. Ha! I thought they were a myth to be honest."

Ysabell slipped her bracers back on and tightened them. As she did Nuthionel turned to Dragar.

"You know of them? What's the gem inlaid in them? How do they work?

"You think I'm a Mage? Best ask Athress when you find him. All I know is that." He pointed at the black gem. "Is not any kind of gem. I'd guess it's made by magic somehow. No idea how."

Nuthionel and Dragar both looked at the bracers. Ysabell picked up the harness for her daggers but Dragar stopped her. "Those are nice blades," he said. "A nice harness too, but they'll do nothing against demons. You might as well fight with sticks." He reached for the rack behind him and took two similar-looking daggers off it. Their blades were split in two points like hers, but they also had diagonal, indented stripes down them -- blood channels. The pommels were black as were the blades, bar a dark blood red stone was set in the base.

"These will never blunt; never need to be sharpened. The Elves made them for fighting summoned creatures, so when fighting demons or elementals, always, and I mean always, use them."

Dragar handed her the weapons, and while she studied them he rumMaged on the shelf behind him. He removed a dusky-grey harness from it. The first dagger positions were the same as on Ysabell's previous harness, but there was a second slot below for two more daggers. It also had no adornments on it at all, and even the buckles were dulled and dark grey.

"That thing looks like it hasn't been cleaned in years," she remarked.

Dragar laughed. Even Nuthionel was grinning. "Last thing you want when trying not to be seen is a shiny buckle or strap marking you as nice easy target, lass," Dragar said. "And black all over is too dark. Makes you look too black but add a bit of grey and you'll be practically invisible as long you keep to the shadows, especially with those bracers on." He handed her the harness. "It has four sheaths, you'll want your own blades in it, as well these. You can never have too many pointy things to stick in your enemy."

Nuthionel looked on as Ysabell took the harness, examined the extra sheath slots on it, and slipped it on. It slid over the leather of her new armour like it wasn't even there. She buckled it up, slotted the two new blades in the top sheath on each side and her old daggers in the lower two. She stretched and dropped into a crouch to see how it felt to hold so many weapons. It was a little uncomfortable on her ribs. Drawing her daggers swiftly from the upper tier for practice, she let the shadows crept up around her, wrapping her in their dark embrace. Nuthionel turned to see Dragar's response, the dwarf gasped. "Drangul's Axe, so it's true!"

A shadowy mist was shrouding Ysabell, it made her hard to see with in it. Ysabell sheathed her blades and stood up again. "Very true."

Nuthionel noted the hint of pride in her voice. She was proud of her new gear. 'She should be, she earned it,' he thought. He looked away to Dragar

"Well, has Bartleby gotten a look at the chests on the cart yet?" Nuthionel asked.

Dragar stepped away from Ysabell, staring for a few moments at her shadowy enchantment, before leading them out of the cage. They went up a set of stairs into a large office full of crates and work areas where people were appraising equipment, gems, weapons for their value. An older man sat at the far end with an assortment of gems before him, he looked up as they approached.

"How does it look Bartleby?" Dragar asked him.

"Good finds here," he replied. "Everything is decent quality. Steel blades, nothing magical, but well-made gear and fairly new as well. They must have raided a recent shipment. The gems though... some of these are cut in ways I can't explain. These have come from a ruin somewhere. They are ancient." He held up a large green gemstone. "One of them has an enchantment on it." He waved a wand across it and it lit up with a white haze. "Not sure what it is yet, but, by the age of it, I'd guess first era Elven. They had outposts around this part of the world, they used gems like these for letting them read other languages."

Bartleby reached into a shelf behind the work area and pulled out one of the scrolls. "Second empire Dwarvish this one. Can't read a word of it myself. Been trying to get it translated for weeks." He held the gem to his forehead and started to read. "'And so it was that the law came into being, All below the surface was the property of the dwarves. All above was for the race of men.'" He sighed. "Bah, just another copy of the treaty of the Icevales."

"I wanted a price not a history lesson," Dragar said. "Do you have a fair value on this junk yet?"

Bartleby shook his head at Dragar's lack of academic interest. "Yes, about 1,800 gold the lot. This gem is worth 1,200 on its own. The rest is pretty everyday fayre. Good quality, but hardly rare. This however." He held up the gem-inlaid headband. "I can't price. I'll need Alir to take a look and maybe a Mage. It's got some powerful enchantment on it, but I'm not going to be the one to try it on. It could be a curse. Dragar turned to Nuthionel. "That leaves you about 2500 gold short, my friend. I'll have a hard time explaining to Alir that I had traded 2,500 gold for a horse worth about 60 if you don't make it back."

"You'll get your gold back," Nuthionel said. "If the head piece is worth what I think it is, that'll see us clear. Now, if we're square, take good care of Seren. I will be back for him in few days at most, with Athress by side."

Dragar took his arm. "Be safe my friend, it would wound me enough to lose Athress, but to lose you both? Who'd drink with me and listen to my lies about my adventures without you two?"

"Hah, as long as you buy the ale, I'm sure you'd find someone."

Dragar chuckled and turned to Ysabell. "You won't find a better elf to teach you, lass. You'd have been better off with a dwarf, but for an elf he's pretty good. You watch his back." Dragar's features darkened. "And if that damn Halfling is going with ye, tell her I'll sever her head if she gets you all killed!"

With a final wave of farewell, Dragar headed back into the warehouse without a backwards glance.

The Gang's All Here

Chapter 8

The closer they got to the Mage District, the louder sounds of explosions grew.

"At least some are still living and putting up a fight," Nuthionel said grimly.

They hurried through the lanes and alleys of the city until they reached a crossroad onto a broad street Ysabell recognised. Looking up to their right, she could see the Goblin's Head where they had met Cali. Nuthionel led her on towards the Mage district. At the corner of the next street she recognised the hooded figure of Cali and standing, with her stood a very tall human, in a hooded cloak over the crimson red robes of her goddess. Guinevere the Priestess, Ysabell presumed.

Cali waved in greeting. Guinevere nodded, wincing as she did so.

"Rough night?" Asked Nuthionel. "Can't think of a better use of your Goddess' gift than healing that damn hangover quickly. Athress may be in dire need."

"Don't worry about me elf," Guinevere said. "Even hung-over I'll still banish more demons than you." She grinned. "In fact, myself and Cali have a little bet going. Care to buy in?"

"We don't know how much time we have. We don't even know Athress is still alive, but you two want to make bets?"

Their cheeks went red with embarrassment.

"We are going to reach him, and we can decide what comes next at that point," Nuthionel continued. "The journey out will be a lot easier if he is with us. If he is... if he is dead, then we will find who is behind this and... and take it from there."

Ysabell watched him, concerned as he stumbled over his words. He was always so confident. Athress clearly meant a lot to him. "We are with you Nuthionel, no matter what." she assured him.

Cali drew her axe. "Just point and I'll cut its head off!"

Guinevere placed a hand on his shoulder and muttered a prayer. His demeanor instantly changed. He glared at her, but she held her hands in the air, a gentle smile on her face. "Merely a prayer of hope my friend. We will meet little success if you wear defeat on your face before we have even drawn our blades."

The Elf nodded his thanks and turned to Ysabell. "We three have fought together many times. You have only fought with me alone. Keep an eye on your allies. A friend's blade is just as lethal as an enemy's."

Ysabell nodded her understanding. Nerves ate at her, still sore from their last misadventure. She was nervous at the thought of fighting again.

Nuthionel led them to the western gate of the Mage district. Cali explained to Ysabell that it was because of fears of this kind of incident that the whole district is walled off with large gates that could be sealed if anything dangerous should happen. Well, Cali really said that it was because, "Those looney bastard Mages couldn't be trusted". A laughing Guinevere countered that it was for safety, both for the city if anything should be summoned and out of control and also in case of anti-Mage riots like those that happened in the Northern cities fifty years ago.

After some incident in the twin cities, the people blamed the Mages and tried to get rid of them. Or so Guinevere was told. There were no survivors to ask. Those cities learned the power of Mages the hard way. The towers were blown apart, killing everyone in the cities and leaving nothing more than ruins for miles around them. The Palace in Carraigbán made the decision to close off the district if something similar ever happened, ensuring peace was maintained for the sake of all involved.

The Guards at the gate were nervous. Around twenty of them faced it, rather than the street. Some looked as young as Ysabell or younger. They were terrified, staring at the gates in fear.

Nuthionel approached the captain of the unit and informed him they were looking to access the district.

He looked at them as if in disbelief. "You want to go in? Do you know what's in there? There's nothing human left. It's overrun with demons!"

Suddenly, a large explosion shook the ground. The captain winced and half ducked. Nuthionel didn't react, instead maintaining eye contact with the Guard. "It sounds like someone in there is still fighting," he said, "and by the size of that explosion doing a good job of it. No one is asking you to go in and rescue them. All I want is for you to let us pass, so that *we* can. If we fail, it's no skin off your nose. If we succeed, well, we might find out what's caused this and be able to put a stop to it."

The Guard Captain thought it over, his forehead glistening with sweat. He was young, probably newly promoted, not a scratch or a dent on his armour. She felt sorry for him. He had been handed a rough assignment.

Finally, he nodded his agreement and let them through. The gates clanged shut behind them, bars locking into place. Ysabell couldn't stop thinking about the Guard Captain's face as he had let them pass, like he thought them dead the moment they passed through the arch.

"What?" Cali questioned. "Where's the damn demons? Those bastards said there were hordes? My axe is out, all oiled up and ready for blood and what, nothing? A bunch of bloody trees and empty streets!"

Another explosion shook the ground as soon as she finished. They all turned to look east towards the Mage tower, from a window near the top a fireball formed and flew, exploding near the base of the tower.

Guinevere smiled. "You can be damn sure Athress is alive, if there's still fight in those Mages, he's in the thick of it, blasting the hell spawn back through the planes!" Even Nuthionel cheered up upon seeing the fireballs.

As they watched, Nuthionel spotted a demon striding between the buildings ahead, searching for anything living to kill. "A Drudir!" he shouted. The thing was large, muscular, well armoured, and wielding a massive broadsword. The strangest thing about its appearance to Ysabell was that its face had no eyes, or eye sockets. 'How does it see?'

Nuthionel signalled to the others.

Cali drew a small, wicked-looking crossbow. She selected a thick bolt from a small quiver strapped to her thigh. She loaded and took aim. As she did, her left hand cracked a flint off the tip of the bolt. A strange, pale, blue flame ignited around it. Seeing Ysabell staring at the flame she said, "Finest triple distilled whiskey there is. Shame to waste on the likes of him but wait till you see it burn!"

Without another word she fired, the blue flame brightening as it streaked through the air. It struck the Drudir in the lower back. The whiskey splashed all over, setting the demon's entire back alight. It swung its massive sword at whatever foe challenged him, but there was no one there.

It's searching face found them quickly. Cali helped by waving. As it strode towards them she taunted, "Ohh, blue's a great colour on you! Just lookin' fabulous!"

She laughed as a second flaming bolt shot from her hand and exploded on the demon's chest. It didn't stop the thing. One hand flapped at its chest trying to put out the flames as it approached them. Nuthionel drew his daggers. Guinevere stepped back and began to recite a prayer, her hands open to the skies. Ysabell followed Nuthionel's example and drew her new blades.

A third bolt fired from Cali's crossbow. This one missed, but it was enough to get the demon running. It raised its great sword above its head as it charged. Cali calmly clipped the crossbow back on her belt and drew her axe. When it was no more than a handful of feet away she let out a blood curdling scream. She ducked under its sword, sweeping her axe at the demon's legs. He was too swift. He leapt over her axe and swung his sword at Guinevere who was still unarmed, calling her prayers to the sky. Ysabell moved faster than she ever had to try and reach her in time to block it. Nuthionel's daggers flew past her head in fast succession, both piercing the demons armour. It barely slowed. Then, Guinevere's chest lit up with a bright light that exploded out from her in a perfect sphere. It struck the demon, flinging the blade from its hands and throwing its body through the air to crash to ground.

There was silence. A perfect moment, where nothing and no one moved or spoke. Then the Demon rolled and rose to his feet. Ysabell stared in disbelief. *'How can it still live?'* Fear tightened her stomach. Nuthionel's daggers protruded from the creatures armour still. Ysabell handed Nuthionel one of her daggers. Took a deep breath to try and calm herself then side by side, they ran in. Cali was up again and running towards it too. Guinevere was recovering from the spell that had left her drained.

Nuthionel reached the Drudir first, spinning to the right at the last moment and slashing a blade across the waist-line weak point in the demons armour. Ysabell, a moment behind him, mimicked his maneuver to the left. But the demon was a fast learner. Mid spin, Ysabell found herself raised into the air by the throat. She could feel the heat beneath the demon's glove burning at her skin. It squeezed, crushing her neck and sealing off her breath. Her vision almost went black before Nuthionel drew his own daggers from the demon's armour, exposing two holes from which the smoke inside began to seep.

It dropped her, and, at seeing Ysabell fall, the rage of the others was like a tsunami crashing over the demon. Guinevere came sprinting in to join the fight, her mace crashed into its face where its eyes would have been had it any. Simultaneously Cali's axe bit deep into its lower spine, a blow that would have crippled if not killed a human. Nuthionel's daggers entered its neck last, one on either side. He levered its helmet off, exposing the neck and head, and slashed through it. Smoke plumed from the demon and it fell, dead or banished... whatever happened to them when killed in this plane.

Guinevere ran to Ysabell's body, she was still alive, though barely, blood leaked from her mouth, her throat was completely crushed, and she was suffocating. Ysabell's last sight was the Priests hands raised in prayer, a white glow radiating through her body. Then all went dark.

Shadows meets Flame

Chapter 9

Gently Ysabell opened her eyes, her throat felt sore, dry and burning. She found herself looking into the concerned faces of her friends.

"How?" She croaked.

Nuthionel, not normally a tactile person, pulled her up into a warm hug, when he let her go she could see the tell-tale signs of tears in his eyes. Cali was smiling on her other side.

"Brave, I'll give ye that, but running at a Drudir with only a single knife in your hand? Head on? You're madder than me!"

It was Guinevere who answered her; "A poor Priestess I would be if I couldn't cast healing spells. The only worry was if it would heal in time for you to get air before your brain died. A word of advice, you are not Nuthionel; he might be stupid enough to try a frontal charge on a Drudir, he might even be lucky enough to survive it. For the rest of us, what you did was suicide."

They helped Ysabell to her feet and Nuthionel returned her blades to her. As they dusted themselves off and prepared to continue on their way, the sky to the east lit up again. A multi-coloured storm of light bolts surrounded the tower. Explosions rang out, followed by the sounds of falling masonry and an unearthly scream. Ysabell had never heard anything like it. Still a little shaken, and feeling tender all over, she worried what else was in store for them. If that was just one. *'Dragar said the district was overrun with them. How many more will we face?'*

As they set off towards the fireworks in the east, a huge creature walked straight out in front of them from behind a row of trees. It scuttled along on four giant, multi-jointed legs similar to a spider's. Based on what Nuthionel had taught her, it had to be a Lasairlaoch, but she never expected something so terrifying. Above its bulbous body and legs was a muscular torso, six arms protruded from its sides, its body encased in leather like armour. She couldn't tell if it was wearing it, or it was the creature's skin.

It turned and saw them immediately. The two lowest of its six arms, coming from just above its front legs, at its lower torso, pulled up to hold two large round shields. The four arms above those, each held a short sword. It drew the top two arms back poised ready to strike and the middle two arms spread out wide, almost inviting them to attack it.

Before the rest of them could even react, Cali sprang at it, screaming obscenities. "Come on ye chargrilled, shite-eat'n bastard! I'll rip your tonkers off!"

The sight of her tearing across the road shook the others into action. Guinevere drew her massive mace from under her cloak with her right hand. Ysabell reckoned the mace probably weighed as much as she did, yet Guinevere wielded it with ease, her left hand raised in prayer as she charged forward.

Nuthionel gave a reassuring nod to Ysabell, then ran in after them, his twin daggers drawn. Cali reached the creature first, her initial axe swing deflecting off the creature's right-hand shield. Its left highest arms shot down, the point of its sword aimed at her head, but she was no novice. She rolled clear to the Lasairlaoch's right, striking a fierce blow as she rose to her feet straight into the thing's right foreleg. Her axe bit into one of the, well, what Ysabell supposed were knees. It rose up with an unearthly screaming, rearing back and swinging to find Cali, but she was already gone, rolling past it to its left-hand side. As it turned again to find the Halfling, it left its hind quarters open to a crashing blow from a Mace. Flames leapt from the split in its armour, and Guinevere's left hand whipped down as she finished her prayer.

The skies opened, and a shaft of bright light shone down on the creature. It screamed again as if burned and when the light extinguished, a dull glow remained along all the weak points in its armour. Guinevere leapt back before it could turn to swing at her again. Cali's axe swept into another leg from behind it. The creature swung wildly at Guinevere, then spun to search for Cali. As it did Nuthionel lightly leapt up on its back where the armour had been cracked by Guinevere's mace. His twin blades slashing between the Lasairlaoch armour at the joins of its lower set of arms, breaking the armour and exposing the magical 'skin' that held the creature together. It bucked wildly, throwing him from its back. A leg behind it kicked out flattening Guinevere, at the same time it found Cali and blocked her swing with one shield then struck her hard with other sending her rolling across the cobbles.

While this was happening, Ysabell tried to use Dragar's advice. She didn't want a repeat of the fight with the Drudir. She dove into the shadows by the trees, crouched and drew her blades. She still couldn't see it, but in her adrenaline-fuelled state she was sure she could feel the shadows wrapping around her, a cold embrace, as she ran, light-footed and silently along the tree line.

The Lasairlaoch was spinning in a frenzy, swords and shields flashing on all sides. Guinevere was casting a healing prayer on Cali who was bleeding from a dozen places but still swinging her axe like she had lost her mind. Nuthionel engaged three arms at once, furiously trying to find a way through the creature's defence. The Lasairlaoch looked confused for a moment, Ysabell knew why, it was wondering what the hazy shadow moving along the tree line was. *'Won't be wondering for long.'* She launched off a tree trunk flying towards the creature's neck.

Before the creature's confusion had worn off, and much too late to try and defend against the twin black blades spinning for its neck, a scream rose in its throat, but never made it to the ears of the group fighting it. Ysabell's enchanted daggers severed the skin across its neck, Flames erupted from the gaping hole between its shoulders and it crumpled to the ground, its skin shriveling up, the flames withering and its armour falling apart, clattering to the ground.

Ysabell landed on her shoulder and attempted to roll to her feet. Her momentum was a little more than she anticipated. She couldn't stop and landed on her shoulder again, hitting hard this time and sliding to a stop. Guinevere offered her a hand. Her right shoulder was throbbing, and she couldn't move her arm. The priestess sat her down and started to cast a prayer of healing on the affected area. Ysabell watched the crumpled armour and smoldering skin of the fire elemental as she did.

Nuthionel limped over to them. Several cuts adorned his torso and he was bleeding on his left leg, just above the knee, from where the edge of a shield had struck him. All of them were staring at Ysabell. She was sure they wanted to know why she delayed; why she didn't just charge in like the rest of them

"By all the Holy Crap Guinevere believes, that was easily the best thing I've EVER SEEN!" Cali exclaimed, breaking the silence. "A fucking shadow. A flying fucking shadow streaking through the air cuttin' its insides out!"

Nuthionel was smiling now. "I am impressed. That wasn't an easy move to pull off."

Guinevere was the last to offer her opinion. "Well, you're a dark horse aren't you. Quiet as a mouse and then you only go and beat three bells of shite out of your first elemental. As soon as we are out of here, you and I are going drinking!"

Ysabell was shocked. She was sure they'd be annoyed with her overly cautious approach to the fight. Nuthionel offered her a last piece of wisdom as Guinevere healed his leg. "The shadows suit you. You only hit one blow in that fight, but it was the only one that mattered. I am proud of you Ysabell."

He left it at that and looked away to check on his leg. He thanked Guinevere when he found it was almost as good as new, though she said he would have a scar.

They took a few more minutes to get themselves cleaned up and sorted out, and then moved on.

"If there are many more of those, how much of a chance do we really have of making through to the tower?" Ysabell asked.

Nuthionel looked worried but didn't answer her; neither did Guinevere, she just glanced at Nuthionel.

"Depends really." Cali, the more garrulous of the group, was than happy to respond.

"If the Mages are blasting the crap out of them up there around the tower, we might get in with only a scrape or two. If the tower is sealed, which is likely, I don't know what we'll do. 'Thion usually has a plan or two up his sleeve."

This answer did nothing to allay Ysabell's fears. The burning in her throat was still fresh, as was the throbbing of her shoulder. She was starting to question whether Nuthionel's judgement was sound when it came to Athress.

They reached the edge of the clearing around the tower. There were several Drudir visible between them and the tower. Fire elementals stalked around the clearing here and there. The ground was littered with bodies of Mages, some badly dismembered, and others burnt or crushed. There was no guarantee Athress was even alive. Ysabell contemplated all this as she watched the Drudir stand impassively. They were willing to play the waiting game. She knew that even if Athress' body were lying in front of them, they would have to take this course. Nuthionel's rage would see to that, but even without that, now had come this far, could they really walk away and leave whatever Mages were alive in there to their fate?

Nuthionel turned and looked at each of them in turn, his face blank and impossible to read. "Well? Idea's or suggestions. Anyone who wants to turn back, I won't blame you. It's the smart choice. The odds of us getting any further are slimmer than I could calculate."

Cali, her face cheerful as always, grunted, "And what of you? Are you turnin' back? If I was to face odds like that, if any one of us here were to face those odds, would you walk away? No, you bloody wouldn't! So, shut up your maudlin whining and tell us the plan." Her swift but heartfelt rebuttal put a smile on everyone's face, except the Elf's.

"There is no plan Cali. We can't sneak past, we can't ambush, and we can't count on help from the tower. We step beyond these trees and there's no going back. The two creatures we faced getting here will be a gentle warm up compared to what awaits us out there. Athress is like a father to me, I cannot walk away, but you all can."

Before either of the others could speak Ysabell heard her own voice, no one more surprised than herself. "No. I can't walk away. Even if you weren't here, and

Athress never existed." She thought back to the goblin attack on her village and how she had sprung to action to help her people without giving it a second thought. "I can hear the screams from that tower. I didn't learn to use these blades to run when it got dangerous. In the ruins of Cloch Dubh we nearly both died, for what? To get your gear back from some bandits and a pair of bracers and some gems? How can I justify being willing to risk my life for that and yet walk away now? No, I will fight and, if I die, so be it. I regret nothing!"

Nuthionel's brow creased as he studied her.

Cali clapped Ysabell on the back. "That's my girl! Sisters in it together. I'll bash 'em and keep their attention forward while you cut their tonkers off from behind."

Guinevere placed a gentle hand Nuthionel's shoulder. "We are all in. We'll make it through this, we always do." She turned to Ysabell. "How can we not when we have Ysabell killing Lasairlaoch's with a single blow? She'll have the field cleared of enemies in no time!"

Ysabell was glad of the jest to lighten the mood slightly; she knew they had little chance of surviving, but was strangely calm. The knot of fear in her stomach was gone, it was an odd feeling at the edge of a battlefield. About to charge in, probably to her death, yet she was completely at peace in that moment, maybe for the first time in her life. She looked around the group. They all seemed to be in a similar mood, accepting of whatever was to come.

For Ysabell, it was partially about making Nuthionel proud. She'd craved the attention of a parent all her life. She was not going to let him down, not even if it killed her!

With one final glance at each other, the small group of friends rose as one, turned and strode into the clearing.

A Stroll in the Valley of Death

Chapter 10

As they cleared the trees, the group spread out. Ysabell drew her daggers and slipped into her cloak of shadows. Nuthionel let his blades slide into his hands, stretching his neck and shoulders. Cali grinned maniacally, counting how many notches she would get to add to her axe by the end, and Guinevere, a head and shoulders above them, drew her massive mace. With a silent prayer it ignited in holy fire, a white flame which Ysabell could feel the heat of from ten feet away.

The two Drudir nearest them turned as they approached. They appeared confused, as if looking for more. Seeing no one else, they drew their weapons and headed to meet the group. Behind them, a Lasairlaoch scuttled to catch up. Its shields bashed together, and its blades raised, ready for the fight.

Nuthionel nodded to Cali. She took off sprinting at the Drudir on the right. As she ran she drew her crossbow and fired a bolt into the forehead of the Drudir on the left. Dropping the crossbow, she grasped her axe with both hands just in time to roll under a demon's great sword. She embedded her axe firmly in its left leg, just below the buttocks, smashing through its armour and knocking it off its feet. A shaft of holy light from the heavens blasted down and slammed the Drudir back to the ground as it tried to rise. It gave Cali enough time to recover. With her axe still stuck in the demon's flesh, her left hand reached to grab the hatchet from her waist. She swung it around hard and fast, cutting the creature's head off in one go.

At the same time, Nuthionel sprinted at the second Drudir, his daggers held in a reverse grip. The crossbow bolt Cali had fired smashed into its forehead as it tried to swing at him, snapping its head back. Nuthionel dove forward, arms bent up at the elbows so both blades plunged through the demon's chest plate. His weight drove them deep and forced the Drudir backwards to the ground.

He rolled clear, but his blades didn't come loose. The Drudir rose to its feet, plucked Nuthionel's daggers from its chest and cast them aside. Foul-smelling smoke streaming from its wounds, it took a step towards Nuthionel, swung in surprise as the shaft of holy fire hit the other Drudir, bathing the battle in light. The distraction let Guinevere take her shot from behind it. The back of its helmet was crushed by a swing of Guin's mace. Holy fire spread from her weapon and seared the helmet, cracking the metal.

Nuthionel grabbed his blades from the ground and joined Cali in a race to Ysabell's aid. She was moving by instinct, much like her fight under the bandit camp, her daggers moved fast, blocking some of the elementals' strikes, dodging others, the Shadows around her making her a hard target to hit.

Cali took advantage of the flame creature's focus on Ysabell, ran in under its legs from its left-hand side. Even the little Halfling had to duck the creature was so low to the ground in comparison to its huge stature. As she passed its legs, her axe in one hand and hatchet in the other, she reached out with both and hacked them hard into the creature's upper leg joints. The Lasairlaoch stumbled to its left and screamed. Ysabell, grateful for the slight respite Cali had brought her, took the chance to step back and draw a breath.

To her left, the remaining Drudir was on its feet and engaging Guin, the priest used her holy shield, granted by prayer, in her left hand, over her as the demon rained mighty blows upon it with its huge sword. The blows would have decapitated a man, but Guin stood firm, her legs planted solidly apart, her great strength yielding nothing to the creature. How she could withstand it Ysabell couldn't imagine, but she knew with Guin's shield using her left hand, she couldn't perform the prayers she normally used in combat.

Nuthionel turned and ran back towards them daggers poised. At the last moment he threw himself into a roll behind the Drudir. Both daggers penetrating their mark behind its knees, exiting the front of its knees, shattering its armour. As it stumbled back, off balance, Nuthionel crouched in its way. Guin dispelled her shield, gathered her mace in both hands and swung a blow that could have felled a tree straight into the creature's face. Its helm shattered, completely crushing what remained of the head inside, its body thrown back over Nuthionel behind its legs. It hit the ground hard, shoulders first; the elf rolled out from under it and grabbed for his daggers even as Guin's mace landed its final blow on the creature's neck line. The blow tore the flattened twisted metal of the helm away from the body, a cloud of smoke plumed from the chest, and it was dead.

Ysabell was drawn back to her own fight as a second Lasairlaoch and a Drudir joined the fight. With a glance, she saw Guinevere running to their aid. Nuthionel's lithe form shot past her; he swung from a large pouch in his cloak his folding short bow. He snapped it into position as he ran, drawing two arrows from the same pouch, the arrows bent as he drew them out; flexible and light, they wouldn't break should he fall or roll on them. Without even slowing he fired two arrows in rapid succession, both hit their marks.

The injured Lasairlaoch lost a shield and a short sword from its left side, as arrows from nowhere plunged through its armour at the wrists. The creature reared back in shock. Ysabell, battling to just to stay alive, wasted no time in capitalising on the distraction. Spinning to her right, her right blade raised up and her left reversed pointing down, she swept them out, the right-hand blade removing the elemental's top hand on its left, her left-hand blade severing the shield hand. Flames spouted from both wrists.

The creature reacted faster than Ysabell could have imagined. Its front left leg shooting out and kicking her hard in the gut, winding her and knocking her back, its right shield hand swung hard, smashing the shield into Ysabell lifting her off her feet. She flew 10 feet or more back from the creature, tried to roll as she hit the ground, came back up onto her feet and collapsed again, unsure of even which direction the Lasairlaoch was in.

Ysabell forced herself to her feet, her lower ribs aching and a deep throbbing in her upper back where she had hit the ground. She still managed to hold onto her daggers. Shaking herself from her daze, she saw the elemental limping towards her again. In sheer rage she screamed at it, "DIE! JUST DIE!" and ran straight for it. Two more arrows slammed into the creature while she did. It swung its head to find the source of the arrows and as it did Ysabell ducked under its right shield arm, rammed both her blades into its flesh above and below a long scale of armour in its torso, and ripped them to the right. A narrow strip of the creatures armour was shredded off its body, leaving its abdomen exposed. Ysabell threw herself clear before the creature had to time to strike her.

A streak of colour she recognised as Nuthionel leapt over her body. His bow bounced on the ground next to her as he drew both daggers and slashed two more strips of the creatures armour loose.

The Lasairlaoch was too fast this time though. It had lost its armour but caught Nuthionel with its shield arm and bashed him to its right, sending him hurtling to smash headlong into a tree. It reared again, screaming, intent on crushing its attackers, but as it dropped to all fours again Guin's mace, swung with both hands and ablaze with holy light, smashed straight through the hole already made in the elemental's armour by her friends.

Holy fire quenched the elemental flames it found, and the mace drove so hard it exited the creature's back. She almost cut it in half, the creature was soon just a smoldering wreck of armour pieces on the ground. There was no time to catch their breath. Cali was fighting for her life against another elemental, and two Drudir were about to join in. Ysabell and the others raced to her aid.

Cali had chopped one of its legs off and shattered the armour on two of its arms and lower abdomen, but she was being pressed. When the Drudir arrived on the right side of the elemental, she raised her axe and charged the Lasairlaoch. Her axe never landed. A glancing blow from the side of a Drudir's blade sent her crashing sideways to the ground. She looked up at the greatsword swinging down from above her.

The sword flew from the demon's hands over her head as a giant blazing white mace smashed through its ribs, crushing the armour and hurling the demon off its feet. The Lasairlaoch was so focused on seeing Cali die tha it looked up too late and gave the shadowy, hazy figure that was Ysabell, her chance. She launched off the back of a Drudir to plunge dual blades into the creature's eyes. Ysabell wrapped her legs around the giant elemental's torso and carved a new hole in its head. Flames spewed out, scorching her arms and face. She slammed to the ground as the Lasairlaoch collapsed in a smoking heap.

She rolled to her side and saw Cali leap to her feet, grab her axe and run to the aid of Nuthionel. The Drudir Ysabell had used as a stepping stone was fighting him in the tree line. It was leaking smoke badly already, but he was struggling, striking no more, focused on dodging the fevered swings of its two hellish blades. Unlike the others, this one wielded two bastard swords. One hit would be enough to cut the elf in half.

Nuthionel threw himself backwards out of the reach of a swinging blade, rolled to his feet, looking shocked to see his foe was gone. In the bushes past him, Ysabell could see a cloud of black smoke rose and a small grinning figure strolled out of it, marking another notch in the haft of her axe. She shook her head, got to her feet and looking around to check on the status of her friends. Guin was casting healing spells as fast as she could, staring at the fast approach of two more Drudir, with two Lasairlaoch behind them.

The companions shook themselves out and prepared for the fight. They were all clearly exhausted, but there was no rest to be had now. If they survived this group, there didn't appear to be any more. Ysabell started to believe they might actually win this.

The demons suddenly stopped, waiting. Ysabell glanced at the others, confused. The ground began to shake beneath them. A huge streak of flames and shadows spread across the grass between them and the demons. As it spread it grew at the edges, curling up into a huge, flaming portal of some sort.

"That's a planar gateway to the abyss!" Guinevere shouted over the howling winds and shaking earth.

Ysabell had read ancient stories about creatures from other planes coming to this world through portals and wiping out the older civilisations. All that remained were the ruins adventurers now raided.

"Nuthionel we cannot face this, we flee or die, trust me on this!" Guin added.

Nuthionel's features darkened, then his face suddenly lit up. "We aren't alone!" he yelled, pointing past her. The door to the tower was open. Several Mages appeared, casting spells to keep the Drudir and elementals at bay.

The companions sprinted for the tower. As soon as they were in, the Mages followed. One of the acolytes waiting at the door slammed it behind them. Two additional blue-robed Mages then casted what Ysabell assumed had to be spells of defence and sealing on it.

To the tower, flee!
Chapter 11

Guin started to thank the Mages who had rescued them, but Nuthionel interrupted her. "Athress! Tell me he lives?"

One of the Mages leaning against the wall, trying to recover after the fight outside, nodded. "Upstairs, exhausted from casting."

Another muttered. "Like us all."

"They butchered so many," the first spoke again. "Where is the City Guard?"

Ysabell and Cali exchanged a worried look. How could they tell these people trapped in here fighting for their lives that the Guards had sealed the district and abandoned it and everyone in it? They stayed silent, Guinevere answered.

"Expect no help from outside. The Guards are struggling as it is just to keep this infestation to this one district. They aren't prepared to deal with summoned creatures such as these." She turned to the first Mage who spoke. "Can you take us to Athress please? Or point the way."

The Mage nodded. He picked up his staff and headed off through an arch before turning left down a long, straight corridor. Ysabell felt something was wrong with this immediately. How was the corridor straight in a round tower? How was it so long? The tower didn't appear that wide and there had been another corridor heading in the opposite direction as well. She turned to Cali and saw a familiar look of concern on her face as she glanced back the way they had come at the other corridor. Cali said nothing as they walked but loosened her axe on her belt. Ysabell knew the halfling's feelings on magic. She noticed with a smirk Cali's hands frequently wandering to the haft of her axe.

They turned off the corridor after about twenty feet into a small round chamber with a spiral staircase. It was stone, but definitely not natural. The steps looked like they had simply grown out of the central column, which itself appeared to be a single cylinder of stone heading up through the ceiling.

Ysabell heard Guinevere and the Mage talking as they started to climb. "..Mage tower riots," the Mage said. "We never discovered who summoned the demons in the twin Cities before their destruction, but the pattern matches. We all saw what happened then. The Mage towers are capable of massive destruction if threatened. So far, we have not activated the defences of this one. The City has encroached too close like in the twin Cities. This park was designed to be five times bigger than this. So, if we activated the dawn star it would destroy only what threatened the tower, well, and the park obviously, well, theoretically at least."

Guinevere interrupted the Mage. "So, you could end this invasion? This tower has the capability to destroy all those demons?"

The Mage, continued. "Oh yes, with ease. The problem is that it would destroy most of the City. At the very least, no one's ever survived its use to report, so it could wipe out the whole city like up North. It can only be a last resort if the Tower is doomed to fall, or the city overrun. Athress has ordered us to try and make contact with the City Guard so we might learn when that point arrives. So far, we have not managed to do that. Something is blocking our attempts to communicate."

"Attempts at communication?" Ysabell asked. "What do you mean?"

Guinevere looked surprised by Ysabell finding her voice. A few hours earlier she would have still been a little intimidated around her and Cali, and certainly around a strange Mage, but the fights outside had inspired a confidence and certainty in herself she had lost back in Farrowfields. The overwhelming new life she had chosen was beginning to feel more normal to her.

The Mage nodded. "Yes, we use astral projection."

She stared at him blankly.

"An iMage of their selves is projected elsewhere and can speak and listen as if they are physically there," Guin explained.

"Yes, but since the attack started, not one of us has been able to," said the blue-robed Mage. "It's like a shield or barrier was put up around the district, and none of us can get our projection through. Athress has been trying since the attack started last night. He's gotten close and from what I heard from one the others, he seems to have found the cause of the barrier. If we can't get through it soon, we have to assume the demons have made it out of the district and that we will have to activate the dawn star." He looked miserable. "A hard choice. Do nothing and risk losing the City, or chose to kill every man, woman and child in a massive unknown radius and hope it was necessary."

Endren led them out of the staircase on to another floor. Ysabell looked out a window to see they were far above the city. The tower was maybe ten stories high, the tallest building in the City by far, but the view from the window suggested they were much higher than that. At least twice as high, yet the stairs they had walked up no more than twenty steps.

She turned to see if Cali had noticed. The Halfling was looking abnormally pale as she too stopped to stare out the window.

Nuthionel poked her. "Come on," he whispered.

Guinevere nodded to their guide to lead on. They traversed multiple winding corridors, and up another short staircase into a huge circular chamber lined with windows and doors out onto a balcony that wound around the tower. Lecterns, chairs, tables, and shelves were everywhere. Every flat surface had grimoires and spell books open, tired, dishevelled Mages poring over them.

On a large dais in the centre of the room an old human Mage sat on a throne-like chair at a circular table. Twelve other Mages sat around the table with him, engaged in a serious discussion. Ysabell could overhear their argument.

"Phantasmal flow plots show a widening of a crack is possible," one of the Mages there said. "It would take a weakening of the source, but we could break through."

Another tall, powerful-looking man with skin as black as Ysabell had ever seen interjected. "Irrelevant! The portal below must be stopped. We know what horrors can come from it. It must be closed, but we cannot close it from this side without an astronomical release of energy. The Dawn Star is the only means we have of doing that and even then, it may not be enough!" He glanced at the elderly Mage in the large chair. "We have no choice!"

The old Mage in the throne raised a hand. "Enough! We cannot bicker back and forth. Unless you have another suggestion of how to close the damn portal, then Vaaldreth is correct. The Dawn Star is our only option. I lament the loss of life, but if sacrificing a few thousand lives saves a million, then that is the price we must pay!" He slumped in his chair. He looked weary beyond measure and Ysabell had never seen a human as old. He must have been over one hundred.

"Athress!" Nuthionel broke from the group and ran toward the dais. The old Mage in charge smiled and stood to welcome Nuthionel.

"Well, well, I should have known you'd be in the middle of this," Athress said, managing a tired grin. "Never could keep yourself out of trouble, could you?"

Nuthionel walked up the steps to reach him and shrugged. He placed his hands on the Mage's shoulders. "It is good to find you alive old friend. Tell us what we can do to help, and we will get it done."

Athress' shoulders sagged, and his face appeared even more aged, the initial happiness at seeing Nuthionel wiped away. "You should not have come. There is really only one thing we can do at this point. That portal out there threatens the entire kingdom and the others around it. Armies will pour from it, armies of demons and demon lords compared to which Drudir are but foot soldiers. We cannot allow it to remain open. But it is held open from the other side. To close it from this side, we may end up destroying the entire city too."

Athress paused for a moment, his eyes lowered

He gazed at Nuthionel, the elf's face frozen in horror. "I cannot see another way 'Thion. I wish I could. I would sacrifice myself a hundred times rather than do this, but I see no alternative. We'd need an army to go through the portal to close it from the other side," His voice was almost pleading, as if begging for another solution.

Ysabell stepped up onto the dais next to Nuthionel, her hand coming to rest on her teacher's shoulder. "But it can be closed from the other side?"

Behind her, Ysabell could hear Cali laugh and comment to Guinevere, "Why haven't we travelled with her before now? She'll get us in more trouble than I do!"

Nuthionel turned to Ysabell. "Do you know what you are suggesting Ysabell?"

"It's simple logic Nuthionel. The solution we have right now is killing ourselves and everyone in a massive radius. The end result is the portal closed, us dead, and half the kingdom dead with us. If we could go through the portal and close it, the end result would be the portal closed and us dead, maybe ten thousand others' lives spared. Either way, nothing changes for us, we are dead regardless. What have we got to lose trying?"

She looked around at the others, her face perfectly calm. She faced the old Mage.

"Well? Am I correct?" Athress looked up.

"You are correct. This, this is possible. But it will be no easy feat. If you manage it..." He looked off into the distance for a moment. He looked directly at Ysabell, she felt a shiver in her spine at the intensity of his gaze: "There are far worse things than death in some of the planes. Things you cannot imagine. Be sure of your decision." Ysabell looked him square in the eye.

"It's better to die fighting than sit and wait to die in some spell."

Guinevere and Cali stepped up onto the dais,

"So Athress, you coming with us or you finally too old?" Cali spoke with her usual deference, or complete lack of it. "You don't want to miss this one, travelling across the planes into hell? They'll be singing songs about us!" She grinned.

Guinevere turned to Ysabell. "Well, I couldn't have picked a nicer bunch to go to hell with. That drink will have to wait."

Nuthionel looked at Athress; "So, what do we need to do? Can we just run straight through the portal? Is there any way to know what we will run into on the other side? It will be a short trip if these armies you speak of are standing in formation on the other side."

"That is why we couldn't take this course, Mage's power is immense but short lived, without rest we would be powerless. One of the reasons I was trying to reach the City Guard. A squad of well-armed troops would be able to protect a few Mages long enough to shut it down. But we are out of time."

Athress waved to the tall, dark-skinned Mage who was arguing for the use of the Dawn Star earlier: "Vaaldreth, what can you do to ease their passage?"

Vaaldreth walked over them, his pointed beard and long moustache making him look evil. "Not to fear." He regarded each of them. "The way will be cleared, I and some of the others will help you fight to the portal. Once we reach it, we will send a spell ahead of you into it, and all you will find on the other side is the incinerated remains of whatever was gathering there. But it will not be clear for long. A portal like this one has not been opened in many centuries, at least on this world. The demons will have sensed it, they will be coming in great numbers to try and reach it. As soon as you are through, you must find the source of the portal's power. I wish I could be more specific, but no one has even seen what that is."

His face darkened, "At least, no one has ever survived to report back."

Now I Lay me Down to Sleep
Chapter 12

The Mages showed them to a bedroom, with three sets of bunks in it. It had belonged to some of the Mage acolytes who didn't make it back to the tower during the attack. A large fire burned in the grate on one wall. The beds stood in rows against the opposite.

Nuthionel lay quietly on one of the upper bunks, staring at the roof above him, tracing the grain in the beams of darkened and aged wood that crossed it. This was not how he had planned things. He should never have brought the others, always they followed him, always they trusted in him and now he had led them to their deaths. He knew he had lost his focus, had been affected by his personal feelings for his mentor and surrogate father Athress, he had abandoned reason and brought them all to this. Worse, he knew Ysabell was here for the same reason, her feeling for him as a father figure, mentor, had led her to follow him here.

They must succeed, at any cost, but if there was cost he could pay to ensure the others returned. He would pay it and gladly, if that was what the Gods wanted of him to let his friends live, then that is what the Gods would get. He'd never been one for prayer, never aligned himself with a god or goddess. He knew little of the Gods of his own people, his parents killed by humans when he was still young. Then the human raiders killed singlehandedly by a young Mage.

He looked around; Cali and Guinevere were asleep already. Ysabell sat by the fire alone, staring into the flames lost in her thoughts. He felt the need to try and explain to her why coming to find Athress was so important to him. He needed her to understand if only, so he could justify what they all now faced. He had led her here. Probably to her death. He owed her an explanation. He rose from his bed and joined her at the fire.

"Thinking of the past or future?"

Ysabell didn't move her gaze from the flames. "Past, probably not the best time to be making plans for a future,"

"Want to talk?" he asked. "I feel the need to speak."

Ysabell nodded her consent.

"First time I met Athress I was a kid. I knew I was dead, my parents, our neighbours, all dead, I was the last one surviving. There was no one left to help me. I was just a kid. Then a voice, out of the trees, a shadow in Mage's robes, a glowing staff in his hands..."

"'Leave the boy be and be on your way,' he said.

The raiders turned, seemed to assess their chances: the Mage walked forward towards them. When he cleared the shadows, I could see he was young, only in his twenties. The leader of the raiders laughed at him. 'Are you stupid Mage?' He turned to the others. 'Kill the idiot, his staff will be worth something.' He turned back to me, drew a dagger and said, 'I'm going to slice out your pretty little almond eyes and leave you out here to starve boy.'"

"I took a deep breath and waited for death, but it never came, lightning flew through the air, fire erupted from the ground, the elements rose and blew, roared and attacked, all at the bidding of this human Mage. To my seven-year-old elven eyes, he looked like a god. The raiders attacked, the Mage tore into them. I was blinded by the brightness and terrified of the explosions, just covered my face and crouched down. Scared witless. Then it was over. A voice, a quiet voice called:

'Boy? Can you understand me? They are dead. Please, I need your help, can you sew wounds?'"

"I looked up, all was quiet, flames still flicked on one of the blackened and charred corpses. Past them lay the Mage, his grey robes, soaked in blood from his side. I went to help him. As the Mage had saved me, I had to try save him."

He looked across at Ysabell, she was watching him now, sadness in her eyes and understanding.

"He raised me, taught me everything I know, made me what I am. I owe him everything."

Ysabell reached across and took his hand.

"I'm glad we could help you come to his aid. Whatever happens tomorrow, do not second guess or feel guilty for bringing us here. I have no desire to be anywhere else. No regrets."

<><><>

With that, Nuthionel rose and headed back to lie down and sleep. Ysabell did not. She sat staring at the fire. It made more sense now. Nuthionel would risk everything to save them man who raised him, saved him. *'Funny thing is, I see Nuthionel as that person to me. What would I do in his shoes? Probably the exact same.'*

Tomorrow they would march through the portal and fight through the gods knew how many demons to try and reach the power source. How would they survive? If only there was another way.

Ysabell started to strip off her armour, bracers first, she held them and looked at them. *'Magical, mysterious. They make me practically invisible in the shadows. With the new dark armour, I could probably sneak past anything. How much my life has changed, how much I've changed. I..'*

She froze staring at the bracers.

'Could it be that simple, could I save Nuthionel and the others?'

Her mind made up in an instant Ysabell rose and strapped her bracers back on. She didn't have much time. She grabbed a sheet of parchment and a pencil, a short letter of explanation was the least she owed her father. When she was done, she sealed it in an envelope and laid it on the table. A quick rumMage through their supplies resulted in a canteen of water and a coiled rope. She stood at the bedroom door, took one last look at her comrades and concentrated. The shadows rose up around her, and she quietly slipped out the door. She slunk through the corridors back to the stairs down. Halfway down she turned off onto a lower floor. Closed doors lined it. Creeping silently along the hallway she kept going until she found a room with an open door and no occupant.

Ysabell swiftly closed the door behind her and checked that the window opened; it did. Looking out, it was a lot lower than the previous floor she had been on. But still maybe three stories high. Hopefully the rope would reach. One end tied to the bed, she threw the other end out the window. It didn't quite reach, she'd have a drop at the end, but less than the height of two men. *For the best really, unlikely a demon will climb back up then.*

She clambered out the window, it was small even for her, an awkward exit. Though it put her mind at ease. *No bloody way a demon is getting in this window.* She grasped the rope as she let go of the window frame, slowly she descended, her hands moving from knot to knot, her feet against the wall of the tower. *Please don't let anything see me, I'm a sitting duck up here.*

Once on the ground, she scanned the area around her. It was clear, most of the demons were gathering out the front of the tower, near the portal. Satisfied she was still unseen, she ran for the trees. She moved in away from the tree line to ensure she was hidden from view in the darker shadows. Only then did she stop to take stock and plan her next move. She had to get to the portal unseen. With demons still coming through it, there was no chance of approaching from the front. But from behind... *Can you go through a portal from behind? Crap, I should have asked more questions earlier. Fuck it. Only one way to find out.*

She set off swiftly, lightly running around the clearing until she was near the portal. The night was cloudy so little or no moonlight lit the clearing, but the portal gave off a light itself from the flames it was wreathed in. The rear of it was clear of demons mostly, bar a single Drudir was standing there. Still as a statue, facing the trees. Now was the real test, as they didn't see with eyes, would her shadows have any effect? If not, she could be in for a serious fight. There was no time for that. Any delay could result in more demons coming. The clouds parted, and moonlight flooded the portal. It looked different; it was smaller, its colouring had changed and it was flickering. She wasn't sure what it meant for the portal, but for her it meant the Demons were distracted.

Ysabell took a deep breath, if he saw her she intended to be through the portal before he could react, even he followed her, she might have time to hide on the other side before he caught up. She watched the sky, a large cloud moved across and covered the moon once again. As it did she rose from her crouched position and sprinted straight at the portal. The Drudir's head turned at the noise of her feet, his hands flew to his sword, but she was past him. She didn't look back and dove forward into the portal.

For a moment she thought it hadn't worked. Her body crashed onto the ground. She had expected a journey of some kind through the planes. The ground was hard, stone. Ysabell looked down and saw slabs of cut stone beneath her. She was through. Swiftly she looked around. Demons were teeming all around below her. She was on a raised dais, the portal behind her. It looked like some kind of pyramid, and she was at the top. Keeping low she scuttled around behind the portal. A small stone crypt or mausoleum type building stood there, it had a single entrance, surrounded by creepy looking carvings. Dashing through it she found a stairway leading down.

It was pitch black inside. Reaching into the small pack at her waist, Ysabell took out her lantern, clipped it to her armour and lit it. She dropped the thin mesh flap over it, so the light was dim, barely enough to see by. A quick check of her daggers and she started her trek downwards. The portal sat atop this structure, between two huge metal columns. They must draw their power from something down below. She would find it and somehow break it. She had no plans for what to do after that, but she didn't think getting back to her own plane was going to be an option. But she would make damn sure she wasn't taken alive. She would complete her task then wait for the demons to come. She would fight until she was killed.

Strange I'm so calm about that. She crept down the stairs to an empty, dusty stone hallway. There were tracks in the dust, several beings had wandered these halls recently, and at least one was humanoid. Clear boot prints stood out among the claw prints in the dust. *Perhaps they have human allies.* All the tracks headed left. So she did too. Despite initial fears that the place might be like a maze, like the catacombs under Cloch Dubh, there were no options to turn off the path. Each floor had but one winding path leading her, through many twists and turns, to the next stars down. *How deep does this go? I'm far below the ground level outside already.*

About seven floors down, she saw her first signs of life, or death. Several smouldering remains of demons scattered in the hallway in front of her. They couldn't have been there for more than an hour or two. *Someone else was here, and they were killing demons. Who?* More wary now she continued on, occasionally finding more remains. Nine floors down, at least six of them were below ground level. There was vibration in the stone down here; it was slight, but it was constant. Ysabell was unsure what it was, but fairly confident it was something to do with whatever was powering this place.

It was eerie walking the dusty, dark hallways. The air had no movement and felt stale and lifeless. The whole place seemed lifeless, apart from the subtle hum from below it was completely silent too. *Not sure if I'd actually prefer a few demons in my way, just to give this place some life...* She had limited time, when the others awoke it wouldn't take them long to figure out what she'd done and try to follow her. That would make all this pointless. She had to get to the power source and shut it off before that happened.

The humming was getting louder, she had moved down another flight of stairs. The vibrations were everywhere now, no more tracks on the floor, the dust was practically dancing beneath her feet. It was loud too. Not suddenly, but it had grown in volume slowly as she had come down, getting louder and louder, until it was no longer a background noise. There was something else, an oppressive, heaviness to the darkness. Like it wasn't merely the absence of light, it was the opposite of light.

Something is watching me

The thought came unbidden, but as soon as she had it, she knew it was right. That feeling of eyes upon you. She couldn't tell from where. But she was definitely not alone. She concentrated and made sure her cloak of shadows was still around her, then slowly and as silently as she could she eased her daggers from their harness. Reaching to her chest she suddenly lifted the mesh, bathing the hall in front of her in light. A shape stood in the corridor ahead. A man... but there was something odd. His eyes were completely black, no whites, no iris, just solid black. His skin was a greyish-green tinged, dull, dead looking. He was dressed in flowing black robes; they seemed to be the source of the darkness. The anti-light. It was hard to make out his shape due to them. Only his head was clear.

He raised a limb, an arm she presumed, and pointed it at her. Ysabell wasn't about to find out what it could do. She hurled herself to the side, rolling on her shoulder. She carried through back onto her feet and sprinted at him, an explosion shook the corridor. A blast of dark light came from behind her where she had been standing. *Please let the lantern stay lit.* As she got close he twirled to one side, his robes raised, their darkness fell over everything, even her light. She wasn't sure where he was, her light wasn't doing much good against the darkness he seemed to emit. Another blast shook the corridor, this one she felt heat streak by her head to head the wall behind. Ysabell dived forward and rolled back to her feet. *So he can see me, but I can't see him. Either he's shit at aiming or my bracers are making me hard to hit.*

Then it hit her.

To see in the light, you needed shadow to give things contrast, so everything wasn't just bright too bright to see. What if to see in his darkness he needed light to give a contrast. Her mind made up, Ysabell doused her lantern. Plunging the corridor into utter darkness. She could see nothing, and by the stumbling to her left, it seemed neither could he. She heard the scuffling of a body hitting a wall softly trying to find its way. That was all she needed. Estimating his height from her mind and trying to remember how far she was from that wall. Ysabell twisted towards the sound, ducking as she did. A blast of heat flew over her head as he reacted to the sound. That provided her distance and she lunged, burying her dagger in flesh. An unearthly scream rang through the hallway. She jumped back and fumbled in the dark for her flint. The corridor lit up instantly. Against the wall the strange looking man was leaning, black looking blood seeping between his fingers where they clutched at his chest. The Darkness coming from his robes had dissipated.

I'm alone here, can't afford to take chances.

She stepped forward and finished him, her dagger sinking deep into his eye socket. She stepped back and just stood, catching her breath and trying to come to grips with what just happened. Not least the fact that she had stabbed a dying man in the eye. If he was a man. *The skin, the blood, the darkness and power, maybe he was a different sort of demon. It's not like I know much about them.* She cleaned her blades and sheathed them, then turned away and continued her search.

Less than a hundred paces on she found the corridor's end. Two huge ornate doors stood in front of her, wooden with brass inlaid designs. Swirls, drawings and some language she couldn't read covered the doors from the ground to the top near the ceiling. Ysabell steeled herself, wrapped herself in shadow and pushed the great doors inwards.

They made no sound as they easily pushed open. It was as if they were light as feathers. If she thought the doors were impressive, what lay beyond was far more so. The room was huge, a great hall. At intervals along the walls were metal staves, topped with crystal orbs. Lightning leapt between them, feeding up great metal ropes to the ceiling. A giant crystalline inverted dome filled the centre of the ceiling. It was filled with crackling lightning.

Ysabell traced the cables back in the other direction. They were being fed from a collection of similar staves around a dais in the middle of the room. Upon it was a plinth. She approached the dais to see what was inside the circle of staves feeding their power.

"NO!" Ysabell froze. "It can't be..."

Into the Maw of Hell
Chapter 13

As dawn began to break, Nuthionel arose. It was time to prepare. He sat up and looked around, Guinevere was still snoring, Cali was already sharpening her axe. There was no sign of Ysabell. *Must be gone for food or something.* He got up and dressed, then walked across the room to their armour and weapons.

Fuck.

Ysabell's armour and weapons were gone. Her small strap on pack that carried her lantern, oil stone and flint too. He spun around and scanned the room, there was no sign of the equipment anywhere.

"Cali. Ysabell, was she here when you woke?" he asked, apprehension in his voice.

"No. Haven't seen her, must have been up well early," the halfling responded.

Nuthionel swept from the room without another word. *She couldn't have, she wouldn't have. It would be stupid. Why? Why would she even think of something like that?* He raced down the corridor and burst into the large room at the top of the tower. It was in chaos. Mages shouting at each other, the air thick with fear and panic. He scanned the room for Athress. He wasn't there, but in his chair sat the black giant Vaaldreth from last night.

"Vaaldreth?" he called. "Where is Athress? We have a problem, a big one."

The Mage turned to look at him, concern and anxiety in his eyes.

"Bigger than you know." The Mage's voice was deep and resonant. It was stressed and frustrated too. "She wasn't the only one with the bright idea to sneak in alone. Athress is missing. He left a note for you."

"What? How?" Nuthionel came to a dead stop. He shook his head. "No, they wouldn't have, Ysabell wouldn't plan something with a stranger she'd just met, and

Athress would never put someone so young in that kind of danger. There must be another explanation." He looked at Vaaldreth for some confirmation. He had to be right.

"I agree." The Mage's voice was cold and emotionless. "That's what makes it such a problem. They probably went separately and unaware of each other."

Cold realisation hit Nuthionel. The Mage watched his face for a moment then stood and roared above the din.

"Silence!" His voice was commanding and firm. It brooked no argument. The room fell quiet, all eyes on Vaaldreth. "You know what to do. The same thing you've been doing for days. Fight, keep the demons at bay. Find a way to get communication out." He looked at Nuthionel again. "We will accompany the mercenaries to the portal immediately. They WILL close the portal and if possible bring back the girl and Athress. We must hold the tower. We will contain this threat."

With that he strode across the room, joined Nuthionel and they strode from the room to gather the others.

Back in the groups chamber Nuthionel explained to the others what had happened and that they would be going in to try and salvage the mission. Cali and Guinevere had no questions. They understood the gravity of the situation. In minutes all three were ready, they joined Vaaldreth on the way down to the tower door. No jokes and laughter now. For once even Cali seemed serious.

Vaaldreth broke the tense silence. "During the night a lot more reinforcements came through the portal. As they were not attacking the tower, I let most of the Mages rest, so they would be ready for today. I will aid them, and we will clear the way to the portal. Once the path is clear, you run for it. Don't stop to fight. There is no time."

The others nodded. They reached the tower entrance and found a dozen or more Mages waiting at the door. All of them older, senior looking Mages. Men and women of great power. Sombre and serious, focusing on the task ahead. As they approached, Vaaldreth gave a nod and two of the Mages stepped forward, dispelling the wards and protections on the doors. They swung the doors open.

A crashing wave of noise hit their ears, the screams of elementals and demons filling the air. Looking past the Mages, a wave of despair washed over the companions. More than forty or fifty of the creatures had come through last night and were waiting between them and the portal. There was no way they would even reach it.

Still, Vaaldreth seemed unconcerned. He stepped forward through the door. Four other older, red-robed Mages followed him through. He was chanting his first spell as he passed the arch. Dozens of spears flew at him, but the Mages accompanying him cast shield spells that diverted them all into the walls of the tower. The Drudir then began to charge, the companions moved to help but a Mage they recognised as the door keeper from the previous day stopped them.

"Save your strength for the far side of that gateway; you'll be in hell soon and there will be plenty to fight there."

Vaaldreth raised his staff above his head and swept it down. As he did, a glowing spark of amber flame leapt from the tip. It shot skyward and grew as it rose, then, like the breath of a dragon, it swept down and over the demons and elementals alike in the clearing. It blasted everything in its path. Some of the demons disintegrated right there, others were thrown aside violently.

Vaaldreth wasn't finished yet. The other four Mages moved up to stand beside him. All of them chanted together, the base of their staffs slamming to the ground at the same time. A crack appeared before their feet, spreading forward at an incredible pace, widening until a yawning chasm opened across the clearing. Molten rock far below the surface illuminated the crevice, spewing smoke and flames up into the sky. Demons and Elementals alike tumbled into it, then, with a wave of his hand, Vaaldreth sealed the earth again. The gap narrowed until the earth re-joined, leaving only a scorched scar across the surface where it had been.

Two of the Mages with him stepped out beyond him while he leaned on his staff to catch his breath. Both moved their hands as if they were drawing an imaginary shape in the air. It wasn't imaginary for long. A huge human-shaped creature formed in the air. Pieces of the earth clawed their way up the ghostly apparition, wrapping it in skin made of dirt and rock. With a final blast of magic, the two Mages morphed the creature into what appeared to be solid rock.

The creature lumbered forward, looked around before charging straight at a group of Lasairlaoch which had escaped Vaaldreth's wrath. The flame elementals attacked it from all sides, but their weapons bounced off the rock elemental's stony skin. Its giant fist crushed one six-armed elemental from its head down with ease. Flames exploded from it, leaving a steaming heap of mangled metal armour and weapons on the earth beneath it.

Nuthionel watched in awe as the Mages' creation tore the creatures apart, in some cases limb from limb. Then they split up, two Mages on the left, two on the right and Vaaldreth in the middle. They started chanting again, staffs held vertically before them... Waving his hands in a fast, circular motion, he called a small globe of flame into being between his hands and shot it straight at the portal.

Nuthionel turned to his companions, wondering what was happening now. They all appeared equally baffled. Vaaldreth's voice caught their attention: "Get ready to run!"

Nuthionel exchanged one last look with his companions and headed toward it. The dark surface of the portal rippled suddenly, as something came through. Some twenty feet above them, a long, black, green and red snout pushed through.

"A Demon Lord!" Guinevere screamed over the noise of the battle. "We cannot fight this 'Thion!"

They had many names across the planes, in this world they had no name, as they had been seen only once on this plane, centuries before. They were all but forgotten except to those who studied magic or the priesthood.

Vaaldreth screamed "GO NOW! We will handle this!"

They ran straight at the creature, it wasn't fully through the portal yet. Nuthionel glanced back once and saw Vaaldreth collapse, he had spent all the power he had to clear their path. But Mages were pouring out of the tower now, and other were casting from the windows and balconies at this new threat. Several young acolytes picked up Vaaldreth's limp form and carried it in. *I hope he makes it.* With that he dove into the portal after Cali and Guin.

The blast of heat told Nuthionel he was in hell. Guinevere grabbed him and pulled him to his feet. In front of them, no more than twenty feet away, was an army, a horde, *What the hell do you call that many?* Thousands of demonic creatures. Nuthionel had no idea what most of them were. Some Drudir were amongst them but most of the demons were huge winged creatures, red and black in colour, bipedal, horns, huge muscular arms and legs, each bearing an enormous sword. They were of varying sizes, but all looked a lot tougher than what they had faced before.

Dozens of charred and smoking demon's corpses already littered the ground around the portal. Vaaldreth's spell had worked well, but there was no shortage remaining. Nuthionel's eyes scanned the landscape around them, trying to find what was powering the portal. He gasped, and then groaned.

"It's underneath," he said. "In this construction."

Cali shouted from behind the Portal. They rushed around to her, a crypt like structure stood there. Horrific scenes were etched into the stonework around a large door. What looked like blood was seeping from the carvings of tortured humans. Knowing they could be seen at any moment, Nuthionel shoved the door, it swung open easily, the trio ducked inside.

Guinevere slammed the door closed behind them. Then spun to the others.

"A bar, something!" She screamed. "We have to jam the door now!"

It was too late; even as she said it, she was thrown violently forward as the door splintered in pieces. A huge red and black skinned demon ducked its horned head under the threshold. Its hooves echoing through the hallway as it stepped in. This close to the portal a battle would alert more, Nuthionel grabbed Guinevere and dragged her to her feet as he turned and ran down the stairs before them.

They stumbled off the stair, Cali swinging to face the demon immediately on reaching the floor. Her battle axe spun in one hand, her hatchet twirled in the other. Nuthionel shoved Guin past her, then turned to stand beside her. He snapped out his bow and drew several arrows. The winged demon was restricted on the stairway. *It can't fight properly on the stairs. It mustn't reach us.*

"Don't let it reach flat ground!" He called to the others. "It dies on the steps!"

With that he let an arrow fly, his aim was true, the shaft sank into the creature's right thigh. More arrows followed in quick succession as he tried to slow its descent. He could hear Guinevere's voice chanting behind him. A wave of light washed over him, it felt refreshing, lending speed and strength to his arms. It continued on and struck the demon differently. The creature was knocked back as if struck a blow. As it stumbled Cali took her chance and ran forward clearing the steps two at a time, She swung her axe at the cloven feet before her. But the demon was faster, it lashed out catching her in the midriff. She flew through the air, crashing into Nuthionel. The two of them landed hard in a crumpled heap on the ground.

The demon used its advantage, rising and clearing the steps into the hallway they stood in. It was wider here, easily as wide as two carts and as high as a man and a half. The demon's head was almost at the roof even so. It towered over them. Roaring in rage, huge muscular arms raised the broadsword to swing. But the blow never fell. Guinevere stepped in over her comrades and grasped the demon's wrists. Her arms swelled with the strain, muscles bulged, and her face grew red. But the demon couldn't drive through her despite his great strength.

Cali swiftly rolled out from under the two titans, retrieved her axe, Nuthionel got to his knees, but before he could stand, Cali used him to launch upwards, her foot slammed into his shoulder. As she rose she swung her axe hard, severing the demon's right arm across its bicep. The arm fell and landed by Nuthionel, Cali came crashing to the ground beside it. The demon screamed in pain and pulled back from Guinevere. With her sudden advantage, the towering priestess drew her long-handled mace and swung it hard in both hands. The heavy bladed end of the mace crushed the demon's skull in a single blow, splattering the walls in blood, brains and shards of bone. Its carcass crashed to the ground.

Nuthionel sank to his knees again breathing a sigh of relief. The body didn't smoke or burn or vaporise. *Must be as we are already in hell. This is where its body belongs.* Cali picked herself up and promptly fell over again, still dazed. Guinevere came to join them and sat on the ground cradling her mace.

"That was close!" she panted. "We can't beat those things 'Thion. Another one could kill us all, we got lucky that time. We have to stop them reaching our plane."

"The city would fall in a day." Nuthionel agreed. "The world would follow. We need to find Athress and Ysabell. They may have found out what powers the portal by now." He looked down the hallway to the left of the stairs into the darkness. "If they still live."

Crystal Rain

Chapter 14

She rushed forward to aid Athress, strapped to the plinth inside the circle of staves, he looked close to death. Blood was seeping from wounds all over his body. Strange crystals were embedded in his flesh. They looked as though they had been stabbed into him. The lightning power was coming from them. Slowly his head turned to the side to see her. There was great pain in his eyes, His visage was the face of torment. Ysabell rushed forward to help him.

"No!" he croaked, coughing, blood wetting his lips. "Stay back, the power will kill you." He gasped for breath, straining with effort. "You must kill me. That will seal the portal. The only way. "

"Not a chance Athress." she retorted defiantly. "Nuthionel would never forgive me. There has to be a way to save you!"

"The power drain is too much." He lay back again, breathing seemed difficult for him. "If you step in here it will kill you, With the portal open, I am stuck, and I am the key to closing the portal. There is no other option."

Ysabell shook her head. *No, there had to be another way.* She couldn't return without Athress and face Nuthionel. Especially knowing their past. She'd rather try to pull him clear anyway, whatever the risk. It was strange, like when she had lay dying on the roadside after the fight with that first Drudir. She felt at peace, no regrets. For the first time in her life she felt she had a role to play. She wasn't just existing, she was living. She had a purpose. If it all ended here, so be it. It would still be better than living to be a wrinkled, old barmaid, married to some village drunk back in Farrowfields.

She looked around desperately; there must be something, there had to be another way. *What would Nuthionel do?* The Orbs were alive with lightning, if she got too close she could be caught like Athress. It would take forever to break them all, there were too many. Her eyes rose to stare at the dome above them. Drawing all that power away to the portal.

'The power drain is too much!' he said. *What if I can stop it? Before pulling him out? And close the damn portal at the same time!*

She had it. She stepped back from the dais wondering if it was even possible. She'd have to be quick, incredibly quick, or she'd kill him anyway. *Not going to know anymore just staring at it.* Ysabell drew her non-magical blades and carefully weighed them in her hands. Then looking up at the Dome again, she leaned back and hurled the blades one after the other, straight up. As they flew she ran up onto the dais, knocked two staves out of her way and grabbed Athress. The pain hit her like an avalanche, the orbs around the dais feeding off her life force. Through the pain she heard the shattering of the crystal dome above.

The pain stopped as abruptly as it started. Without a moment's pause, she hauled Athress bodily from the dais and the two of them rolled off onto the floor. Shards of crystal rained from the ceiling, bolts of lightning leapt between them. It was breath taking. *The whole building shook. Hope that's the portal closing. Hope Athress survives to tell me how to get out of this mess.* Even as the thought crossed her mind, Athress' breathing grew more ragged. He had to have lost a lot of blood. Ysabell didn't know what to do. Remove the crystals and bandage? Or leave them in to plug the holes? She was no healer.

Footsteps... Running. Several people... Or demons.

She forced herself up and concentrated on her bracers, the chill of the shadows a welcome feeling. Ysabell turned to face the door, ready to face what came. *Guess we both die anyway. At least we finished our task.* Tears welled in her eyes. This wasn't the end she had imagined. A group came running through the door and stopped, Ysabell realised they were staring at the crystals raining down on the dais. They hadn't noticed her yet.

"Bloody hellfire what's that?" Cali's voice rang out across the room.

Ysabell couldn't believe it, a wave of relief washed over her. Crashing into her, she collapsed to her knees as the tension, the fear and adrenaline of the last few hours drained from her. She couldn't speak, but through tear-filled eyes she saw the trio of friends running to them. Nuthionel took her arm and helped her up. Guinevere wasted no time in aiding Athress. One hand glowing with holy light she held it over each wound after she removed the crystals one by one. Ysabell watched over Nuthionel's shoulder. Athress' breathing eased and some colour returned to his face as Guinevere worked.

Pull yourself together! We have to get out of here. Ysabell pulled away from Nuthionel and smiled a thank you.

"Guin?" Ysabell asked, "How is he?"

"He'll live." She replied. "He's lost a lot of blood and is weak. I've stopped the bleeding, but it will take time for his body to recover."

"The one thing we don't have." Nuthionel's voice was calm but Ysabell could hear the concern in it. "One of the demons followed us in here, its dead, but if more came after we'll have a fight on our hands. A fight we might not be able to win."

Ysabell looked around, none of them seemed to have realised the biggest problem, or they just weren't saying it.

"We've closed the portal." She said. "Where would we flee to? We are trapped."

Her eyes dropped to Athress, lying on the cold floor, sleeping or unconscious. He seemed to be genuinely resting now. Guinevere had worked miracles on him. He still looked thinner and weaker, and scars had formed all over him where the crystals had been. Guinevere had stacked them all in a neat pile to one side. "Unless he can do something." Ysabell looked up at the others, her eyes searching for some hope. "Could he? Make a portal or something?" "We won't know until he wakes." Nuthionel answered. "Even if it is something he is capable of, he may be too weak now." He looked up at Guin and Cali. "We need to prepare for a fight. We must not be taken by surprise."

The light in the room was fading as the crystal orbs around the perimeter lost their charge and faded. Ysabell took out her flint to relight her lantern. Before she could, Guinevere recited a simple prayer, causing her mace to light up with holy fire again. The glow gave far more light than the little lantern. *Great for seeing, going to make us easy to see too though.*

Guinevere returned to Athress, trying to wake him, they needed him to be able to walk. This room had only the one door. It was a death trap if they were found here. Nuthionel helped Ysabell search for her thrown daggers among the shattered crystals scattered across the dais.

"What happened?" He asked. "How was he hurt?"

"I found him here when I got here." Ysabell picked up a dagger as she spoke. "He told me the energy drain would kill us both if I tried to move him."

"Here's the other," Nuthionel answered. He joined her and handed her the second dagger. "So how did you get him out?"

"I smashed the energy collector in the ceiling so there'd be no drain." Her confidence growing as she told him. "Threw the daggers at it, grabbed him and rolled away before the shards landed."

Nuthionel's eyebrows rose in surprise. Ysabell glowed. His opinion meant so much to her. She had made him proud. Nuthionel nodded at her in silent approval. She could see he was impressed. Cali was listening in too. She wasn't as subtle as Nuthionel.

"Didn't think ye had the tonkers. Sneaking off like that, going to the hells alone, saving Athress? You've balls like a beòthail dragon!"

No idea what that is, but I think she's impressed too. Ysabell never felt so proud. Nuthionel was like the father she had always wanted. She craved his praise, his approval. Though she was still worried. Her plan was to prevent the others from having to enter. Now they were all stuck here anyway and Athress too. She looked over and saw that Guinevere had Athress on his feet. The old Mage was looking shaken and weak, but he beckoned Ysabell over.

"Do you realise what might have happened?" His voice was weak but stern. "Smashing that dome with that much energy stored in it? Do you have any idea what it might have done?"

"No. I. I just." Ysabell stumbled over her words.

"Me neither," Athress said with a grin. "I was so worried about what 'might' happen, I never thought of the obvious solution. Thank you. I won't forget what you did for me. Now, we must get out of here. I can open a temporary portal back to our world for us. But not down here. The Orbs here would drain any power I use I'm afraid."

It felt like the weight of the world was lifted off Ysabell's shoulders. *He can do it, we can get home. All of us.* She looked excitedly at the others. The mood had certainly brightened. Except for Athress. His face was grave.

"We shall have to be outside to do it, once I start, we will be spotted." His eyes moved from face to face. "You will have to defend me while I cast. When we go through it, you will have to hold it against anything that would follow until I close it again."

Guinevere was the first to react.

"What? Out there?" Her voice shook with disbelief. "Have you seen what is outside? There are thousands, tens of thousands. Just one of them nearly killed the three of us."

"I'll fight anything, anywhere, whatever the odds!" Cali voice cut across them. "But Guin's right. This is just suicide. Ye won't open any portal. We'll barely get out the door before we're dead!"

Athress' face remained calm. He held up his hand for silence.

"I doubt there is an army outside still. When I arrived here, another was trapped in that contraption feeding the portal. I made a deal." He turned to Guinevere. "Now stay calm, I chose the lesser of two evils, though I ended up betrayed. It may work to our advantage."

The groups exchanged worried glances, what new surprise awaited them?

"The portal was powered by Canavos the Vile," Athress continued. From Guinevere's face, Ysabell knew this was bad, though she had never heard of this Canavos. "I freed him to allow him exact revenge on the creature orchestrating this attack. Also, with him free the portal would have no power to feed it."

"So what went wrong? Nuthionel asked.

"He betrayed me. As I approached, the orbs sapped my strength, he placed me on the plinth and rammed those crystals into my flesh to buy time. The portal would stay open long enough for him to flee undetected, and then as I bled out, it would close with my death. Ysabell's intervention stopped this. So, it would have been closed when he reached the surface. The demons may have bigger fish than us to fry!"

Something crossed Ysabell's mind. Canavos would have had to pass her, and no one did. *Unless there was another path?*

"Nothing passed me," Ysabell spoke up. "In fact, in this whole structure I met only one demon, I killed him in the corridor outside."

"You killed one of those winged critters alone?" Cali was wide eyed.

"No," Ysabell answered. "It was more like a man, but with dead looking skin and an odd darkness that swallowed all my light coming from him."

There was silence for a moment as all their eyes settled on Ysabell. She looked around uncomfortably. *Don't they believe me?* Guinevere was the first to speak.

"'Darkness surrounds him, nothing escapes him, not light, not life'." She quoted. "You killed Canavos the Vile." It was a statement, not a question.

Ysabell wasn't sure what to say; thankfully Nuthionel broke the silence.

"Well." His voice was slightly amused, but also full of pride as he watched Ysabell. "There goes your plan Athress, but if she can kill a demi-god, we might have a chance outside after all."

Guinevere started to object again but Ysabell stepped forward, her hand raised to silence her.

"No! We can do this." Ysabell said abruptly. She wasn't going to let doubt steal away their salvation. Now they had a way. It had to work. "Either we stay here and wait for them to come for us, and we die. Or we get up. We fight, and we survive long enough to get through the portal. On the other side we'll have the Mage tower to help us defend the portal while Athress closes it."

She looked around for disagreement. The others were all looking at her. But no one said a word.

"We are doing this."

With that she turned at stalked towards the door. She could hear the others falling in behind her.

Of a thousand deeds, let him learn but one

Chapter 15

Vaaldreth, his staff held before him and basking in a bright blue haze, groaned and collapsed forward. Mages ran to his aid. They rolled him over and struggled to lift him back to his chair. His eyes opened, and he smiled faintly.

"We are through," he said. "The Palace is sending aid. The City and Palace Guards are on the way." Then he closed his eyes and lost consciousness. Garaveigh, the city's High Priest of Assaurot, stepped forward to tend to him.

"He is fine, nothing some sleep won't cure. Take him to his chambers and lie him down. We must prepare for the armies' arrival. I need Mages paired with healers, and I want a path cleared towards the district's western gate. No excuses! I want the path cleared even if you must call down Armageddon upon the district to do so. Do it! Do it now!"

He looked around the circular room at the top of the Mage tower. He had only been here once before. *Didn't have to fight through an army of demons to get here that time though. A lot of good men, mercenaries and priests died getting here...* He turned away and strode out to the balcony to see how the battle was progressing. It had been a long day and evening, and the night was only half over. Felling the Demon

Lord, which lay burning on the grass far below, had given the defenders a huge surge in confidence. Garaveigh didn't impress easily, but Vaaldreth had power beyond imagination. He briefly wondered what would have happened to the City had Vaaldreth not been here. *Where is Athress?* They had been friends for many years. He found it troubling that the Arch Mage had left at what seemed to be the Cities time of greatest need. *If he died in there...*

"Survive in there old man," he whispered. "We will need your strength again before this is over."

Garaveigh knelt and prayed. He needed to know where the companions and Athress were. He feared they had failed, and kept that fear to himself, but he had to know for sure. The boost to moral was fading fast as hordes of demons streamed through the portal, seemly never-ending. Most of the mercenaries they had brought to aid the Mages were dead, along with a good quarter of his priests, the Gods alone knew how many Mages.

He allowed himself a brief smile. None had run. None had tried to leave. Everyone who died out there had done so with courage; fought to the end with ferocity. His memory strayed to Carabar, a young priest from the Severed Isles. Only two years into his training. When the Mage he was healing fell and he found himself surrounded by Drudir, he picked up a hammer from a dead mercenary. He was impaled from behind by a demon, but with his last breath he swung the hammer and severed its head.

Garaveigh knew there would be time to weep for the fallen later. Their stories, their courage, would not be forgotten. He would see to that. Carraigbán owed every last one of them. He would ensure a monument was built with each of their names engraved on it and how they died. The sacrifices they made to defend the city must be heard.

He cleared his head and focused. He asked his god for a vision of the companions, and his prayer was answered. Before his eyes, through a great fog, he saw Athress, lying on his back. Held to a table of some kind. Wounds all over his body. Garaveigh's heart sank. They were finished.

He made himself continue to watch. Their sacrifice was owed someone to bear witness. The vision blurred and shifted forward. He could see Ysabell... *Alive, alone, but alive, there may still be hope.* He watched her stop, light her lantern and face an enemy. A creature made of shadow. Even through the vision he knew what this was. This creature, this entity. This false god. Canavos the Vile. Once a High Priest of Asetha, he was seduced by evil and corrupted. Through the darkest of rites and human sacrifices he had drawn fel energy into his body and became something else. He was not man, nor demon, and though some cults worshipped him as such, he was no god. But he was not mortal. The girl was brave, but she couldn't fight this thing.

Heart in his throat Garaveigh watched the fight. Something was wrong. Canavos was weak, he seemed drained. He barely had any power. *She might actually do it.* As she plunged her dagger into Canavos' eye and walked away without a second glance at his corpse, Garaveigh sat back; he was breathless. She killed him, she killed Canavos. It scarcely seemed possible. Yet he had seen it with own eyes.

Garaveigh's heart soared. She wasn't dead. Maybe they others still lived too. He couldn't help himself and roared out aloud for all in the tower and in the battle below to hear. "They live yet! GIVE THEM TIME!"

The defenders below were lifted by the news, and their renewed vigour took the demonic legions by surprise. They threw themselves into the fray, hacking and slashing at demons. Spells exploded all across the battlefield. The push didn't last long. After a few minutes the armies of Drudir, winged Demons, Imps and Lasairlaoch soon gained the upper hand again. More and more flooded through the portal to drive the defenders back. For every demon they killed, two seemed to take its place. The portal had widened and dozens more were coming through by the minute.

Suddenly, the lines broke. The defenders were in disarray, and demons rushed forward to take advantage. They pushed hard, defenders falling in their wake, until a wave of sound rolled across the battlefield. Out from the trees, in full armour with shining breastplates and swords raised, two hundred of the City Guard charged into the fray. Behind them fifty Archers stepped out of the bushes and formed their lines. To their right two teams of dwarves hauling two large trebuchets appeared from behind a row of distant buildings.

Garaveigh exhaled. The companions lived, the Carraigbán armies had arrived, hope had returned. He knelt down to re-enter his vision and see what was happening inside the temple. Before he could, a shockwave hit the tower. Books flew from shelves, furniture lurched across the floor. Garaveigh was thrown from his knees to the ground. He scrambled up, holding the wall for support as the building shook, stumbled out onto the balcony again.

The portal was growing, but the flames around it were dying. Vaaldreth appeared at his side.

"It's losing power. Deforming - it can't hold its shape anymore. They've done it, they've gone and done it."

As he spoke the portal exploded, a second massive shockwave threw everything in its path to the ground, defenders, demons, even the Garaveigh and Vaaldreth in the tower. Silence descended for a moment. One perfect moment. Garaveigh rose and looked down below. A scream ended the peace as the defenders rose to their feet and threw themselves forward with renewed courage. The demons would receive no more support. There was still a tough fight ahead, but now, finally, there was a chance.

"Have you news of Athress and the others?" Vaaldreth asked eagerly.

Garaveigh returned inside to where he had been meditating before the fire.

"I will try for more information. If I can remain undisturbed for a time." With that the Priest knelt, bowed his head and focused once again.

<><>

Guinevere's mace swung over Cali's head lifting the Drudir from its feet and slamming it into the wall, its armour shattered at the chest where she struck, she turned her head to check on the others. Nuthionel and Ysabell were back to back tearing two demons apart, their blades a blur. Athress came into view as the vision cleared, alive and fighting. A blow to his chest from a huge winged demon sent his body crashing to the ground, blood spattered from his lips as he hit, the demon standing over him, its blade raised. A tuft of flaming red hair dashed past the others towards the prone Mage; Cali was in a rage. Guinevere following her. The demon's head rolled across the hall in seconds and Guinevere laid her hands on Athress' chest to heal what she could.

His chest moved, and the skin rippled under his robes as broken ribs slowly straightened and snapped back into place. He cried out in pain. She guided a healing light from her hand to some internal injury. Garaveigh watched on anxiously. *I hope it isn't serious. We need him alive.* He watched as she turned back to his ribs, repairing the bone. In minutes she had healed him as best as could be done for now. Garaveigh knew the pain would be excruciating for days. The prayers would heal the worst of it, but the damaged tissue and muscle would not heal as fast.

Athress opened his mouth to speak, when his face turned to horror. Garaveigh screamed a warning in vain, knowing they couldn't hear him. Guinevere turned too late. A Warhammer slammed into her. It would have hit her head, killing her, if not for the warning in Athress' face. Instead she took the full force into her right shoulder.

<><>

Guinevere dragged herself up against the wall and drew her mace, but her arm gave way. The weight was too much. Ysabell watched in horror as the demon spun and swung his hammer again. She had no defence, no time to even utter a prayer. Nuthionel shoved his foe aside and sprinted towards Guinevere and Athress. He launched forward and crashed into her injured shoulder, hurling her out of the path of the hammer. As Guin hit the ground Ysabell screamed. Time slowed as she watched the demon's hammer smash into Nuthionel. She couldn't move. *No! It's not real.*

Nuthionel's twisted body lay on the ground at the Demon's feet, his eyes wide open, seeming to look at Guinevere. But there was no light behind them. He had taken the full force of the demon's hammer into his own chest to save her. He was dead.

Ysabell couldn't feel, couldn't think, her whole world was crashing down around her. '*Try to get the hell out of here, I'll follow,*' his words from the Bandit camp echoed in her mind.

The demon approached Guinevere where she lay. Ysabell tore her gaze from Nuthionel to watch. Guinevere barely seemed to even notice, the fight sapped from her at the sight of Nuthionel. She didn't even resist as the creature raised its hammer. Ysabell snapped, her fear, her doubt was all smothered in hate. Her mind filled with rage. Its weapon fell, with the demon's arm still attached to it, but no longer attached to the demon.

It screamed in agony, swinging to face its foe. Ysabell stood alone before it, her gaze burning with lust for revenge. The demon ran at her swinging its remaining arm to try and crush her, but its huge hand clutched at only air. She was gone, slipping past its missing right arm, and slicing her blades deep into its right knee. As it buckled, she struck again, crossing her daggers as she severed the tendons in its right ankle.

The demon tried to stand but stumbled against the wall, its right foot completely useless. It growled in rage as Ysabell leapt up on its back. She buried both daggers into either side of the spine and dragged them down as hard as she could, screaming as she did. The demon collapsed to the ground as she withdrew her weapons. It was still alive, but paralysed. Ysabell strolled around to its face and crouched to look it in the eye.

"I don't know how you things feed or if you can starve," she said. "I hope not. I hope you need no sustenance and can lie here and spend the rest of eternity watching a wall."

She rose, cleaned and sheathed her blades, and walked over to where Nuthionel lay. She leaned down and closed his eyes, her own welling with tears. Her body shook as she silently sobbed.

Guin and Cali joined her at his body. Athress sat against the wall nearby. He looked catatonic, his eyes streaming, staring at his foster son's body. Cali was at a loss for words. Large tears rolled down her cheeks as she stared down. Guin couldn't speak either. There were no words between them. Ysabell dropped to her knees beside Nuthionel's body.

She looked at the other two, they had known him for, she didn't even know how long, whatever her loss, theirs was worse. Mutilating the demon had lessened her pain none. She was numb as if a great void filled her. She looked back down at Nuthionel one more time, and then stood. His voice still haunting her mind. '*We might have a chance after all outside.*' She grabbed his daggers and put them in her sheath, casting her old ones aside, then, tears in her eyes, she set off down the corridor. She heard the others step in behind her. This would end once and for all.

She would get to the surface and let the armies come. They would all join 'Thion soon enough.

One last hurdle

Chapter 16

Ysabell walked boldly down the corridor of the hellish stronghold. Her insecurities were gone. There was no fear, no hesitation, and no doubts. She wanted to meet more demons, and she wanted them to suffer. Her sorrow over Nuthionel's fate was a quiet pool now, buried somewhere beneath the searing heat of rage and hate burning in her. Cali and Guinevere walked side by side behind her in silence, each lost in their own thoughts and memories. Athress caught up with Ysabell.

For a time, they walked in silence. Then he spoke quietly, his words meant only for her.

"He was proud of you and he believed in you, more than you know."

Athress dropped back to leave her alone with her thoughts.

They had fought five or six of those winged demons, 'Beliar,' Athress called them. They had killed two dozen other demons, small screeching things, like tiny goblins, spindle like arms and legs, with razor sharp claws and rows of needle like teeth. They were called 'Furies'. They were easy to kill but came in groups. Ysabell was covered in cuts and scratches from them. If they met more, the fighting would be all the more difficult without Nuthionel. Ysabell was starting to have her own doubts about whether they could manage this.

Soon they reached the final stairs, much quicker this time. Cali and Guinevere showed them the stairs they had taken down, it was a much more direct route. They paused briefly.

"Well, this is it." Athress was calm, on the outside anyway. "We suffered a great loss, but we have also achieved a great victory. This is one last hurdle."

"We will do this, we'll hold back the tide and buy you time Athress. Just... don't take too long," Guinevere showed no sign of the doubts about this plan she had earlier.

Hearing the calm and confidence in their voices lifted Ysabell and helped to keep her own doubts at bay. Nuthionel's death had affected her badly, but she wouldn't let him down now.

With no further delays, the group walked up the stairway and out the arch that had housed the it, its door shattered from earlier. The portal was gone, they stood atop the pyramid like stone structure, some six floors above the ground level. What had been a massive army below, was now in disarray. In fighting and roaring of demons creating a chaotic scene. Ysabell had no idea of what was happening, but the distraction was good. It would buy them a few minutes hopefully.

Athress wasted no time, as soon as they cleared the building he began to cast. The words were strange, a language Ysabell had never heard. She turned to Guinevere, the priest and Cali were standing, weapons drawn watching for anything approaching them.

"What is that language Mages use?" She asked.

"Haigárish" Guinevere replied, her eyes still scanning the demons below. "It's named after Haigáran, God of Magic. Magic is an energy that flows between all things. Rocks, trees, you and me, even the little things too small to see. It's like a giant web. The Mesh I think they call it." She paused for a moment, watching a great winged creature in the distance. It turned away from them and continued on its way.

"Mages use the language taught to them by Haigáran to tap into it," Guinevere continued. "Tweak it and manipulate the flow of this energy. But it takes enormous inner strength to control it. The energy channels through their body leaving them exhausted. Too much energy means a dead Mage. That's why they need to rest after casting too much."

A crackle of lightning flashed between Athress' hands. The portal was starting to open. Winds whipped up around them, drowning out the sounds of the demons below. Guinevere's face lit up and she clapped Ysabell on the back.

"Looks like we'll make it after all." She shouted.

"They've seen us!" Cali's voice roared above the wind.

Guinevere's face darkened as she and Ysabell spun to see what was coming. Ysabell felt like she was hit when she saw. They were so close and now this. Hundreds of demons were taking flight or running up the steps at the front of the flat-topped Pyramid. Three of them weren't going to protect Athress for long.

The first to reach them was a Beliar, its huge broadsword already in its hands it swung for Guinevere as it landed. She threw herself backwards just in time to avoid the blade, Cali ran in axe swinging. The Beliar beat its wings once, rising over Cali's swing, one of its cloven feet lashing out and felling the halfling with a blow to the head. Guinevere was up and drawing her mace. Knowing the damage she could do with it Ysabell played bait and screamed at the demon, daggers drawn. It turned towards her and raised its sword, she concentrated and summoned her shadow cloak. It took the demon by surprise, letting her dart in under his raised arms and slash a dagger across his gut. She rolled quickly to one side before the Beliar could react. It roared in rage, dropped to the ground, and reached out with a huge hand to try and grab Ysabell as she rose back to her feet.

Guinevere's mace crushed its shoulder before it could. She cursed her aim and made to swing again. The Beliar flapped its wings to avoid her, but before it could leave the ground Cali's hatchet was thrown and embedded into where its wings joined its back. The demon was grounded. Between the three of them they made short work of the now crippled and weakened creature.

There was no time to celebrate, two more landed before them. Guinevere back handed her mace into one, swinging it over Ysabell's head. It gave Ysabell space to move in and help Cali with the second. A Warhammer caught Cali, clipping her back and sending her sprawling to the ground. Past her, Ysabell could see Guinevere struggling with the second. Both wounded. A blinding flash of light illuminated the battle as the portal burst into life. Ysabell dodged a feint from the Beliar in front of her, even as she sidestepped she realised she had been fooled. The demon swiveled and spun its club as she stepped into it. She briefly felt the pain as her left shoulder took the hit. Then everything went blank.

<><><>

Vaaldreth leaned heavily on his staff as he walked. Garaveigh watched him from where he sat resting. He had never used the visions with such regularity before, it was leaving him with a blinding headache and wearing him out fast. *A good man. He nearly killed himself breaking the shield over the district. Yet he still goes on, where others would rest.* The sun had reached its peak and passed it since they last spoke.

"Last I saw they were alive and leaving the temple." He offered. "Athress planned to open a temporary portal once they were clear of it."

Vaaldreth nodded but said no more as Garaveigh was returning to his kneeling position to find out where they were now.

He concentrated on Athress to try and see where he was. The vision came slower this time and more painfully. He wouldn't be able to hold it for long. He could see them, fighting Beliar atop the pyramid temple. Cali was down, lying before a portal, Athress had a portal open.

Garaveigh struggled to hold the connection as voices shouted all around him, feet running by. He pushed on trying to clear his head and see through the fog. He watched as a club smashed Ysabell into her left shoulder. She flew through the air like a rag doll and hit the ground hard. He couldn't see if Cali or Ysabell still lived, but Athress was now free to join the fight. The old Mage stepped forward, as

Guinevere's mace knocked a demon back, he stepped between her and the two beliar they were fighting. Ten or twelve more were landing behind them. Garaveigh heard one word shouted above the chaos.

"Down!"

Guinevere dropped to flatten herself to the ground as Athress threw his arms out wide, his staff in his right-hand jerking down. The etherium shod base slamming into the ground as he spoke.

"Élenthaí sphericaí Val'dath!" He shouted the words into the air and around him the air rippled in a sphere that grew at lightning speed. The demons in its path were hurled from the plateau. Guinevere jumped to her feet and ran to Cali and Ysabell. She picked up Ysabell and slung her over her right shoulder, then grabbed Cali and held her against her side. With Athress she stepped into the portal. Demons were reaching the plateau in their hundreds now, all running, flying, crawling towards the portal as fast as they could.

Garaveigh brought himself back immediately. Tried to stand but staggered.

"Vaaldreth, a portal," He gasped "Athress has opened a portal, they are coming, but demons, an army of them is right on their heels."

"The portal just opened." Vaaldreth replied, "We must defend it till it closes."

Garaveigh's head was a little clearer now, he stumbled out onto the balcony. Vaaldreth pointed at a Beliar still fighting in the clearing below, then cast a spell.

"Fúlcruthíos Syncamus"

As he shouted the words he leapt over the side. Garaveigh ran to rails to see, the demon Vaaldreth had cast at was being pulled up into the air. As Vaaldreth went down, the demon went up, he was using a fulcrum spell of some kind to slow his fall.

The fight below was still in full swing, the defenders had been decimated by the demons. Their fury when the portal had closed had seen countless defenders slaughtered in minutes.

When things were at their darkest, screams filled the air, smoke and foul fumes darkened the sky and a sea of blood threatened to wash away the last of the defender's morale, a citizen's ragtag militia came screaming through the trees, with Dragar, the dwarf who ran Alir's trading post, at their fore and tore into the legions of demons, many died in the first charge. Dragar slew all around, demons falling like leaves from an autumn tree in his wake, though he fell to a Lasairlaoch's blade shortly after.

The opening of a new portal, smaller and wreathed in lightning rather than flames clearly terrified the defenders. From his vantage point, Garaveigh could see fear spread through the ranks. Vaaldreth hit the ground running, calling for aid as he did. Several Mages abandoned their fight to join him running towards the portal. A flash of light burst as several bodies were expelled from it. Guinevere, carrying Cali and Ysabell stumbled out first, she swiftly looked around, laid her friends down and drew her mace, turning to face the portal.

Athress came through next, he moved out of Guinevere's way and immediately began the spell to seal the portal once again. Almost immediately following them the demons started coming. The first one out died instantly as it ran head first into a massive crushing blow from Guinevere's mace. Blood splattered across the ground. As the second appeared it stumbled on the remains of the first, an easy target once again for Guin. As it died, Vaaldreth's scream from behind sent her running to one side as a spinning ball of white hot flame screamed past her into the portal.

Athress' hands swept down with his staff held out. A white glow from the tip attached to the top of the portal and as he drew it down, the light swept down the portal sealing it like it was knitting the fabric of the world back together.

Garaveigh turned and ran for the stairs down. Moments later he burst out the tower door, the battle had been joined by Athress and Vaaldreth, they were wreaking devastation on the demons. With the aid of the militia and City Guards it looked like they were going to win this. He raced across the field to where Guinevere was on her knees over the motionless bodies of her friends. As he approached she looked up, her face streaked with dirt, tears and dried blood.

"They are bad!" Her voice cracking, but stern and harsh. "Barely clinging to life. Help Ysabell."

Without another word she turned back to Cali and began her healing prayers. White glowing lights floated from her hands into Cali's short body. Garaveigh turned his attention to Ysabell, he left shoulder was shattered, but that was nowhere near the worst of it, her collar bone and ribs on that side were crushed too. He closed his eyes and placed his hands over her breast. Probing with his mind he found internal injuries, a collapsed lung, the heart strained and struggling, massive bleeding, torn muscle and sinew.

He cleared his mind and focused first on the bones, they shifted and moved back to where they belonged, grinding and cracking as they did. Once he had them in place, he began to stop the worst of the internal bleeding. He just needed to stabilise her to get her inside where the healers could tend to her properly. He was a priest, regrowing torn muscles and fixing her lung would need a proper healer, a Druid.

Enemies Unmasked
Chapter 17

Garaveigh sat on the shell of a demon's armour outside the tower, watching the survivors sift through the bodies to look for friends and loved ones. There was no celebration. The celebrations were for the politicians and those who were safe outside the walls of this district. Those who had fought knew there was no joy here.

Towards the tower he could see Athress picking his way across the battlefield to join him. Athress sat without a word, took out a pipe and tobacco. He offered the pouch to Garaveigh who thanked him and filled his own pipe. They sat in silence for a time, just watching the scene in front of them. Garaveigh was accepting of death, as a Priest it was part of life, part of the order of things. But even he was affected by this, the sheer scale. Bodies were strewn across the district. Hundreds had died, maybe a thousand. Slaughtered senselessly and they still didn't even know why, or by whom.

"I've seen a lot of war. You too." Garaveigh broke the silence. "I just wasn't prepared to see it here. It's always somewhere far away."

Athress took a deep pull on his pipe, slowly exhaling he watched the smoke rise until the wind took it out across the battle field.

"I'd seen enough death Garaveigh." He took another draw on his pipe. "I came back here to live out my days in peace. After the massacre at Silvan Asúr I swore I'd never fight in another battle."

Garaveigh watched his friend with concern. Silvan Asúr was an Elven city down south. During the last war Athress had been in the fighting there. He had been young then. He had witnessed humanity at its worst. Elven civilians unarmed and defenceless slaughtered. Garaveigh wondered if Nuthionel knew it was Athress' own unit who had slaughtered Nuthionel's family. Athress had killed his own men to save the boy.

"You sought no war or battle my friend." He placed a comforting hand on Athress' shoulder. "They came here to kill and destroy us all. Your conscience is clear."

The old Mage snorted.

"Nuthionel was killed coming to save me, Ysabell and Cali may yet die." Athress sighed. "I was arrogant Garaveigh, I was so sure of my own power I was blinded. Canavos made a fool of me. A weak old fool, who should have put his staff away years ago."

Athress rose, Garaveigh followed suit.

"I will go look in on Ysabell." Athress stretched his aching body as he spoke. His own injuries still paining him. "I understand Haydleth has sent a healer from the druids' grove."

Garaveigh nodded and watched Athress walk away towards the tower. Then he called over a young cleric he recognised. He couldn't remember the young man's name.

"Ah... Brenton isn't it?" He asked as the young man neared him. The cleric nodded. "Do me a favour, find Guinevere. You know her?" Again, a nod. "Send her to me at the temple of Assaurot when she has time. Thank you."

He waved the cleric off on his task and set off to the temple. *I have bad feeling about this. Feels like the calm before a storm.*

<><><>

The tower seemed so peaceful. Many of the Mages were dead, those remaining were mostly resting or under the care of healers. Many had over used their magic. He had lost several to it, others clung to life precariously. He was proud of them though. From the most powerful senior Mages to the acolytes who could barely conjure a flame in their hand. All had faced the enemy the best they could. They had all been willing to give their lives in defence of the city.

The door to Ysabell's room was slightly ajar. She was talking quietly, her voice weak. A small elvish druid sat with her. *The healer Haydleth sent. I must send him my thanks.* He pushed open the door gently and walked in. Ysabell's face turned to him.

"Athress. There was no time before." Ysabell's voice was faint, her face strained, he could see it hurt for her to talk still. "I am sorry, so sorry."

"Thank you." Athress turned away to the hearth, as much to hide his face as to light a fire. He threw a fistful of powder down on the bare hearth.

"Conflagéous." The powder ignited instantly into a blue bone fire.

"I should thank you Ysabell," Athress started. "I would be dead had you not come for me. I made a mistake. I made a deal with a creature of evil. I know better than that."

He turned back to Ysabell and the small druid.

"Thank you," he said.

The flames behind him changed colour as he spoke, with a roar like an explosion they shot up as if oil had been poured on them. Ysabell pushed herself up from the bed, her face white with the pain as she did. Guinevere appeared at the door moments later, mace in hand. The four of them watched the flames. Athress prepared a spell in his mind, if this was an attack he would be ready.

The flames rose to almost the height of the room, and a shape began to form within them. It gained no detail, just a silhouette of a humanoid shape, with huge demonic horns on its head. Its voice rang out, echoing through the halls of the tower. "I expected to find an army had destroyed my portal and routed my forces. Instead I find a young girl, a priest who thinks she's a warrior and a Mage far past his usefulness. Canavos slain and my plans laid to waste. Impressive, but you will not live to enjoy your pathetic victory here. You will be skinned alive and I will torture your souls for eternity. I have existed since before your world came into being and I will be here long after it is all returned to dust. You will learn to fear the name Xelazenivein. I can feel your fear from here, so flee little mortals, run and hide, it will make it all the more fun when I come for you."

Guinevere, Athress and the druid Ériu looked at each other. Athress could see fear in the other's eyes. Except Ysabell's, she was not afraid. She was shaking, her face red and her eyes burned; she finally had a target to lay the blame for Nuthionel's death.

"Run? Hide? I don't think so," Ysabell's voice was low, and cold as the grave. "I'm just getting started. I'm coming for you Xelazenivein, I will trawl all the levels of the infinite abyss to find you if I must."

The demon's figure stepped back as if struck. Ysabell wasn't done with him yet.

"I've a demi-god dead by my hands already. You can feel our fear? Remember that feeling demon, you will know that fear before I am through with you!"

As she uttered the last word, she stepped forward and scattered the ash of the fire across the stone floor with her foot, extinguishing the flames instantly.

Guinevere caught her as she collapsed. With Ériu's help they got back on the bed.

"Your injuries are severe." The druid's gentle voice lilted. "'Trawling all the levels of the infinite abyss will have to wait a few weeks."

Athress hasn't moved. He was still staring at where the apparition had been. Guinevere approached.

"Athress?" She enquired. "Are you ok?"

He spun to face them, his face dark.

"I must go, I need to speak with Garaveigh. We must research before the Assemble meeting this afternoon." His voice was anything but calm. Ysabell had never seen him like this, even when he lay under that crystal dome, he had been calm. Now he was anxious, unnerved.

"Athress? You know of this Xelazenivein?" She asked sharply.

He looked at her, his calm returning slowly. But his eyes were dark as if he had learned some terrible truth.

"Not by name, no. But by what he said. 'I have existed since before your world came into being'. We live in a multiverse, linked planes of existence. Portals can travel between them. They are held within a fabric, like a bag, but of reality. There are others like this, other Multiverses. Travel between them is all but impossible. Even the Gods cannot manage that."

Ysabell and Guinevere exchanged glances, this sounded bad.

"But once, a thousand times a thousand years ago, creatures in one of these other multiverses abused their power so much they destroyed all the planes, everything within their reality. As they fled from their own destruction, they managed, how we will never know, to tear open the fabric of our reality and enter it. They recreated their own worlds here, or shadow replicas of them. We call these the Abyss, the Hells."

Ysabell looked on as fascinated as she was worried, she had never heard of this before.

"Over the millennia all kinds of evil creatures, twisted creations, forgotten gods came to inhabit these planes." Athress continued. "But hidden among the demons all this time has been those who created the hells, who created the demons. Those survivors from 'outside'." Athress sighed heavily.

"If one of these survivors is our enemy, they are far more powerful than the Demon Lords we know of. They are close to being Gods already. We must find out all we can and do all we can to stop this creature's plans. I will ask Garaveigh to have all the High Priests gather and see if any can get more answers from their gods. Here in the tower, we will study the old manuscripts of the Mages that first brought our races to this world, maybe we can learn more through their experiences."

<> <> <>

Athress and Garaveigh sat side by side in the council chambers of the palace, awaiting the Lords Assembly to arrive. They had been summoned once the initial celebration of the victory over the demon armies was over. They were both advisory members of the Assembly. Athress had a bad feeling, something was going on, and going by the last few weeks, it wasn't going to be something good.

The news of Xelazenivein had worried him deeply. If an elder of the abyss was involved, he was unlikely to give up after one attempt. As Athress pondered, a page came in and announced the Assembly. The various Guild leaders, Lords and Ladies, heads of various institutes that made up the ruling assembly of the City filed in and took their seats. As advisors, Garaveigh and Athress' seats were set slightly above the others, but they were not allowed to vote.

Dartag Crawhammer, Head of the Guild of Blacksmiths and current chairman, or chair-dwarf, of the Assembly called for order.

"We have received word from Griffon hunters to the North. A great horde of Goblins has been spotted on the march south. It appears to be heading this way and the reports we have are that it is huge, numbering tens of thousands. Scouts who tried to get a closer look never returned. We also have no idea where they came from. The Northern cities have lain in ruins for near fifty years. The Ice Mountains beyond have never hosted life that we know of, and past them there is nothing but the silent wastes, nothing could live there, or pass through them."

Voices across the chamber gasped in shock. Then the whispering started which grew to murmurs and further until the noise level rose to near shouting. Dartag banged his gavel on the table again. "ORDER!" The assembly quietened under his stern stare until he had silence again.

"We need information before any course of action can be decided upon." He turned to Athress and Garaveigh. "Esteemed advisors to this council. You both have means of ascertaining what we cannot. We have never asked you to involve yourself in civil matters before, but given the recent attack on the Mage district, I have concerns that this may be connected. Our best and bravest are dead in that battle. This city has lasted for centuries without a wall. We are a city of commerce, not war. Yet the defence mounted by you and those who sacrificed themselves in the Mage district, saved every last one of us. We seek your help again." He turned to assembly for approval, voices chorused across the room in agreement.

"Please," he continued, "use whatever means necessary to find out what the hell is going on! If this host does intend to attack this city, what can we do? None of us here are military men or women. Our city guard has more experience in separating drunks than fighting wars. Should we abandon our homes to this horde?"

Athress' head bowed, his hands clasped in his lap. Should he tell them what he knew? Would it strengthen their resolve or cause panic? The decision was taken from him when Garaveigh rested a hand on his shoulder and stood before the assembly.

"You are in more danger than you can imagine, but fleeing will avail us nothing. The armies that invaded this city from the Abyss served a demon lord of unimaginable power. His goal was not the destruction of our city, but the destruction of our world. I will seek a vision from my God to discern the purpose of this army but defeating one demon invasion in the Mage district is not winning the coming war."

Athress rose and Garaveigh allowed him to continue. "This city is ultimately defenceless. That must change. I and the Mage tower can, with the help of the Dwarves from the Underbore, construct walls from stone, earth and magic. It will take many months, but if this army is marching from the ice mountains, we should have enough time. In the meantime, this assembly must see to provisions in case of a siege. We need warehouses filled with non-perishable foods, and we need grain and hay stored for feeding livestock. Most importantly, we need water. An army could dam the river, depriving us of clean water and sealing our sewage and waste in here with us. Either one would be catastrophic. We need to locate all the wells in the city and learn how much water they can draw in a day"

Relics and Regrets

Chapter 18

Guinevere strangely felt alone as she walked through the city towards the temple district. The streets were crowded, revellers crowding around the taverns, spilling out onto the streets, drinks in hand. The city was electric with life as it celebrated the victory in the Mage district. Survivors of the battle coming back to tell tales of their heroism, sowing the seeds for the next generation of soldiers and fighters.

Fireworks exploded over the Palace. The assembly wanted to create a festive atmosphere, show the world life goes on in the city. As much to take people's minds off what had happened as to show traders and merchants that Carraigbán was still open for business. It was an odd feeling for Guinevere, she was generally the one in the midst of any excuse to drink and celebrate. But today she felt no joy or happiness. Revellers celebrated with their loved ones, their families and friends. Guinevere was a mercenary. Her family were Nuthionel and Cali.

She wasn't happy about leaving Cali's bedside to meet Garaveigh. The cheerful halfling hadn't woken yet. Ériu, the Healer treating her and Ysabell, had informed her Cali was in a coma. They had no way of knowing if she would wake. 'Sometimes the body says sleep. We have to trust it knows what's best for Cali's recovery.'

Guinevere sighed. She missed the jokes, inappropriate humour and constant chatter from her friend. She crossed the bán river into the temple district and headed for the Cathedral of Light. Garaveigh had requested she meet him there urgently. As she approached the Cathedral's steps a cleric of Asetha was waiting for her.

"The High Priest awaits you." He spoke nervously. His voice shaking a little.

Guinevere nodded to him and followed the young cleric inside. He looked barely out of his teens, maybe not even. He led her through the Cathedral to an alcove with a stairs leading down to the catacombs. Someone had lit the torches, the normally dark passages were bright. She had been here before as a trainee, many years before, laying the dead to rest. It seemed an odd place for Garaveigh to want to meet her.

They walked past the burial chambers until they came to an ancient gate, Guinevere in her younger days had often wondered what was beyond it. It had always been locked. Now it stood open, the hinges had fresh oil on them, as had the lock.

"I can go no further." The cleric stopped at the gates. "The High Priest was very clear, only you were to go past the gates."

"He didn't happen to mention why?" Guinevere asked, already guessing the answer. Something was going on. Something odd. She had a feeling it had to do with the enemy they had discovered and their fight in hell.

"No ma'am. He told me not to question." The boy was clearly curious, but nervous of Garaveigh. Guinevere wondered was she that nervous of the High Priest when she had been training. Probably. High Priest Kaveath had been a grumpy old codger.

"Ok, thank you." She responded.

She paused for a moment looking down the stairs ahead into the under crypt. Then made her way down the stairs. The torches here had not been lit. But there was a light from further down, she headed towards that. On reaching the bottom of the stairs she found a corridor, with many closed doors on each side. Straight ahead was an open one, at the end of the passage. It was also lit up brightly. Guinevere strode in, Garaveigh was there, but her attention was caught by the room. Unlike the old grey stones of the catacombs, this room was lined in marble, grey marble glittered on the floor, white on the walls and ceiling. She'd never heard of this place; it was like a monument to someone. A beautiful black granite altar stood at the back of the room. On top of it was an ornate brass chest. Everything was covered in thick dust. You could see where Garaveigh had swept aside cobwebs to clear the room. Even through the dirt and dust of centuries, it was an incredible sight.

Garaveigh waited for her to finish taking in the room before speaking.

"I received word from Athress about the encounter with our enemy you had today. A name at last." He looked at her face as if waiting for a reaction. But Guinevere was too drained, emotionally and physically. He continued. "I called you here in connection with that. We, all of us, not just this city. But all of our people on this world now have an enemy who seeks our destruction. For what reason I don't know. But we know what he is. He is Evil. Pure Evil."

"Garaveigh, if Athress is right about what he is, he may be an evil beyond us. I will fight in any way I can, you know that. I believe Ysabell will too, and" she paused to maintain her composure. "And Cali will too. But how much we can do? Can he be physically hurt? If I swing my mace at him can I even injure him?"

A satisfied look spread on Garaveighs face. "Exactly what I wondered. Exactly. What can mere mortals hope to do against an evil as colossal and ancient as this?" His eyes lit up with a fire inside. "That is why you are here tonight. This Cathedral was built to protect this tomb. No person was ever in buried here. But some 'thing' was. It has been guarded and kept secret here for over four hundred years."

He stepped back and indicated the brass chest, approached one side of it and took the handle there.

"Take the other and lift with me." He asked.

Guinevere did as he asked.

"One, two, three, Lift"

The chest lifted, it wasn't a chest really, it had no bottom and had been sat down over something on the altar. As they lifted it light shone out from under it, bright and pure. They lowered the chest to the floor. Guinevere stood and stared. Upon the altar was a mace, sitting in a beautiful cradle of gold and silver, encrusted with diamonds. But stand was nothing to Guinevere, she had eyes only for the mace. A little over half her height, a metal haft, workmanship looked elven, it looked light but strong. The head was a series of diamond shaped wedges around the central ball. The detail engraved into it was incredible. No workman could create such fine detail. No workman had. Guinevere knew what it was immediately. Though she had always believed it was a myth.

<><><>

Ysabell stood beside her bed staring out the window at the city below. It was lit up with festive lanterns, lights in windows, even fireworks. She watched the blazing bursts of colour over the city. They reminded her of the battle to get to the Mage tower. Explosions and fireballs shooting through the air. But no one was screaming out there. There was laughter and singing. The city was celebrating.

Her eyes drifted down to the clearing below. *Well, most of the city.* The clearing had small memorials, flowers and signs placed around it, against the trees, the seats. She watched a man with two girls, no more than eleven or twelve, laying flowers at a small marker, it had incense burning and a statuette to Asetha. The girls sobbing, tears streaming down their faces. She guessed they were saying goodbye to their mother, or brother. They turned into their father and he held them. Protecting them, helping them grieve. Her teeth clenched and she stepped away from the window. *It's not fair.* The bitterness in her was hard to bear. Her eyes wandered to the daggers laid out on her bed table, almost reverently, a candle lit behind them.

Ysabell shivered, the fire had long gone out. Ériu was gone home for the evening. She wasn't bothered lighting a fire just for herself. Strangely in Farrowfields she'd always been alone in one sense. She had no friends, a father who was drunk most of the time and spent many nights sleeping on the tavern floor. But she'd never felt alone before. She stared at the daggers trying to picture the hands that had held them. The hands that had held her as a child and saved her. *Why did you have to leave me? I needed you. I still do.*

A gentle knock at her door made her look up. Athress stood there. He seemed to be looking at the daggers, but his eyes didn't appear particularly focused. They were lost, with nowhere to go, He moved slowly, with no energy or enthusiasm.

"May I join you?" He asked, his voice was quiet. "I have a need to talk to someone."

Ysabell nodded. "Please, come in."

The old Mage, and he was old, shuffled in and sat in a soft chair near the hearth. He seemed older today, *Nuthionel's death hit him hard.* He threw some logs into the fireplace, then raised a hand and spoke a word. The logs caught and burst into flame,

Ysabell moved over and sat in the opposite chair by the fire. They sat in silence for a moment, watching the flames. A small insect ran along the length of one of the logs, seeking to escape the flames. She watched it reach the end and leap, it fell straight down into the flames below.

"Did he ever tell you how we met?" Athress began.

"He glossed over it once. Said you saved him from raiders." Ysabell answered.

"If only that were the whole of it." Athress stared into the flames a pained expression on his face. "There were no raiders." He sighed. His face a picture of deep regret.

"I fought in the war. Against the elves, I was still young, naive and believed the nonsense the politicians throw at idealistic young men and women to make them die in wars that should never have been fought." Ysabell could see his eyes were distant now, he was seeing across fifty years or more. "My unit, my squad in the army were good men, when we left our homes we were all good men. We believed we were the army of light going to end the threat of the evil elves." He snorted in derision. "But war has a way of changing you. I saw men who at home were loyal husbands, devoted fathers. Yet out there, the constant death, watching your friends die. I saw once good men rape, torture and maim. I watched innocents die. Our army so full of righteous fury we believed it was ok if we did it. We fought on the side of light."

"You regret joining the war?" Ysabell asked. "Do you believe it was unjust?"

"Unjust? Ah Ysabell. The Elves were never a threat; we were the invaders. Slaughtering a peaceful people so our politicians could gain more wealth." His fist was clenching the arm of his chair now. His mouth twisted in a bitter sneer. "Army of Light, we were the evil barbarians who came to slaughter the innocent. Nuthionel's family weren't killed by raiders. They were killed by my squad. My comrades." His voice raised. Ysabell could hear the pain in it.

"Did Nuthionel know that?" She enquired softly.

"No. How I could tell him that?" He was almost pleading. "I stood by, I let it happen. I will never forgive that I didn't step in earlier. His family butchered, his sister raped and I, I a coward, I did nothing." A solitary tear escaped his left eye and slowly traced a path down his cheek into his beard. He hung his head down before continuing.

"He thought me a hero. But I was no hero. I was a coward Ysabell. I had not the strength to stand up to my commanding officer and squad. Worse, when I finally found my courage, I buried my sin. I killed them all before they could hurt Nuthionel. My own brothers in arms. Not one of them lived. I could have merely incapacitated them. I was powerful enough even then. But I killed them. To cover my own guilt."

He raised his head and looked at Ysabell. "In all the years I never told him. I never had the strength to confess. I so wanted to be the man he thought I was." He sighed.

Ysabell was shocked at what Athress had been, but she saw his pain and regret.

"You may not have been that man back then. But you are now." She reached across and held his hand in hers. "Nuthionel would judge you not on what you once were. But on what and who you are now. You risked everything to save others from having to venture through the portal. Now you lead the defence of a city of innocents. You could walk away. You could be that young Athress once again and turn a blind eye. But you won't."

They stayed like that in silence for a few moments. Then Athress rose. Took a deep breath and looked down at Ysabell in her chair.

"Thank you Ysabell. For listening to the regrets of an old man." His eyes looked to the daggers on the table again. "I will leave you to your peace. Get some rest. You have a lot of recovering left to do."

With that, he walked slowly from the room. Ysabell sat alone again. She stared into the dancing flames, wondering what Nuthionel would have thought had he known the truth. There were voices coming from Cali's room next door. *No, not voices, a voice.* Carefully she eased herself upright, her left side was still in a lot of pain. Moving out into the corridor, she leant on the wall outside Cali's room and listened.

"Remember that tavern in Glanmyrdwyrr? The elf with the attitude about halflings? Ha, he learned a valuable lesson. Wonder if he ever got the use of that leg back." It was Guinevere talking to Cali. Ysabell didn't want to intrude on her privacy. But didn't want to walk in until Guinevere had finished.

"And the bartender had to bar us, you kept telling everyone the food had poisoned you. Just because you drank too much Dwarven spirits and were sick for two days... Remember Cali? .. Cali? Don't go. Please? Don't leave me."

Ysabell could hear Guinevere's loneliness, the emotion in her cracking voice. It had never occurred to her that this band of misfits only really had each other. Now they had lost Nuthionel, all Guin had left was Cali. She pushed off the wall and walked to the door coughing as she did to give Guinevere a warning. She knocked and waited for Guin to call.

"Come in"

Guinevere was sitting beside Cali's bed. *She's been crying.*

"Mind if I join you?" Ysabell asked softly.

Guin smiled, her face still strained. "Of course not, come in. Company would be welcome, Cali's not her usual talkative self tonight." Her face almost winced as she made the light-hearted joke. Ysabell entered the room and took a seat beside Guin's at Cali's bedside.

"I'm only next door, but I'm being kept out of the loop. I think Ériu wants to keep me from getting stressed or worried. But it means I have no idea how Cali's doing? Has she told you anything?"

"Not a lot." Guinevere replied. "All she'll say is that Cali needs to sleep, the daMage was really bad and her mind sent her to sleep while it tries to repair everything. Nothing to do but wait."

Ysabell watched Guin's face crease with worry as she spoke. Her hands wringing as she spoke. *Not a side I ever thought to see of Guinevere. She always seemed so strong.* Ysabell reached across and put her hand on Guinevere's.

"She's strong, stronger than anyone I've ever known. She'll get through this." She squeezed and let Guin's hands go again, leaning back into her chair. She figured Guin knew as well as she did, Cali's odds were 50/50 at best. But they had to stay positive, losing Nuthionel was bad enough.

They sat in silence for a few minutes. It was strangely comfortable. Ysabell knew a boundary had been crossed tonight, they were closer, more friends than they had been. Most of the time they had spent together until now, they had spent fighting for their lives. Movement caught her eye, she watched Guin reach down the other side of her seat and draw out a huge battle mace. Some five feet long, beautifully crafted and detailed. As Guin lifted it, a faint glow traced along its edges.

"The Mace of Asetha. The High Priest led me to it earlier this evening. It was created by the Goddess herself. Garaveigh believes our part in this is not over yet and I will have need of this." Her face darkened as she looked down at Cali's tiny form. "I pray he is right, those responsible will pay in kind."

The City Walls
Chapter 19

The rain seemed reluctant to be here. Falling slowly, more mist like than rain. It soaked through everything. The skies were dull, grey and lifeless. Just like him. Ysabell watched the priest Garaveigh speak, but she couldn't focus on his words. Just noises on the wind. They didn't even have a body to lay to rest. Just a stone to mark the passing of a friend, a father figure, a hero. The cemetery was empty, at Athress' request Garaveigh had kept the ceremony only for those who had known Nuthionel, despite the protests of the Lords who wished to be seen attending.

A handful of mercenaries, misfits and friends gathered in the mist to remember Nuthionel, the blade master and the mercenary. Ysabell glanced around the small group. Guinevere stood beside her, cloak pulled tightly around her. Her face was solemn and calm. Like the ocean, calm on the surface, but rolling and unstoppable below.

"….A few words?" Ysabell snapped her attention back to Garaveigh, he was looking directly at her, his eyebrows raised in query. When she didn't answer, he shifted his gaze to Athress. "Athress..?"

The old Mage was leaning heavily on his staff, he stepped forward slowly. His deep and calm voice sounded old, so old and weary.

"To those who didn't know him, perhaps all they saw was a mercenary." His eyes slowly scanned the group, lingering on Guinevere and then Ysabell. "But to those who stood and fought by his side, who travelled with him and saw him truly. Nuthionel was a man of principal, of honour. Yes, he worked for pay, but when faced with a choice of what was right, and what was profitable, he never faltered. No one paid him to fight his way to the Mage tower, no one paid him to risk everything and come to the abyss. His loyalty to his friends, his sense of honour compelled him to.

He chose, he fought and died willingly to save others. He died as he had lived. A friend, a hero, a ..son.." Athress voice cracked and faltered into silence as emotion overwhelmed him. Another voice came to his aid.

"A brother and a father figure. A saviour to all who needed saving." Ysabell stood, her tears mingling with the rain streaming down her face as she spoke. "He was whatever we needed him to be. If he had known of what he faced in the abyss, he would still have chosen to go. All that is left for us is to be worthy of his sacrifice. He bought us our lives, what time we have, with his life." She walked forward and placed a hand on the memorial stone. "We will not waste it." Ysabell leaned in to whisper directly to the stone. "That bastard will die, I promise you. The last thing he sees will be your blades as they cut his heart out."

<><><>

Ysabell sat on her bed, Nuthionel's daggers in her hands. *What now and where to?* She asked herself, trying to figure the first step in finding this demon creature that was responsible for Nuthionel's death, when a shout from next door propelled her to her feet. Ready for battle, she ran from the room towards the cry.

"Cali! Can you hear me?" Guinevere's was a mix of elation and fear. Cali was still lying in her bed, but Ysabell could see her eyes were open and aware. She looked weak but awake.

"Guinevere, please." Ériu gently, but firmly, pushed Guin back into her chair and turned to Cali. "Take your time, you've been through a lot." Cali's face was contorted, anger, no, rage radiating from it. Her eyes found Ysabell's, a question burning in them.

"Yes. We are going after the one who caused this." Ysabell's voice was cold. "We're going to cut his insides out and show them to him." The strain in Cali's face faded and she lay back to rest.

<><><>

Athress gathered his Mages and walked out of the Mage district. The dwarven stone carvers were ready to start work. The approach to building a wall around Carraigbán would be novel. To Athress' knowledge it had never been tried, but he could think of no way of getting defences ready in time other than this. What worried him was the sheer size of the city. Certain areas would have to be sacrificed. The Northern Avenues of trees, the Eastern Aspen Row, behind the palace where several of more affluent residents of the city lived and some of the southern road. Even at that, it would be a tough task to complete the walls in time.

They crossed the bán river and headed down through the poorer districts onto the southern road. Up ahead Athress could see a group of some sixty or seventy Dwarves, and a handful of human apprentices being trained up. Dagen was the charge hand. A good Dwarf, solid, no slacking around him. He nodded at Athress.

"Mage, you really think you can do this?" he asked.

"Can you really finish it?" Athress shot back.

They both chuckled at the enormity of what they were about to attempt. The dwarves stepped back and Athress and the Mages lined up, staffs ready. Athress began to cast his spell with the other Mages like mirrors of him. The ground shook beneath them. The Dwarves looked with concerned glances at the buildings around them. They had all been evacuated at this end of the road but Athress had warned this might happen if the bedrock was solid.

Across the road, stone broke the surface and rose up, earth spilling to one side, cobbles bouncing down the slopes. In a line all along the row of Mages the same thing was happening. Sweat poured from the Mages, but they held the line.

It grew steadily, solid stone erupting from below the ground. For more than an hour they held, focusing their power into the living rock. Buildings that were in the way collapsed as the wall of rock surged from underneath them, leaving great piles of bricks and rubble lying at the base in many places. Eventually Athress halted, and all the Mages along the line followed suit. Several collapsing to the ground in exhaustion. Athress leaned on his staff and admired at their handiwork. He heard approaching footsteps of Dagen behind him.

"I'm impressed, Mage," he said. "Never have I seen such a thing. Taller than five men easily, over a hundred paces long. Go rest, you'll need it. Only fifty times more of that at least to do yet. I'll get my teams to work straight away. How long before you lot are ready to do the next section?"

Athress studied at the row of tired Mages. They would need time. "I have two teams. This group will need a week to recover. How soon before you will be ready to start on the next section?"

Dagen stared up at the wall of rock before him. "Ten days at least. We have to cut a gateway into this one, but non-gated sections, about six maybe seven days."

Athress nodded. "Four days' time I will bring the second team down to raise the next section. We will try to keep them rotating slightly ahead of your work so you won't need to wait for us." He regarded the river in the distance. "Have you thought about the river yet?"

"I still reckon our only chance there is Druids. It's too open, we can't protect it all. I've checked the spring at the temple district. Our water supply is safe, but they can damn it at any point leaving the city and poison us all with our own waste. Druids could fix that, open a channel or redirect it, or something. Those tree huggers are far better at that stuff than us. Has the assembly contacted the circle?"

"Not yet." Athress frowned. "They are still dwelling on the floods from ten years ago. I've tried to tell them those mercenaries attacked the Druids grove first and they merely defended themselves, but the privileged attitude of some of the Lords is beyond belief. They seem to think they have the right to do anything and no one should ever fight back. Fools. If they do not, I will make contact with the Circle myself and ask for help. The defence of the city was handed to myself and Garaveigh to oversee. If they want that to continue, they can damn well do as we say."

Athress nodded to the dwarf, he watched Dagen walk away and wave his team forward to get started cutting into the stone. The craftsmen in the Artisan District were already working on the gate that would sit in the opening once they'd carved it. Giant wooden doors with oaken beams three-foot-thick, lined in iron and banded with steel. Once it was done the Mages would enchant it to resist blunt force as well. The blacksmiths guild would also mould the thick bars to seal it - two-foot square, twelve-foot-long beams of solid steel.

<><><>

Garaveigh waited for Athress to join him in the Park near the Mage's District. The meeting with the assembly had not gone well. Lord Varilane was against asking the Druids circle for help. His son, Faros, had been one of those who attacked the Druids grove ten years ago hoping to drive them out so the forest in that area could be cleared. Faros died in the fight and the Druids created floods that destroyed the farmlands north of the City as a warning.

Garaveigh felt the Druids were right. They had been attacked, and their attackers paid the price. But it would seem from the arguments raised at the assembly many of the Council members were among those who had been illegally funding the group of mercenaries who attacked the druids and were still sore about their losses. Thankfully, Athress was a strong force to deal with. He had told them either they agreed to it, or the Mages and Priests would cease all work on the city's defences and leave them to their fate. That led Dartag to immediately call a vote. He declared that any who voted against the measure were clearly involved in funding the mercenaries who had attacked the grove, and their finances would be examined in detail.

After that, nobody voted against the measure to ask for help from the Circle, though several abstained. Once he had their approval, Athress sent a missive to the Druid's Circle, explaining the situation and offering them a Park in the City to set up a branch of the Circle in exchange for their aid. The Park would be theirs, from this day on and he would enshrine that in the City Charter to ensure no overzealous Lords tried to get their hands on it.

Garaveigh watched Athress walked across the grass to join him, he turned to Athress as he approached.

"Here? Will it be acceptable to them?" Garaveigh asked. "There are no trees, it's open on all sides to the streets and I wouldn't put it past some members of the assembly to send a few goons here."

"Yes here," Athress said. "Don't worry about the Druid's Circle. They are aware of the... political situation. As for trees, well I'm sure they will take care of those themselves. Ah... Here they come."

A shoot grew at an unnatural rate from the ground, some ten feet in front of them. It quickly developed from a seedling to a sapling, from a sapling to a small tree, then a large oak tree, and then a massive oak tree. Additional shoots began to spring from the ground around them.

Soon Athress and Garaveigh were standing in a small clearing in the centre of a dense growth of mature oak, ash, yew and rowan trees. Twisted roots began grow out of the grass in a circle around them, at the edge of the clearing. Garaveigh looked at Athress for reassurance, the Mage merely smiled. The roots thickened and grew up to man-height and formed into tall cone-shapes before stopping. These started to crack open and out stepped the Druids.

An elderly one was first. He was well built, with long grey hair turning white and a beard to match. His robes were a brownish-green and he held a staff. It wasn't carved, but instead looked to be grown from vines. Garaveigh recognised him as Haydleth. He didn't know much about the man, but he knew Athress and the old Druid had known each other years.

"We came as soon as we were able," he said. "This threat would destroy us all, not just this city. Have you seen the army up close yet?"

Athress nodded. "Yes. It is hard to believe a horde of goblins that large could have bred unnoticed. The mountains are barren wastelands and there is nothing there to feed them. This is no coincidence."

"There is more," Garaveigh cut in. "We have received an answer from our prayers to Assaurot. There is more beneath that mountain than just the Goblins. We don't know what, but he has told us what is hidden there could mean the difference between our destruction and our salvation. He sent a vision, which has left me confused. I saw the Heroes of Carraigbán, the three survivors, the Mage Vaaldreth and an Elven druidess with them, marching across the snow wastes towards the Mountains.

A Timely Intervention

Chapter 20

Ysabell trained hard with Cali and Guin in the Mages courtyard. Both herself and Cali were healing well, and the daily training was helping both their recovery physically and mentally. Blades moved fast and aggressively as they ran through their warm up manoeuvres. A small group of civilians gathered at the edges of the courtyard to watch the display. A sudden explosion from the Mage tower spun them around. They glanced at each other and ran in through the open door, weapons in hand heading towards the shouting.

They burst into the chambers of Vaaldreth, thick smoke billowed from a bone fire in the centre of the room. Vaaldreth was lying on the ground beyond it, flapping out flames on his robes. His face frantic as he turned to see them enter, words tumbled out.

"I intercepted a message of the enemy, from within Carraigbán. We have a traitor. He intends to kill the assembly as they meet today!" Before the last words left his lips Ysabell was hurtling down the corridor, she plunged down the stairs 3 steps at a time, Guin and Cali at her heels.

They reached palace in less than fifteen minutes. The gate guards were both dead, their throats slit. The group sprinted on, Ysabell praying they weren't too late. She took the steps up to the palace reception hall two at a time until she burst through the doors. A lone Palace Guard was attempting to defend himself from three well-armoured attackers. They toyed with him for sport, the corpses around the chamber showing his brothers in arms were all slaughtered.

Their heads swung when they heard the doors, and saw Ysabell and the others barge through. Before they had time to react, the first fell to a throwing dagger in his eye from Ysabell and the second to Cali's hatchet smashing through his chest plate. The last managed to get his sword raised to defend himself, but Ysabell didn't slow her pace. She parried his blade to one side with her left-hand blade, her other dagger plunging through his throat simultaneously.

The Palace guard slumped to his knees. "Thank you," he panted. "The chambers... they've gone into the chambers... you must help... I think.." His eyes scanned the room in shock. "I'm the only guard left!"

Ysabell turned from him, bolting up the steps to the assembly chambers.

<><><>

Athress rose to speak, "My Lords and Ladies, I have the latest updates on our defences. With the Druids work, our water supplies are safe, as is our sewage exiting the city. No one can dam either. I have some thoughts on strengthening our forces..."

Lord Varilane rose and interrupted. "There is no need Athress. No need at all. You see you are dead, all of you who defy my Lord Xelazenivein, are dead." As he spoke, mercenary soldiers in the armour of House Varilane entered the chambers. They arranged themselves around the table in a circle, swords drawn. One stepped up to the raised seats of Garaveigh and Athress and shouted at them to get down. Athress' face grew dark with anger, he raised his hand to cast but was struck from behind, a heavy blow to the head with the pommel of a sword. He fell forward and was caught by Garaveigh.

Varilane continued on, smirking at Athress; "My life is worth more than all of yours, anointed by a new God, I am the divinely chosen King of this land. Your mutterings and attempts to cast will achieve nothing. I am protected by the power of my God!"

"Let's test that theory!" Said a voice from the chamber doors, the voice was low, just enough to carry around the room, confident, completely cold and devoid of emotion. There, in the doorway, with the hall behind filled by the bloodied bodies of Varilane's dead guards, stood a figure. It was hard to make it out, clouds of shadows, almost like black smoke wisped and swept around it. The assembled lords and ladies of the council were unsure whether this was a saviour or something worse. Athress smiled, and prepared to begin casting, while Garaveigh lowered his head and began muttering a prayer. Lord Varilane turned pale at the apparition; this creature had apparently killed several of his guards, without a sound, in only seconds since the rest of his troops had entered the chamber.

He swung to his Guards, "Kill it, Kill it now!!" His voice rose several octaves with fear. The Guards on either side of the door moved towards the figure, too slow, it moved in a blur, like the shadow of a dancer seen through a sheet, no clear shapes, nothing defined, but smooth confident movements. Both guards fell dead, one with his hands clutching his slit throat, the other with a hole in his breastplate spewing blood.

Ysabell leapt onto the table and cleared it, slamming feet first into Lord Varilane as he screamed for his guards. Several guards ran forward only to find themselves attacked from behind, a deranged ginger Halfling had already killed two before they knew they were under attack, and a huge Priestess, taller than any of the soldiers, strode into the room swinging a giant mace that crushed the skulls of any who came in reach. Athress cast a shield over the council members to protect them, and ushered them to the far side of the room. All but Dartag, the dwarven blacksmith, who swept up a sword from one of the dead Guards and tore into Varilane's forces. Athress and Garaveigh entered the fight, lightning blasting from Athress' fingertips and Holy Fire erupting from random mercenaries as Garaveigh cast. As Ysabell rose from Varilane's chest, three guards charging at her, swords raised, the first died with a throwing dagger in his throat, she ran at the second, dropped to her knees and she slid past him, her right-hand blade slicing up to into his groin severing the artery, she tumbled forward, rising to her feet and skewering the last guard in the chest with both blades as she did so.

The fight was over in minutes. Guinevere tied Lord Varilane to a chair for questioning as palace guard reinforcements arrived just in time to drag the dead bodies out.

Varilane screamed at them "You've already lost fools. You face a second army, coming from the Northern Mountains. They have already set off. Thirty thousand strong. A demon servant of my Lord now rules the Goblins and has unified the tribes as their King, he has sent a general to lead them, A Demon that has led armies for millennia and never known defeat. You are all dead! More will be coming too, demons, and creatures of the abyss! You cannot stop this."

Athress watched him and nodded to himself as the palace Guards dragged Varilane from the room. He stood and signalled Ysabell to join him. They walked back to the seats reserved for the Council advisors. Athress asked one of the guards to bring a third chair to the raised platform. Once it was in place, he indicated Ysabell should sit, then called for order. Garaveigh re-joined them and the entire assembly took their places.

Guinevere and Cali stood either side of the door, remaining on-guard in case Xelazenivein, or his traitorous followers, had any other surprises in store.

"So" Athress voice was weary as he nodded towards Varilane. "Another horde of Goblins have left the Mountains and are making their way here. We will face nearly twice what we had though then, with only four and half thousand or so defenders." His eyes scanned the room, worried faces stared up at him from the council.

"The Mage tower, the Priests quarter, and now the druids, will have an impact on evening the odds, but being realistic..."

He regarded Garaveigh, then Ysabell and then the two companions standing at the door. His face thoughtful as he paused. "Being realistic we have no way of defending against such a number. They will wear us down with simple attrition."

Gasps of shock came from his captive audience. Heads sank into hands as councilors realised they and their families were now trapped. The city with its new impenetrable walls was no longer a safe, defensible location, it was a death trap.

Athress raised his hand for attention. "We have one option still," he said. "If the Goblins fight because of this demon, who has risen as a king, uniting all the tribes. They must believe this 'king' to be an incredibly strong and powerful goblin. They would not follow a demon knowingly. It is my belief that if this treachery would become known, they would turn back to their mountain holes seeking retribution against the demon, or break down to fighting amongst themselves. Or if this Demon was slain and his demonic General, they would see their great leader defeated and flee. Either way, the city would no longer be their goal."

Lady Carale interrupted. "How exactly do we get them to realise their leader is a demon? Just send out a messenger to tell them? Why would they believe us?"

The others raised their voices in agreement. *If I say it now, I put Ysabell and the others in an awkward position. But I need a plan agreed on now.* Athress sighed to himself and lifted his hand once more and silence fell over the hall.

"We have but one option," he said. "We need a small group to travel to the Northern Mountains as fast as possible. Once there, they must find where the Goblins are coming from, a cave, a ruin or something. They must have a settlement somewhere. Track down this false king and expose him or kill him. Let the goblins see their great king as he truly is or dead and his body evaporate as only a demon's will. Either they will realise their error in following a demon or they will see the King they worship slaughtered. Either option works. With luck, then they will flee back into their caves and deep places. In the meantime, we hold as long as we can. We will arm every man and woman able, and send them to defend the walls. We will also send missives to Deep Crag and Glanmyrdwyrr to ask for aid. ... I see no other way." Athress sat down heavily. It was a lot to ask, but he saw no other options. He turned to Ysabell.

"You are the most suited to lead this group if you are willing. I know you have suffered, lost a great deal, not least almost your own lives for a city that is not your own already. I beg for your aid once again."

Ysabell's eyes wandered to Cali and Guin. The concern and worry plain in them.

"You wish to find Xelazenivein, you wish retribution?" Athress continued. "I have no leads for you, but the demon leading those Goblins is his servant. That is your best hope, our best hope for information."

A Flicker of Hope

Chapter 21

Ysabell told the others she'd meet them back at the Goblin's Head that evening. She needed some time to clear her head and get her thoughts together. She walked through the streets, watching crowds gather in places, neighbours talking, worrying, fear spreading like a plague. The news of the second army was out. Some houses had carts outside, the occupants packing up what belongings they had to try finding safety to the south while the road was still open. Squads of guardsmen jogged by regularly, in training for the city defence. She stared at the size and strength of the new city walls, astonished by their magnitude. She heard from passers-by how the stone rose by magic, was carved and shaped by Dwarven Stone masons.

How could it all be for nothing? she asked herself. All these people, doing everything they could, and it was all pointless, buying themselves a few extra days or weeks in a siege.

As she reached the Mage district gates, she found a boy of no more than six or seven sitting on the road outside. His clothes were clean but thin and worn. His shoes had nearly no sole left. He looked ashamed, sitting with his cap held out in front of him hoping for a few coins. She sat beside him and asked him where his parents were.

"Dead." He nodded to the Mage district. Ysabell waited for more, but he went silent again.

"Who do you live with?" She asked "Who looks after you now?"

"My sister." He looked at her suspiciously. "Why do you want to know all this?"

Ysabell sighed. Orphans on the streets, the city it seemed was glad of its citizen's sacrifices, but not thankful enough to care for those left behind. She reached to her waist and took a coin pouch from it with 2 gold pieces and several silver in it. She handed it to the boy.

"Go straight home to your sister. Talk to no one; let no one know you have that. You will be robbed if anyone finds out. Go now."

She rose and walked away, behind her she heard a quiet "Thank you." And then hurried footsteps as he ran away.

She wished she could be there to see the girl's face when he handed her what would be a year's salary to an average household in the poorer districts.

She headed to the Mage tower, to see how Vaaldreth was doing. In the park outside the tower she found him seated on a bench, stretched out enjoying the sun, his hands heavily bandaged. Her shadow moved across him, he opened his eyes, an annoyed look in them, until he saw her smiling down.

"Ah, Ysabell," he said. "I hear you swooped in to save the day in a most dramatic fashion."

"Oh you know I love to make an entrance...You've heard then?"

Vaal's face grew serious. "Aye. They want to send you off on some crazy suicide mission into the Northern Mountains to kill a demon, spoil Xelazenivein's plans and save the city. That about sum it up?"

<><><>

Ysabell looked away into the distance, towards the north. She couldn't see the mountains from the city. It would take weeks to reach them. Vaaldreth could see the conflict in her face, she wanted to tell the city no. Ysabell was clearly still distraught over seeing Nuthionel die. She had almost lost Cali and herself. She clearly wanted to find a way to get back to Xelazenivein and this was a distraction. Vaaldreth thought it only made sense; she'd never had any time to grieve. Unlike Cali and Guinevere, and to a lesser extent himself, she had never suffered this kind of loss before, seeing a companion; a friend die in front of you isn't easy. At the same time, he knew she wanted to do this, or part of her did, she was split in three, the part that wanted to pack it in, that hated what she had become, a cold-hearted killer, sit in a tavern and drink till it all went away, the part wanted to do 'the right thing' and be the hero people wanted her to be and that last part, the part that maybe frightened her a little. The part that enjoyed the fighting in the abyss, that enjoyed the bloodshed and killing. Ysabell was young, it would be hard for her to understand, it was in our nature to revel in such things. You couldn't fight it, you just accepted it and made sure you never sought battle just to satisfy that urge but at the same time, never fled for fear of that urge.

"You could pack up, head south with the refugees and leave Carraigbán and its people to their fate. Then when the goblin armies come south, you could travel west to the dwarven cities, and then when the Goblin armies arrive there… Well, at some point you will have to fight or accept death. For me, I would rather die facing my enemies, I will join whatever group heads north. If I die, I won't go alone" Vaaldreth stood and looked off to the North as well. They stared at the horizon in silence. After a few minutes he spoke again. "Those Northern Mountains look as good a place to die as any other." He grinned at Ysabell. "Maybe even better than most."

Ysabell smiled back at him. "Not quite what I expected the adventurer's life to be like. I had visions of exciting raids into underground tombs finding treasure every other day." She looked down, a deep sadness in her eyes. "Not watching your friends die, unable to save them."

"Ysabell, you three are the only flicker of hope this city has left. You may not feel like a hero." He snorted. "I'm not sure any hero ever does. It's not how you feel that really matters I think. It's that you try, that these people get to see you standing up and fighting, they get to see someone willing to face this enemy. That, that is what gives your average person the strength to fight on. You are not a person to them, you are a symbol. Without that symbol, they have already lost. Think on it."

He rose and led her inside to her chamber to rest. Athress arrived back not long after and spoke with Vaaldreth as they both stood at the door of her room, while she slept.

"Will she do it? Will they all do it?" He asked.

Vaaldreth turned sternly to Athress, anger in his eyes;

"Athress, she is a seventeen-year-old girl. Already having saved this city twice, has lost the closest thing she had to family in the abyss, now expected to lead her remaining closest friends to, likely, their death, alone and isolated under the Mountains. She may as well be going back into the abyss for all the help she will find there. I believe she will do it, but try to bear in mind what it is you ask of her." Vaaldreth left to head to his own study, he had much preparing to do.

In a vault, far below the ground. Sealed for a thousand years lay a tome, a grimoire. It had belonged to a Mage, Marveth. One of, if not the most powerful that had ever lived. He had been man-kinds saviour, once. But then had turned to evil as his lust for power grew and he tried to challenge the Gods. Vaaldreth would make a new staff, using spells from Marveth's spell book. He would memorise what he could from it. They would need stronger magics, forbidden magics. He strode down the ancient stairs that led to the vaults. Before long he stood before a door. It wasn't particularly impressive. A small wooden door set in the old stone of the walls. But he knew better to judge by appearances. This door was sealed by ancient and powerful magics, wards and seals were carved into it. Closing his eyes he viewed it with his mind instead, he could see the mesh as it wrapped around it, around the walls beyond it. It was not going to be easy to breach.

< >< >< >

Several hours later, Ysabell awoke, it took her a moment to realise where she was. She stared at the ceiling as if hoping for divine inspiration when a voice broke the silence.

"I forget, sometimes, that you are new to this life, that you are still so young and that you also felt his loss. I know what I ask of you is selfish, it is unfair, and it may seem ungrateful for all you and your companions have done thus far. The burden of leadership is a heavy one, and sometimes we take decisions that cost us dearly. My decisions sent the closest thing I've ever had to a son into that portal. I sent him to his death. That weighs heavy on me, but perhaps a heaver weight is the knowledge that I would do it again."

Ysabell sat up in shock, looking at Athress. The old man sat in the chair she had sat in, in what seemed like a different lifetime, writing a letter to her father. His eyes showed the tell-tale signs that he had wept and he appeared so much older than he had only months before when they left. He looked back at her defiantly.

"Yes, you heard me, I would do it again. I accept the responsibility to defend this city and defend it I will, in any way I can. I cannot condemn the tens of thousands living here to death because of my personal feelings. It broke my heart to lose him, but the choice was still the right one, my attempt to close that portal could have saved more lives than I could count. The fact that I failed doesn't change that the decision was the best one available to me at that time." He looked off out the window and quietly intoned, almost like it was a learned verse, "Leaders bear the hard choices so others don't have to."

Athress hung his head. She could see these months had taken their toll on him too. She realised they weren't the only ones to have suffered. She'd seen the plaque erected outside listing the names of those who fought in the clearing, and who died there. *Was their sacrifice any less than Nuthionel's? Was his sacrifice to be in vain? If here what would he do?* Ysabell shook her head. That was an easy question. *He would do what is right. He would go, as will Cali and Guin. He wouldn't think twice about it with all these lives in the balance, neither would they.*

"I will go," Ysabell said, rising as she spoke and heading for the door.

"Because you believe it is the right thing to do?" Athress asked watching her closely. "Or because it's what he would have done?"

Ysabell paused for a moment, then without answering, she continued out of the room and didn't look back. She made her way to the Goblin's Head to meet the others.

Ysabell moved through the city crowd with ease. People moved aside when they saw her. Word had spread; everyone knew who she was. To Ysabell, people seemed more afraid of her than anything else.

117

She greeted her friends with a nod and Cali disappeared to get her a drink. They sat in the same booth at the back where she had first met Cali. They drank in silence, each of them filled with memories. Finally, Ysabell spoke.

"I'm going north, I've agreed to try this … this suicide mission. What the hell, I survived the last one." Her attempt to sound light hearted didn't seem to fool the others. Guinevere reached across the table and took Ysabell's hand.

"We will be glad to have you with us. As I know Vaaldreth will be. We need to know where we are going, so a guide will join us. Several members of the Druids circle have been scouting to the North tracking the movements of the army, and tracing them back to the mountains. One of these druids is coming with us." She looked at Ysabell. "There is hope Ysabell, we can do this and we can return alive. We've been through worse."

Ysabell looked up at Guinevere, smiled, and squeezed her hand back. But her eyes showed no hope. *We've been through worse.... but we had Nuthionel to lead us then...*

A Guide in the Night
Chapter 22

Athress organised rooms at the palace for the four companions to allow them rest and ready themselves. Ysabell was anxious to be on their way, the optimism of the others and the knowledge that Vaaldreth would be with them had raised her confidence. But they had to wait. The druid circle scouts had only just returned to the city after several weeks away and needed time to recuperate and fill Athress in on what the situation was. Athress had come to them that morning to say the news wasn't good. The first army was making better time than they had anticipated. They would likely reach the walls in a day or less. He had also voiced his concerns that the approaching army had stopped to cut wood two days ago, to make ladders and equipment for tackling a wall. They shouldn't yet know there was a wall, so Athress had fears another traitor in the city was in contact. He warned the companions to be on their guard, trust no one.

Moonlight flitted in through a crack in the heavy curtains, sending a silver shaft of light across Ysabell's room. In its path were backpacks and weapons, to the sides, beds, each one with a mound under the covers, it was two in the morning, and not a sound stirred those sleeping in the palace. The shaft of light was briefly broken, as a slim shape moved among the bags, silently across the room. The silence shattered, the curtains ripped aside and moonlight flooded the room.

The creeping stranger froze in shock, the crack in the curtains had been intentional. It had ruined her night sight and made the shadows in the corners deeper. The mounds in each bed were blankets made to look like people, each corner of the room had the occupants hidden in the shadows, fully armed, bows, spells and daggers pointing at their night visitor. She turned to face the moonlight, so it lit up her face. Guinevere, Cali and Ysabell burst out laughing.

"Aye druid, not so stealthy as ye thought are ye? Cali laughed.

Guinevere, still chuckling commented. "Dangerous risk sneaking up on us in the dark."

The small and slender druid smiled. She was smaller than all but Cali with dark hair that was curly, but weighed down by its length to seem wavier. Her voice was soft and warm, her face smiling. "Well, I figured with you here Cali, I could have marched in with a brass band and still not wake you. I should have suspected when I didn't hear your subtle foghorn of a snore I had to listen to while healing you."

The Druid turned to Ysabell and Vaaldreth. "I have come to lead you out of here. Athress sent me. He said to tell you his fears are realised. The enemy will be at the wall in a few hours, and they already have advance scouts at all known exits to the city. It would seem they know of your mission. The traitor has been busy. We need to leave now, if we are to leave at all."

The companions were ready to go. After Athress' warning that day, Ysabell had insisted they have everything ready to leave at a moment's notice. They grabbed their gear and followed Ériu out of the room and through the dark corridors of the palace. They avoided the palace guard, choosing to trust no one like instructed.

Ériu led them through the corridors until they reached an empty council chamber on the second floor. They crept inside and closed the door. The window was open. Ysabell went over to check outside and found, to her a surprise, a thick vine rising from the ground to the window. There were plants nearby, but nothing it could have come from. She realised it must have been how Ériu had come in undetected.

The companions carefully climbed down the vine, passing bags and gear down to each other until they were all on the ground. Ériu was the last out the window. When she reached the ground, she touched the vine and it shrank back down into the ground. She turned to the others, her finger to her lips, and then led the way through the palace gardens to the wall. When they stood at the wall, sheltered from view by a screen of undergrowth, Ériu spoke again.

"The gates are watched. I don't trust the Guards here, we have reason to suspect at least one, maybe more, are in contact with the enemy. Several Guard's bodies were found disposed of over the walls, stripped of their uniforms. I would guess, those uniforms will be worn by either the Guards taking the next shift in defending your room, or waiting for Athress in the morning as he leaves the Mage tower to come to the Assembly." She smirked. "Athress is already with the Druids circle. I think those 'guards' will find more than they bargained for."

After she filled them in, Ériu knelt on the ground and pushed her hands down into the soil. She closed her eyes. For a few moments, nothing happened. Ysabell glanced at the others, but they were all watching the little druid. Then Ysabell felt slight tremors in the ground. Small growths appeared in several spots around them, growing into acorn shaped pods made of roots. They bent to open doorway into each pod. Inside was enough room for a single person to stand.

Ériu stood and motioned that they should enter. Ysabell wasn't at all feeling trusting enough to step into a pod that had clawed its way from the ground, but the others all did without a word and Ériu had healed her and Cali. Likely saved their lives, so she followed the others, hoping she wasn't going to regret this.

The roots tightened up and sealed the entrance behind her. Ysabell became aware of a sensation of movement and a strange earthy noise it went on for some twenty or more minutes, it was hard to know. The pod shuddered and came to a stop. Its root walls shrivelled and opened again. Ysabell hurriedly stepped out before it shrunk into the ground.

She looked around and found that they were in a clearing in a wooded area. Several Druids were there, as was Athress. The others all stood around looking disorientated, like she probably looked as well. The night was still not over, and the area was lit only by moonlight.

Athress came forward to greet them. "Excellent, you are all here. We hoped Ériu would reach you before anything happened."

"Athress, we cannot tarry here," Ériu interrupted. "The enemy are all around. If a trailing scout for the lead army should double back or an advance scout for the second army should find this place, our trip will end rather swiftly."

Athress looked suitably chastised. "I'm sorry. I do like to talk a bit more than I should, too much time spent alone in my study I think. But yes, Ériu is correct, you are outside the City now. This was the only way the enemy had not anticipated. Arcane magics are traceable, nature's magic is not. The city is now surrounded to all intents and purposes, the bulk of the army is even now reaching the walls. The Druids have the only secret ways in and out. They have taken you as far as they are able, approximately thirty miles north of Carraigbán. The only advice I can give you is trust Ériu. She knows the roads, and the paths of the wilds well. Keep off the main roads, let no one see you and leave no survivors or witnesses if it comes to that. Leave no sign of your passing. Hopefully that will give you the edge of surprise when you reach the mountains. We intended you to leave on horseback, but that's out of the question now. You'd be an easy target. Move as fast as you can, when you are close to the mountains Ériu has an idea on getting you through the last leg faster."

He clasped Ysabell's hands in his. "So many owe you so much already. I am sorry we had to ask this of all of you." He smiled but the sadness in his eyes betrayed him. Ysabell could see he was worried they wouldn't survive, like she was. If it came to it, she resolved to send the others home and stealth her way to the demon alone. Not an ideal solution, but at least her friends would live to see another tomorrow. As if he could read her mind Athress spoke once more.

"No one of you could hope to complete this task alone, but together, you have a chance and no more than that. The thoughts, prayers and hopes of a nation go with you."

With that, he turned. Joined by the other druids, they stepped into more pods rising from the ground. In minutes the five companions stood alone in the clearing, the song of birds told them it was dawn, before the first light breaking over the horizon had begun to filter through the trees, giving an eerie, green glow to the forest floor. Birds sung their songs, and the buzz of insects wasn't far behind it.

"We should move as soon as possible; we have little time and a lot of ground to cover." Ysabell spoke with confidence and determination. "Ériu? Do we know if it's safe to set out yet?"

"There's nothing close to us now, the Druids scouted this area before we gathered here." Ériu's soft and gentle voice was calm and reassuring. "The sooner we set off the better."

Needing nothing else to assure her, Ysabell turned and start off into the trees heading North, towards the distant mountains. The others stepped in behind and followed. They marched for most of the remaining darkness and well into the next day. Ysabell wanted to cover as much ground as they could each march, at regular intervals Ériu would lag behind and call to woodland creatures to come trample and obscure their trail. They stopped once to eat after about four hours' march, then continued for another five hours before stopping. It was a little after midday.

"We should stop and make camp, it is better that we move as much as we can under the cover of darkness." Ériu stated. "If we make camp now and get some rest we can set off again during the night. I can lead the way; my Elvish night vision will insure we take the best path through the forest."

Ysabell could see the sense in that and agreed, the other the same. They quickly set up a cold camp, no fire to mark their location. They all had dried meat and fruits in their bags so cooking wasn't needed. There was little talk while they ate. Ysabell watched her companions, each caught up in their own thoughts as they sat around the ground. Only Cali seemed completely as ease.

"We should set up a watch." Ysabell offered. "Just to be sure. I'll take first."

Swiftly they arranged a watch order and those not on watch lay down to sleep. Soon Ysabell was alone with her thoughts in the still forest. Green filtered light shone down in beams through their dappled shade. *Looks almost magical.*

Ériu took the last watch, sitting in meditation she connected herself to the living, breathing forest around her. She could feel every creature for miles, the heartbeats, the breaths, the deaths of small animals in the jaws of the fox, the elation of the hawk as it plucked its prey from the leaves. Ériu was young for a Druid with her power, but she had a connection to Nature few humans would ever manage, even among her own people, the elves, it was rare that one so young could connect so deeply with the world around her. Ériu pushed at the limits of her power, stretching her awareness as far as she could in all directions. It took a lot of effort. She was sweating and strained looking.

Ysabell and the others awoke to find Ériu sitting in meditation, sweating and strained-looking. Guinevere put Ysabell's mind at rest.

"She is scouting," she said. "Linking herself to the plants and animals around us, she will sense anything that walks, crawls or flies in the vicinity. Though she looks under strain, I hope she isn't trying to push too far."

While they waited, they ate and prepared to travel again. It would be dark soon.

Night Terrors

Chapter 23

Ériu slumped forward, waking from her meditation suddenly. She was visibly distressed.

"Goblins, two squads. They are seeking us," she said. "Athress was correct, we are betrayed."

Ysabell rose immediately and started packing up her equipment.

"Everyone ready to leave in five minutes," she said. "Ériu can you do anything to cover our spoil? I don't want our camp site left as a clear marker to where we are or were."

The Druid nodded. "Once we have cleared the area I will erase our signs here. You have a plan?"

Ysabell was already hoisting her pack, ready to go. "Yes. We get the hell out of here and put as much distance as we can between them and us. If they are tracking us, that won't be enough as they know which way we're headed. So once dark, I will seek them and see if they are as afraid as they should be." Her face darkened as she smiled at Ériu. The smile was not a pleasant one. It was cold and deadly. "Bad things come out of the shadows at night."

They cleared the campsite quickly and then the companions headed off to the north. Ériu lingered till they were clear and then knelt, her hands pushing down through the earth like it was water. Ysabell wondered how she did that. The earth here was undisturbed, and packed hard, she would've needed a spade to get into it. The little druid's eyes closed and her face relaxed, the others watched from the trees.

After a few moments, small shoots crept up from the ground. These changed from small shoots into small ferns, which became big ferns. The area they had camped in was now overgrown and looked as though it hadn't been disturbed in years. Ysabell stared in wonder at the druid's power.

The group moved on through the woods, travelling in single file to disguise their numbers and reduce the tracks they left. By the time it was dark, it'd been several hours, Ysabell signaled the group to stop and rest. Whilst the others set about getting food out and prepared to rest for a bit, Ysabell checked her dual pairs of blades. Then, leaving all the rest of her gear with the camp, she set off into the woods alone, her mind remembering what seemed a lifetime ago, Nuthionel creeping towards the bandit's camp. Moving like a ghost. As she disappeared from the view of her companions, she let the shadows swirl up around her, wrapping her in their cold embrace. She melted into the darkness of the woods, just another shadow flitting through the half-light.

<><><>

The leader of the Goblin patrol didn't seem to live up to the reputation for stupidity. He led his troops carefully and quietly. These were no blundering band of gormless goblins. They walked in single file, carefully. Their leader picking out the trail ahead. Ysabell had watched them a while now, they had lost the trail several times where Ériu had covered it, but always he found it again. No doubt it helped that he knew where they were headed.

They were gaining on the companions, so Ysabell wasted no time. The odds were far too high for her to attack them. But in single file, they created an opportunity to spread a little fear as well as lower their numbers. *Careful now, don't blow this. Remember Nuthionel in the ruins, two Goblins, dead before they knew he was there. You can do this.*

The last Goblin in line was clearly a scout, he was moving side to side across their trail, looking for any signs of their prey. It made it all the easier for Ysabell, she waited until he strayed off to the left, out of sight of the patrol briefly. But long enough for a shadow to step out from behind a tree beside him and open his throat, a second blade slid between his armour straps at his side, up into his lungs. He made no sound as she let him drop gently to the forest floor.

Ysabell dragged him quietly in under some ferns. She didn't want him easy to find if the patrol went looking. Once she was sure he was well hidden, she hurried back after the patrol. Two more Goblins died silently in the dark. Their bodies vanishing. As she approached to find a fourth victim, the patrol leader shouted out a name. Ysabell leaned back against a tree, about twenty paces off the trail, in dark shadows, and waited.

"Oc'Jar? Come!" The patrol stopped, but no one came forward. He called again, louder. "Oc'Jar! Where is Oc'Jar?" He stood back and looked thoughtful for a moment. Then in common he shouted to his squads.

"Everyone, in formation, now!" he ordered. "In line!" He walked down the lines of Goblins counting. Out of sixteen goblins, Ysabell knew they were now only thirteen. Three were missing, yet there had been no cry, no shout, no sign, he wouldn't even know when it had happened. They'd been marching for hours.

She cast her gaze over the now nervous looking patrol. She knew what they were thinking. Something had changed; somehow, they were no longer the hunters... Something was hunting them, and it had taken three already, three well-armed experienced Goblins, gone without a sound or a sign. They would be worried. He barked several orders and all remaining Goblins moved into pairs to march side by side, with him at the lead. It would not be so easy to pick them off when they were in pairs but she wasn't going to let stop her. As they set off, a scream went up from behind them, Ysabell ran right through the middle of his line of troops, two Goblins fell dead as she passed, and then she was gone back into the undergrowth. Before they could even think about following, there was nothing to follow, the darkness swallowed her whole, there was nothing but shadows all around in the undergrowth... The plan was working, the remaining Goblins looked terrified. They probably had no idea what they had just seen. She knew the shadows made her look almost demonic.

Yes! Ysabell watched as the Goblins made a camp, quickly and fearfully, they were jumping at shadows. Forcing them, creatures of the dark, to hide with a fire for light, was going to destroy their morale. But it also made it harder for Ysabell to target them.

Silence descended on the Goblin camp, a fire was lit in the centre, they all huddle as close to it as they could, weapons drawn and looking out into the darkness of the forest. Noises in the darkness caused jumps and grunts of fear and fright, several hours they sat like that, some of them started to nod off, drained by fear and tension. The dawn was coming; their leader was clearly furious. He strode over to a tree to relieve himself, Ysabell moved through the trees to get close. She cracked a twig under foot as she prepared to throw a knife, he turned his head to late, all he saw was the sharp throwing knife entered his right eye sinking deep, into his brain, killing him instantly. He slumped forward against the tree, and collapsed, Ysabell's dark shadowy arms crept around the tree trunk and withdrew the knife. It vanished as quickly as it had appeared.

The other goblins saw him fall, saw the shadow on the tree trunk; it almost looked like it had come out of the tree. Not one of them moved to his aid, they stayed around the fire until the sun rose. Then gathering their belongings, and headed East.

Ysabell was left with a choice, she didn't know where they were headed. If they were heading for reinforcements, they could bring the second army down on top of her and her companions. She contemplated for a while. Ten seemed like too many to charge in and kill, but she couldn't take the risk of giving away their position. She made her decision and ran light footed after the goblin patrol.

It was brighter now, no shadows to hide in, bar her own. When she caught up with them, she hid behind a large oak and watched them for a few minutes. She got a feel for their speed, checking which ones had the bows and who was carrying swords. All the little details that would decide what order they had to die in. It was foolish, and even though she knew it, her emotions overrode her good sense. She still woke nights feeling that creatures tongue on her face. Sweating and shaking. Since Nuthionel's death she didn't even have the comfort of knowing her savior was nearby. Every Goblin she killed made that fear ease for a time.

She took a deep breath and drew two throwing knives, then ran from her cover straight at the goblin patrol. Her wrists flicked. Two fell dead before they knew what hit them. She drew another throwing knife without slowing down to kill a third. The last Goblin's marching partner saw him fall with the knife in his back and let out a roar.

The entire patrol turned and drew their weapons. Ysabell with shadows swirling around her ran through the undergrowth straight at them. She hoped the sight was terrifying them. The goblins froze in confusion; the pause was all Ysabell needed. Her first two daggers flew through the air, killing the two furthest from her, both of whom had bows ready to draw. She drew her two enchanted daggers out of their sheathes and sliced out wide to cut the throat of a goblin on her right as she ran in. The one on her left parried, and with his own second blade opened a deep wound on her shoulder. She spun on the ball of her left foot and plunged her right-hand dagger into its back. Three Goblins still lived. Moving on instinct at this stage, Ysabell hurled threw one dagger into the throat of the goblin behind her. Then she ran at the goblin in front, rolling under his blade, taking a fierce blow to her ribs from his fist, she rose and open his throat from behind. As blood sprayed onto her face she flipped the blade and hurled it straight into the chest of the third. As it struck, the Goblins arrow struck Ysabell in her already wounded arm. Biting deep into the flesh.

The clearing fell silent. Ten dead goblins lay in pools of their own blood. The wounds on her shoulder were both deep and throbbing. She was losing blood fast. Tearing cloth from one of the goblins shirts, she removed the arrow and bound the wounds tight. She retrieved her blades, cleaning them and sheathing them one by one. Once she'd recovered them all she set off on her long walk back to camp

Ysabell jogged back into the camp, looking exhausted and worn. Her leather armour sliced at the shoulder, dried blood caked around the bandages. Guinevere immediately went to check her wounds. Cali frowned. "Not one," she groused. "Not one bloody goblin did you leave for me!" She marched off in a huff. Vaaldreth explained.

"Ériu watched your battle from a wood mouse' eyes. It was foolhardy, dangerous and put our entire mission at risk." His face was dark and angry. "Did you hear nothing of what Athress said? No one of us can do this alone Ysabell. We are a team. You were lucky out there. Luck doesn't last." He walked off to get his belongings cleaned up.

The Battle Begins
Chapter 24

Athress stood before the assembled troops of Carraigbán. They stretched across the courtyard and Gardens of the Palace. His eyes scanned the crowds as they looked up expectantly. The fierce determination on the faces of those in their twenties, thirties and forties. These would be his fiercest fighters, young enough to wield a blade with skill and force, old enough not to be too fool hardy, and holding in their heart their children. Lastly, the eyes of youth, some terrified and red from weeping, some proud and excited.

Athress contemplated on how cruel the world was, and how foolish warriors were with their stories of glory and honor on the battlefield. Few told the truth of blood, and maiming, and dismemberment; the screams of the young and old; the emptying of bladders; the foul stench of rotting corpses. Where's the glory in watching your best friend die in your arms, his entrails spilling from his stomach? Athress hated himself for what he must do, the innocence of a whole generation of Carraigbán's young was about to be lost.

He stepped up onto the plinth, cheers greeting him from the crowds from those who saw him as the stories described him. The Mage who called lightning from the skies and fire from his fingertips, who had travelled the world, fought Demons, Goblins and all manner of evil creature in the Bowels of the Earth. The Mage that would fight with them on the walls until the bitter end. All that was true, but that wouldn't change the fact that they were so vastly outnumbered. Many, if not all of them, would die, and he along with them. If Ysabell and the others failed, nothing would save them. The walls and this ragtag militia were only buying time.

He raised his hands, causing the cheering to rise to a crescendo. Then, whispering a spell, he made his voice echo out over the crowd so all could hear him.

"We stand here today, not to celebrate or to mourn, we gather here, side by side, to show each other and our enemy that despite treachery, despite the forces of hell raised against us, we will not surrender! We will not be broken! AND WE WILL NOT BE DEFEATED!"

The crowd screamed, the sounds of shields and swords clashing together echoing through the city.

"This enemy comes to kill each and every last one of us! They will not stop until even the memory of us is consigned to history! With an army the like of which has never been seen, they think to make us cower; to make us beg before they finish us! They come certain of their victory! THEY ARE WRONG!"

Again, the crowd stirred with cheers and the clashing of iron.

"We WILL hold these walls. We WILL defend this city. We WILL turn this tide! For Carraigbán!"

The chant erupted across the crowds, spreading through every street and avenue. Athress took up his staff and with his entourage of Mages took the steps down from the Plinth to march to his place at the northern wall. The warriors, the women, the men, the mothers, fathers, grandparents and children marched behind him, clanging their swords on their shields. They marched in unison like the beating of war drums as all their voices echoed, "For Carraigbán!" over and over again.

The militia spread into their units and took their assigned posts between the units of the actual Palace and City Guards and Mercenaries. Athress' plan was to split up the civilians as much as possible since they were the weak link. He surrounded them with experienced fighters who would take the pressure off them. He wished their desire to protect those they loved was a substitute for battle experience. He felt the weight of tremendous guilt at how many of these people would likely die.

Athress sighed. Without them, the city would fall on the first day. "We bear difficult choices, so others don't have to..." he whispered as if to convince himself.

As he took his place on the wall, over the north gate, Athress gazed out over the parapet upon the legions of the enemy. He felt relief to see the formations seemed only semi-organised. Even the influence of the demon ruling as their king couldn't change Goblins into a disciplined fighting force. But with forty thousand or so of them facing 4,500 soldiers with another 8000 in untrained civilian militias, they didn't need to be disciplined.

The leader of the goblin forces stood at the front of his army and was giving his final words to his troops. They didn't carry as far as the city. Athress looked over his shoulder at the archers in the streets below. They had their arrows in front of them, bows in their hands, awaiting the command. His eyes strayed to the abandoned warehouse near the gates. If the gates broke he had a backup plan, but it would take a lot of luck and good timing to work. If they broke.

The goblin leader finished his speech and the shouts from the massive army beyond the walls suggested they were soon to charge. Athress turned to his Mages and checked that they were ready. They all nodded. There were no acolytes on the wall for the first day. He needed the strongest and best only to give the enemy something to fear.

The Goblins started forward, an unimaginable black mass of bodies surging forward towards the wall, carrying makeshift ladders that would allow them climb. Dartag Crawhammer, the head of the blacksmiths guild and current chairperson of the City's Assembly, stood on the wall stretching his shoulders. With a huge battle hammer in his hands, he leapt up onto the parapet to be seen by the defenders.

"When the ladders come, work in teams!" he roared. "One of you knocks the ladder, your partner will protect you by stabbing and shield bashing any head that appears at the top of that ladder while you work. If they get a cargo net on the walls, step forward and do not let a single Goblin make the ramparts! One of you takes a blade to the net while the others keep the goblins down." He glanced at the goblin army which was almost in archer range. "SHOW NO MERCY! KILL THEM ALL!"

He leapt down from the parapet and re-joined the line. He was standing with a group of civilians to strengthen their resolve. "Move up a little there me boys," he said to them. "I'll need a wee bit of room to swing this hammer." He grinned from ear to ear, spat in his palms and gave the hammer a few swings to loosen up. "Time to CRACK SOME SKULLS!"

When he was done the first of the ladders slammed against the wall. In minutes a goblin head appeared at the parapet. Dartag's hammer decapitated the creature with one swing, its head flying across the walls towards the next ladder and striking more Goblins on the way up. The Militia around him seemed to grow in confidence and laid into the goblins approaching the wall as well.

Athress and his Mages began to rain fireballs and lightning down on the Goblin forces before they reached the walls, thinning their numbers, but he waited till the Goblin were in full assault before signaling the archers, they would catch hundreds that were stuck between those at the walls and those pushing from behind. He raised his arm and let it drop. Five hundred arrows raced through the air, over the wall to come whistling down onto the attackers.

The Archers fired volley after volley. While they did, Athress and the Mages prepared their surprise for the Goblins. He stood at the front, wearing white robes to make sure the enemy could see him standing out. He raised his staff above his head and chanted the words of one of the spells from Marveth's spellbook which Vaaldreth had recovered from the Vault. He had contemplated destroying the book, so its dark secrets would be lost forever, but for this, he would trust himself and only himself with it. The spell was horrendously strong, too much power for him alone. But with eleven other Mages feeding him power, he was confident it would work.

Clouds darkened above the goblins. They swirled in fast, much too fast to be natural. The Mages kept shields up around Athress as he cast, a spell of this magnitude would take time, and he would be a target for all of it. Winds whipped up like a raging vortex in minutes. Rain poured from the heavens and the rolling crash of thunder sounded overhead.

Athress focused hard on controlling the mesh, the energies he was trying to build up into one blast were overwhelming. But looking down the parapets he could see the defenders were taking heavy losses. This had to work

The exertion caused Athress almost to fall. One of his assistants stepped forward to help him stay upright. Athress' staff looked like it was alive. Tiny, dark, storm clouds with flashes of lightning swirled around it in his hands. His hands burned and his body felt like it would tear asunder from the strain. The Storm clouds on his staff and built up enough, with great effort he slowly began to direct them, edge them all in the same direction towards the top of the staff. It lit up as they reached it, growing brighter and brighter as more arrived. Then, all at once, Athress released a shout across the battle.

He swung his staff towards the goblin's leader, visible in the distance. As he did a massive bolt of lightning tore through the sky, exploding right where the leader stood. Athress's staff exploded in his hands blasting him and his assistant flat. But the shockwave from his target was far greater, it reached as far as the walls, hundreds were knocked from their feet and a smoking crater was all that remained of the leader.

Body parts, blood, and pieces of goblin flew through the air. Countless maimed Goblins lay sprinkled about the smoking crater. The defenders cheered as the enemy fled from the walls, slipping and sliding on blood and the bodies of the fallen.

The skies cleared in minutes. Athress' assistants picked him from the ground where he lay, and loaded him onto a cart that was waiting to get him back to the Mage tower where Garaveigh had healers waiting. Athress knew he might not have survived the spell, and, even though he did, it would put him out of action for days. But the risk paid off. It had worked better than he'd hoped.

Though weak, he was conscious, and he would live. He realized as he was carried away that some of the other Mages who had helped him were dead, consumed by the energy channeled through them. Their sacrifice would be remembered. He hoped Dartag and Garaveigh would see the wall didn't fall while he was gone. They had to hold.

The Frozen North

Chapter 25

Miles of snow and frost stretched in every direction. The forests left far behind them. Cali didn't know what was worse, Ysabell running off and doing all the fighting without her or having to march day after day through this frozen wasteland. The view never changed, white, in all directions. Behind them a tiny darkness that suggested something not covered in snow, ahead the mountains loomed but still seemed so far away.

On the horizon, the ruined twin cities were barely visible. Cali hoped to avoid them. Rumours of hauntings by the spirits of those who had dwelt there and died there when the Mage towers detonated. Killing everything for miles in all directions. Up till now it was believed that the Mages did it in response to an attack on the towers by the city's citizens. But seeing how close Carraigbán had been to doing the same as they could see no other way of closing the portal, Athress and Garaveigh believed these cities were attacked by Xelazenivein's forces in the same way Carraigbán was. They wiped their own cities off the map to save the rest of the world from the invasion from the abyss. It seemed to have worked, they were both destroyed within days of each other, and whatever daMage they had done, it took Xelazenivein fifty-four years to try again.

<><><>

Ysabell was exhausted. The snow was deep in places, up to her knees. Trudging through it was taking its toll. She held her gaze fixed on the distant mountain peaks, intent on reaching them and as quickly as possible. If they didn't manage to speed up, the city would fall by the time they got to the goblin's caves.

They had been travelling weeks with the city under siege all that time. She hoped the walls still held. In the last update Athress informed them that half the citizens militia were dead along with about a third of the Guards and mercenaries. All those thousands dead and they seemed no closer to their goal.

The last few days, the small druid had been constantly scanning the skies, looking more and more concerned. Whenever she caught Ysabell watching her, she quickly tried to appear like she was just looking around. Whatever was bothering her, she didn't want to share just yet. Ysabell had played that game with Nuthionel, she was getting a little impatient with people keeping things to themselves.

"OK, time for a rest, and food," she said. "That rocky outcrop over there looks pretty sheltered."

She pointed a large rock shelf protruding from the ground. The group trudged to it and started getting a camp set up. Vaaldreth lit a magical fire. It was green, but no one cared as long as it was warm. Whilst everyone busied themselves, Ysabell caught Ériu's eye and nodded her off to the side.

"Just give me the bad news," she said. "We'll have no secrets out here." Her tone wasn't angry or confrontational, just weary and resigned.

Ériu seemed startled, clearly not realising just how obvious she had been. She opened her mouth to lie, then sighed. "Griffons. They nest in the southwest ridges of the mountains, but they hunt out here, always have. Every other time I've been up here at least. Once we knew we could not take horses, our plan was to use griffons once we got in range and fly over the ruined cities and the second army. Now they're nowhere to be found. Without them, I have no idea how we will reach the mountains. It will take us weeks to walk."

"Then we need to find out what's happened to the Griffons," Ysabell said. "You scouted here before you joined us. How did you get here and back to the city so fast?" Ériu thought for a moment, as if trying to find a way to explain it.

"Have you heard or maybe even seen how a Mage can spirit travel? How they can project their spirit elsewhere? Ysabell nodded. "Druids can do something similar. We can let our body sleep while our spirit melds with nature. We can move our consciousness from plant to plant, through roots to animals, all the way across great landscapes to reach where we wish to see. It can take days to get where we are going instead of months, and once we reach our destination we can join with any animal we find there to use its eyes and ears. That is how I scouted, but it took me several days to recover from exhaustion after,"

Ysabell had never even heard of this before. She guessed it was a deeper form of what Ériu had done in the forest to track her progress against the Goblin patrol. Whatever it was, it looked to her like they had their answer.

"So, can you do it here?" she asked. "Can you get to those peaks, find the griffons and use one of them to get your spirit back here?"

"I think I can, but it would mean camping here for a few days. I will need protection and my body kept warm. Most importantly, I must be undisturbed. It would disconnect my body and spirit. That would be fatal. But if you can manage to keep my body safe here, I could leave tonight and reach the griffon peaks by the following night."

"That's our plan then." Ysabell smiled at the druid. "You've saved our necks again Ériu."

She turned away to inform the others that they needed to set up a more permanent base camp. Ériu ate and drank, preparing herself for her journey. She said she needed to ensure her body was well hydrated and had an excess of food to reduce her recovery time upon her return. While she did that, the others set about making their camp discrete and sheltered. Snow was piled up to make a wall that leaned in towards the outcrop of rock they camped under. The rock came up out of the ground like a small cliff, leaning out over them. They piled snow up like walls on all but one side, using the rock as a roof. Vaal cast an ice spell on it to harden it, soon they had a solid ice wall reaching up to meet the rock ceiling, a small chimney hole was all they left clear.

Guinevere and Cali collected dead wood and brush from nearby so it would be sheltered. If they could get it good and dry before they burnt it, it would produce less smoke. In the meantime, Vaal warmed the inside of their shelter with another magical fire, it wouldn't last for long, but would give them time to find wood for a real fire. He then went outside to prepare a small wind spell. It blew as much snow as possible onto the top of their shelter and down its walls, making their shelter appear like a large snow drift against a rock. Nobody would be any the wiser that there was a camp beneath it

Once Ériu was prepared, she set up her bedroll in the deepest corner of the ice bower and settled herself in. The roof was low there, only a foot or so above her, but she wouldn't be moving. The others resolved to remain in the shelter as much as possible and only venture outside to fetch more wood if absolutely necessary. An enemy finding them would be a disaster. They had to remain inconspicuous.

Ériu closed her eyes and within minutes they could see was gone. Ysabell crawled next to her and checked she was still breathing. She was, barely. Her spirit was gone. It was an eerie thought that hers was an empty body now; a shell with no life in it that just continued to breathe as it waited on its owner to return.

The days passed by slowly in the ice bower. After the first night's wood collection, they stopped going outside. It was a new experience for most of the companions. Cali and Guin had travelled the roads for years, and Ysabell had been walking the woods even before Nuthionel led her away from home. Only Vaaldreth seemed unfazed by it. He sat in a corner, a blanket behind him against the ice to reflect the heat back at him, and studied his spell books. He seemed quite content.

The other three tried everything they could think of to pass the time. From telling stories, discussing fighting styles and moves, trying each other's weapons, to just bickering.

The second night Ysabell listened as the others told their stories, she knew so little about them. It seemed strange.

"So Vaal, how did you end up with the garish clothes, and a giant hunting knife?" Ysabel asked. "You are the only Mage I've met who can fight physically without magic as well."

"I wasn't always a Mage." Vaaldreth chuckled. "My training started late in life. I grew up far to the south. My people are suspicious of magic. They view it as evil. So, I hid it as long as I could. Like the other young men in my village I trained to be a hunter and a warrior."

He fell silent staring into the fire for a few moments, Ysabell stayed letting him take his time with his memory.

"We were a simple people, we fought for land and water for our cattle with our neighbouring states. Our King was an arrogant man; he threw us into battle on a whim. Many young men died every year to satisfy his greed for power and wealth." Vaaldreth's face grew dark. "Eventually I could take it no more, I spoke out, against his greed, his cowardice, how he hid in his luxury while we fought. He was no leader. I was sentenced to death as were my family. We were to be burnt alive."

He took a deep breath, Ysabell could see the emotion in him. He was angry still after all these decades.

"We were chained to a pyre and it set alight. That was when I first realised just how powerful my magic could be. I focused my anger, my hatred into that fire and twisted, bent it, it flowed like water for me, across the dirt to our great King and burnt him like a torch. But my control was sporadic, my family died in the smoke and flames I could not control. My people were terrified and fled, I managed to work myself free, as I tried to keep the flames at bay as best I could. I escaped but I could not stay there any longer. I was now the devil. So I left. I travelled north until in a small village where I worked chopping wood in exchange for food and shelter, I met a Mage. He knew what I was straight away. He brought me to the tower to train."

He shook himself of his nostalgia, forced a half grimace, half smile. "That's the short version."

Ysabell learnt much of her companions in those few days. Except Cali. She refused point blank to speak of her past. All she would say is, "Nuthionel saved me. He took me and showed me there was a life worth living." After that she clammed up and her face became dark if anyone pushed to find out more. Guinevere was open about training through her youth to be a Priestess, about her adventures, her lovers.

She held nothing back. Ysabell was as shocked by Guinevere's language as she was by her promiscuity. She saw just how sheltered a life she had led in Farrowfields.

On the fourth day Cali warned she was going to crack someone's head if something didn't happen soon when they heard a shriek like that of a hawk or eagle, but far louder. The Companions froze, wondering should they go look, or stay hidden and let whatever it is pass them by.

As they sat in silence staring at the roof towards the sound, Ériu's eyes flickering open and she gasped. Guinevere grabbed a water skin and held it up to the druid's lips. After five or six sips, she spoke. "Griffon...outside, needs our help... Goblins holding more." Then she lay back down coughing.

Ysabell had some broth heating on the fire for her in minutes and Guinevere helped her out of her bedroll and up to the fire. She clutched the water skin and sipped at it slowly. The warm broth did her good and before long she could speak again properly.

"The Goblins," she said. "I should have known. They have captured several of the Griffons. It wouldn't surprise me if they seek to use them to get over the walls of Carraigbán. The those left cannot aid us as they need to protect what remains of their nests and eggs, but also they don't wish to anger the goblins in case the captured ones suffer for it.. One agreed to fly back here so that I could return faster with the news. If we want to get over these mountains and to the valley that leads to the Goblin caves, we need to free the captured Gryphons. They are being held only a few miles northwest from here."

Ysabell cursed inwardly. She knew her plan couldn't have been as easy as it sounded. Nothing was ever easy, why should it start now? Only Cali seemed pleased with the news.

"So, there's maybe a chance we might have to kill a few wee Goblins then?" she exclaimed. "Maybe a few little heads that need separating from their necks? Well done druid, I don't care what they say about you softy nature types, you're okay by me!"

Too close for comfort

Chapter 26

After another day and nights rest to allow Ériu to recover, the group packed up and set off once again. Vaaldreth sealed the entrance to their bower with ice in case they passed this way again on their return and needed shelter. It would also prevent anyone tracking them from realising where they had camped and for how long they were there. Unfortunately, a lack of foresight meant they had dark grey travel cloaks, great for being hidden in the forest but making them far too conspicuous on the trek through the snow to the goblin camp holding the Griffons.

As they walked Ysabell tried to think up a plan for when they got there. If the goblins were holding a dozen or so griffons, they would need plenty of guards. She didn't know much about griffons, but she knew they were fiercely aggressive and dangerous to get in a fight with. The hind legs and quarters were like those of a lion, with large claws and powerful limbs. The front half was like that of a huge bird of prey. Wicked, curved talons, huge wings and a razor-sharp beak.

Ysabell mulled over options for reaching the Griffons, making a plan, changing it, making another and so on. By nightfall they were close enough to see the camp. The Goblins had it well-lit with torches. The group stamped down a hollow in the snow and crouched into it. Their dark cloaks, combined with the darkness, would make them look like no more than a rock in the snow.

"I've been thinking," Ysabell said. "We know there will be no shortage of Goblins in this camp. Holding twelve Griffons can't be an easy job. If we go in loud, we'll have them all on us, it might be better if I–"

"Not a flaming hope!" Cali interrupted. "I'm not missing the fun again. You go in, we all go in!"

Ériu held up a hand to quiet them both and the soft-spoken druid suggested an alternative. "It's night time, the Goblins night vision is gone from the torches, and there may be no need to fight at all. If Ysabell and I can sneak in to the corral, we could simple cut the bonds holding the Griffons, they could fly off, while the Goblins watch them go, we sneak back out. No one is any the wiser, no sign we were ever here, no risk of alerting the enemy we are coming."

"There'll likely be more Goblins than even you know what to do with in those caves Cali," Ysabell added. "Right now we need the element of surprise or it's all been for nothing. If we can get through this without a fight, it's the better option."

She waited for Cali's response. The Halfling looked pissed, but she nodded her agreement. She had to know it made sense; but Ysabell knew Cali would hate any plan that didn't involve lots of killing.

So, the plan was hatched. It was pitch black when they set off, several hours off dawn. The others were to watch for signs of a fight, if one started, they could come in blasting with everything they had in them.

Ériu impressed Ysabell at how quietly she could move and how well she blended into her surroundings. It was an unusual experience for Ysabell to find herself as the loud one when creeping through the shadows.

The closer they got to the camp, the less snow they had to trudge through. Most of it anywhere near the camp had been well trampled. They stayed at the outskirts, beyond the reach of the torches, trying to find out where the Griffons were. There didn't seem to be any pens or enclosures to keep griffons in. She hoped they hadn't ended up as food, or already sent off to link up with the army. Ériu tapped her arm suddenly and leaned in.

"Up on the top of that cliff, behind the camp, on the plateau, there is a huge pit. They keep the Griffons there, with rope netting over the top to prevent their escape," she whispered. "That passage in the rock face at the back of the camp leads to the bottom of the pit. We can't go that way, but we could climb the rock face, and get to the pit from above?"

She looked back at the passage in the rock face that led from the Goblin camp into the pit. "We need to get the others here now. When we start cutting that netting, there's a chance the goblins will be alerted. If they are, we'll need to hold that passage against them until whoever is doing the cutting finishes, then the Griffons can fly us out. It will be a big risk, but I can see no other way." Ysabell nodded. It did seem like the only solution... at least Cali would be happy.

"It'll be nearly dawn by the time we get back to them and return. That's going to make it even trickier. We'll be sitting ducks in the air for their archers."

Ériu once again had a solution to ease Ysabell's worries. "We don't need to go back. Watch."

Ériu faced the companions remaining back in the dip in the snow. She cupped her hands and blew into them. In seconds a light was twinkling in the palm of her hand. Holding it in her right hand, she covered it and uncovered it a series of times, sometimes long pauses, sometimes short. Ysabell realised Ériu was using a code with the light to speak to the others. A single short flash responded. Ériu extinguished her light and turned back to Ysabell grinning.

"They are on the way," she said.

Ysabell waiting for fifty minutes or so until the other came into view and joined them, they explained the plan, as expected Cali grinned with anticipation. Vaaldreth and Ériu discussed ways of sealing the passage once they were ready to mount the Griffons, buying them time to mount and escape. If they sealed it too early, the Goblins would move up the cliff and gain the high ground. If they kept them engaged at the passage, with luck, they wouldn't be smart enough to consider going up and around to flank the companions. Cali's taunts were likely to help in that respect. She had insulting enemies down to a fine art. Ysabell reminded them that the ideal plan was still to not be noticed at all. But they had to be prepared just in case.

The group moved as quietly as possible to the west of the Goblin camp and climbed the rock face leading to the plateau above. In the middle of the plateau was a deep crater, the pit containing the Griffons. As they approached it, Ériu dropped and signaled to the others to do the same. She beckoned Ysabell to her.

"Up ahead to the right, at the edge of the basin, is a single Goblin," she said, her elvish eyes seeing something the rest of them couldn't yet. "He seems to be patrolling the rim. He's alone, but one shout before we are in place and ready would blow this whole attempt. Can you take care of him?"

Ysabell nodded. She crept forward, her blades drawn, a shadow cloaked by night. Her moccasins helped her feet fall without a sound across the rocky surface. She closed in on her prey.

He was walking towards her, so she stayed motionless and let him approach. Once he was passed she slipped in behind him. Her left hand sank its dagger into his lungs from behind, at the same time as her right-hand dagger drew a faint red line across his throat. He barely struggled, his hands clutching his neck as he slid to the ground against her. His body twitched while she cleaned her blades on his tunic, and then waved to Ériu to move the group up.

As soon as the group reached her at the rim of the pit, Ysabell heard a gasp from behind her. A goblin had just climbed a ladder from the pit and seen the body of his fellow along with Ysabell and the others. Before they could react, he took off across the plateau. Vaaldreth sent a spell shooting after him. Whatever it was, it connected but didn't seem to do anything, Ysabell spun back to the others.

"There must be another patrol or a ladder down again on the other side," she said. "He must not reach it alive and he must not make a sound!"

"He is silenced, he will make no sound," Vaaldreth's deep voice reassured her.

The group set off after the Goblin as fast as they could. A light flared up ahead when he reached a camp of two bedrolls and two more goblins. He had them awake but was unable to speak as he tried to make them understand. They couldn't let that happen, one shout would ruin it all.

Cali wound her crossbow as she ran. The bolt cocked and she nodded to Ysabell who returned the gesture. She fired at the Goblin on the right, the Goblin on the left turned in shock, opened his mouth, but two throwing knives embedded in his throat kept him from screaming. The silenced Goblin turned to face the approaching group, a look of terror on his face. It wasn't long lived. Guinevere ran in and smashed his head cleanly from his shoulders. They were alone again.

On the Wings of the Night
Chapter 27

Ériu looked over the edge where the camp's ladder was, her night vision showing her clearly what lay below. She leaned back and nodded.

"All is clear," she said. "Only the Griffons are down there. The passage leading to the main camp is to the left when we reach the bottom. We need a plan."

Cali immediately announced she would hold the passage if anything came through it and Guinevere suggested that she help Ériu calm the Griffons.

"Okay as soon as I cut the nets, I'll drop." Said Ysabell "You see me climbing down, Ériu, and there's a fight at that passage, then you and Vaal' try and seal it for a few moments to buy us time to mount and escape."

There were no questions. It all sounded so simple and matter of fact. But they were taking on thirty or more Goblins, if the tents were sleeping much more, there could be as many as fifty. Ultimately, they couldn't hope to defeat that many, at least not without taking losses themselves, even with the passage to funnel the Goblins and stop them being swamped. But they didn't need to; they just needed to hold them long enough. If anything went wrong, one mistake, they were all dead. Which meant Carraigbán was dead.

Ériu climbed down first. She would need to keep the Griffons calm and make them understand what was going to happen. After her was Cali, upon reaching the Ground she headed straight for the passage in the pit wall that lead to the Goblin camp. Close behind her followed Vaaldreth, with Guin bringing up the rear.

Ysabell watched them until she could no longer see them in the dark, gave them another minute to be sure they were in position, and then started cutting the away the netting. She headed to the far side of the pit first and slashed as swiftly as she could, making her away around the edge towards where the others had descended. Her blades carved easily through the ropes that attached the huge, hand-woven nets to metal pegs hammered into the stone. She was about halfway through when the alarm was raised. A goblin walked into the narrow passage into the 'pen' and found a relaxed looking Halfling, with a mop of flaming red hair, leaning against the wall, rubbing the blade of an axe with an oil stone.

"Oh, are ye out for a wee walk?" Cali said. "'Tis a lovely night for it sure enough. Well? Go on, call yer friends ye halfwit, I haven't got all night!" Cali leapt up and brandished her axe. The creature yelped and ran screaming for aid back into the camp.

Ysabell heard the cries and started sprinting, her blade down and slicing as she ran. Once she was nearly back, she sheathed her weapon and started dragging the netting back towards her. It was a lot heavier than she'd imagined, but slowly it pulled back and she dropped it down into the pit, piled in a heap.

She ran forward without taking the time to catch her breath and climbed down the ladder, falling the last few steps in her hurry. Ériu must have seen her. Light flashed as Vaaldreth's fireball flew through the air. She spun to look at the passage and saw Cali sprinting back towards them. An earth-shaking explosion tore through the night and a huge rolling wave of flames followed Cali out of the passage sending her sprawling.

Ériu sprinted past her towards the flames, buried her hands in the ground and began her work. Slowly, roots forced their way through the ground and out of cracks in the sides of the passageway. They crossed over each other, in multiple layers, building a tangled wall of living roots and vines. It would buy them enough time, Ysabell was sure.

Ériu came back and guided each of the companions onto the back of a Griffon, before the one that had asked for their aid flew down to pick her up. She called to the others to hold on tight, and then her griffon leapt gracefully from the ground and took flight, the others followed.

Ysabell's breath was taken away at the speed they moved from standing to airborne. She couldn't believe she was actually flying! The scenery was dark below, but she could see the shadows and shapes whizzing by as they flew! The wings of the griffons beat only to gain height, then swept back at an angle causing them to shoot forward through the sky like arrows. It was like nothing Ysabell had ever experienced. Guinevere seemed to be loving it as well, as she was laughing off to the right. To her left she could hear Cali cursing, clearly not a fan of heights.

The first rays of light swept across the mountains to her left as the sun rose and lit up the snowy peaks. They were spectacular. The view of the mountains, feeling the air on her face, and shooting through the skies on a griffons back... She didn't want it to end.

Ériu's griffon, in the lead, banked left to head over the mountains. The Goblin caverns were in a valley in the middle of the mountain range. Looking from up there, Ysabell realised the scale of what they had been trying to achieve on foot. It would have taken them another three or four weeks at least to walk around the mountains.

Ysabell watched Ériu's griffon dive into a wide snowy valley in the mountain range, sealed on one end and open on the other. She guessed this was it. The other Griffons all followed. The snow on the ground was dirty and looked like it had been trampled. Her hands wandered to the hilts of her blades when she saw movement. Goblins were moving around, twelve to fifteen by the looks of it.

The griffons all dove fast towards the ground. Again, Ysabell couldn't catch her breath they were going so fast. Ériu's griffon up ahead landed on a sentry goblin and with one swift movement tore its head off with its beak. The other griffons followed. Ysabell was nearly shaken off as hers shredded one of the goblins.

She leapt lightly to the ground, drawing her blades as she did. Her back pack restricted her movements somewhat, putting her a little off balance. Her griffon lashed out at another goblin to protect her, ripping its right arm off. Ysabell's dropped her backpack to the ground, and before it hit, she disembowelled the one-armed goblin and slit his throat.

She moved toward the others with speed born of the anger, and hatred of these creatures. Cali fell from her Griffon, landing hard on her backpack, like an overturned turtle. Two Goblins ran at her. She flung her hatchet hard into one's face. Ysabell kicked the second back and grabbed Cali, trying to pull her up and shield her from attack. Something strange happened, she felt her shadows extending, spreading onto Cali. She had no time to think on it then, dragging Cali to her feet, she turned fast, parried a blow from the goblins short sword with her left-hand dagger, while drawing the second from its sheath and burying it up to the hilt in the Goblins chest.

Vaaldreth was fighting three Goblins single-handed. One was stuck in a patch of ice that grasped its lower legs, a second was screaming as flames fanned from Vaal's right hand into its face, and the third was hacking at Vaal as he attempted to block with his own blade. Ysabell flipped and flung a dagger. It embedded itself in the creature's neck, protruding out through the front of its throat. As she ran forward to retrieve it, Vaal turned his full attention to the burning Goblin in front of him, stabbing it in the gut with his dagger. Then he turned to the third and cast a small but effective shadow orb at it, a sphere of blue and black shadows, flickering with lightning, and a tail like a meteor trailing it, flew from his palm to slam into the Goblin. It died in seconds.

Fourteen Goblins were dead, many killed by the Griffons. Nobody was injured. Cali got down on her knees and kissed the ground. Guinevere rolled her eyes and kicked the halfling as she passed.

"Get up you," she said. "What are you, a warrior or a babe? Scared of a little ride on an overgrown bird!"

Cali glowered at her and got to her feet, grumbling, "If the Gods intended us to fly, they'd have given us wings."

Ériu thanked the Griffons for their help and sent them on their way. They would keep a watch for the companions return. The thrill of flying waned fast as the companions checked their gear and prepared themselves for combat. Backpacks were loosened so they would drop easily, blades oiled to slide from sheathes without noise. Before long, they were all ready.

Ysabell took a deep breath and stepped into the entrance of the cave.

Down the rabbit hole

Chapter 28

The cave was dark and musty. The smell reminded Ysabell of the ruins under Cloch Dubh. She drew her daggers and headed deeper into the darkness. There was little to no light, so Vaaldreth cast a small glow spell. A wisp like ball of light floated above them. It was a soft light, just enough to see by.

Ysabell's eyes became accustomed to the reduced light quickly. The cave appeared natural only for the first thirty or so feet, after which the walls were carved with precision and care. Wide corridors, with huge metal braces fitted into the walls for holding braziers. This was no Goblins handiwork.

"Dwarven," Vaaldreth confirmed her suspicions. "Goblins can't mine or work stone like this. Like most Goblin colonies, this is a dwarven ruin they've claimed. But something isn't right here. This stone wasn't carved in ages past. This is recent, less than a hundred years. Ysabell?" She turned to face him. "We may have another issue to deal with here. Goblins keep slaves. This work was either done by Dwarven slaves, or the Dwarves who lived here were captured or killed by the Goblins so they could seize this place. We need to know which. If they are alive, their release would cause a major headache for the Goblins and give us a huge distraction to find their 'king'."

"It would also mean that Dwarves held as slaves in this stinking cesspit would be free," Guin added. "To either escape or try to take their home back. An infinitely better prospect than living as these creature's slaves. It is the right thing to do."

Ysabell nodded in agreement at them both. "We keep an eye out for any sign of captives. If we can get a goblin alive, we can question it." She turned back to the passage and continued leading them forward. The once solid stone had been carved into a passage, patterns with brick shapes and Dwarvish runes embellishing the sides and ceiling. Air moved in this corridor, which suggested something up ahead.

She waved for the others to be silent. The passage ended in an archway, with light emanating from beyond it. A patrol or a communal room, Ysabell presumed. Either one would not be good for their attempts at stealth.

The group made their way to the arch, keeping to the sides of the passage. They peered in and gasped. It was a huge cavern with an enormous stone staircase leading down to the floor. It looked as though it had been expanded and shaped beautifully, with walls that had shards of crystal either placed in them, or were mined specifically to make use of them. Great braziers were lit on the streets, yes streets, below, which were lined with dwarven-built stone houses and buildings. The light of the braziers reflected in the crystals of the cavern diffusing the light to spread it evenly across the cavern. There must have been a community of dwarves living and mining here for several decades for so much work to be done.

As Ysabell's eyes took in the scene, they began to see things that signaled something wasn't right. Piles of rubbish lay in the streets, the buildings were dirty, doors just left open. It didn't look abandoned. Far from it. It looked very much lived in... by goblins.

It would be a half an hour or so to march across the cavern, through filthy, goblin infested, well-lit streets. No doubt somewhere down there was the demon and a few legions of his soldiers too. Getting caught would be all but certain. Ysabell might be able to sneak through this, maybe even Ériu, but the others? No way. Yet there was no other path but down the stairs. She looked at Vaaldreth.

"Any ideas?" she asked. "You have anything in that spell book that may be of use?"

Vaaldreth seemed to be weighing up the odds, before shaking his head. "No, but you may. I saw your shadows spread to Cali when you touched outside. It wouldn't hide us, but if we are swift, we would at least be less conspicuous. We would need to take the stairs fast and get in cover again. Our prey may well be in this cavern, finding him will be tricky. Seeking dwarven survivors may be our best bet."

Ysabell nodded, then instructed everyone to be ready to move fast. She pointed to a building below them at the end of the stairs. "That's where we head to. We must maintain contact for this to work, so stick close together as we move. Once in there we can plan our next move."

Ysabell let her shadow cloak envelop her. She waited until her friends had all linked up to each other and her, then she concentrated, like when she had first learned to summon the shadows, but this time on hiding them all. The shadows crept from form to form. Once they were enveloped, Cali shuddered at the strange cold feeling, Ysabell took the lead and set a good pace and led the dark cloud of shadow down. There were several hundred steps down to the cavern floor, but it didn't take long to clear them.

Upon reaching the bottom, they entered the building. The group let go of each other and the shadows dissipated as quickly as they had appeared. The group all looked a little shook from the experience.

"Does it feel like that every time?" Cali enquired. Shaking the feeling from her arms. Ysabell smiled and nodded then spoke.

"Guin and Cali, you hold the door. Anyone who comes in gets put to sleep. Don't kill them, we have questions. Ériu, you and Vaaldreth look around the rest of the building; I don't want any surprises creeping up on us. I will sneak out the back and try to get a captive to drag back here. I won't be long, but Vaaldreth, can you track me? Or you Ériu? So, if anything happens, you'll know?"

Ériu shook her head. "The stone is too dense here for me. I can feel nothing through it."

"I cannot track you," Vaaldreth said, "but I can put a trace spell on a stone or something similar and you can carry it. It means if anything happens I will be able to locate you."

"Can't you put the trace spell on me?" Ysabell asked.

With a shake if his head Vaaldreth explained. "No, well not without killing you. The spell makes a physical change to its target. It would kill a living target."

"Ok, let's not try that, the stone sounds good." Ysabell turned back to the others. "I won't be long, if I don't come swiftly, come looking for me, but stay out of sight and quiet, anyone sees you, silence them and capture them, or they die, quietly!" She glared at Cali as she emphasised the last word.

Ysabell couldn't find a rear door but slipped quietly out a window that opened onto an alleyway behind the house. She drew her blades and crept off in the shadows of the alley to seek her prey.

The alley was clean compared to the main streets. She guessed the Goblins weren't bothered with the back alleys since there wouldn't be much wealth in them. She felt sorry for the dwarves who had lived here. If they saw what had become of their homes, she was sure they'd be heart broken. If they lived, they deserved to be freed.

The end of the alley was approaching, and she spotted one of the large braziers ahead. It was a huge basin of metal atop a stone block. As she got closer she could see a lever which allowed the bottom of the brazier to open and drop ash and waste down into whatever lay below. It gave her an idea.

She crept to edge of the alley and watched and waited. It was a quiet street, but occasionally a goblin would wander in or out of a doorway. She waited until there was no one in sight then quickly dashed to the brazier, pulled its lever and ran back to her hiding place. The fire vanished immediately. From the sound, she guessed there was a passage beneath taking the ash away to, an empty cavern or stream or something. Either way, the area was no longer well-lit.

Ysabell felt safer stalking the streets in the darkness. She dumped two more braziers, leaving this section of the cavern in twilight. It made her shadows more effective at keeping her hidden. To top it off, she'd also finally found a suitable goblin to question; her main problem was how to get it back to the safe house undetected.

<><><>

Ing'Luk was happy; she had found a hidden box in one of the houses, full of glittering stones and gold, she had to be careful no one else found out, in case they came to steal them. Gold and glittering stones would buy her a better position in the Great Kings Army! The Dwarves had lots of riches, she had bribed one of them with extra food rations to find out where this gold was and it had paid off, more than she had imagined. She reckoned if she bribed a few more she could get rich, quick. She checked no one was watching her, it was darker than usual, she thought that was good, made it harder for other Goblins to see her. When she was sure she was alone, she snuck down an alley behind the street to get to her hiding place for all her treasure. She wondered briefly why it was so very dark. Then she saw something move, a shadow, detaching itself from a wall, she stared, closed her eyes and shook her head to try and shake the strange sight out of her eyes. It worked, when she opened her eyes it was gone. Then something struck her from behind, hard. The Goblin fell senseless to the ground.

<><><>

Ysabell stood over her captive. The goblin was small, female, and carrying a canvas sack that spilled out gold and precious gems when it fell. She was stealing from the dwarves' homes.

Ysabell bound her hands and feet and gagged her in case she awoke on the journey back. With the dimmed lights, Ysabell made her way back much quicker. As she approached the safe house she noticed that there was light coming from the windows. Something was wrong. The others wouldn't be so stupid to draw attention to themselves like that.

She laid her captive down and crept up to the window she had exited from earlier. Goblins, all armed to the teeth were searching the building. Ysabell cursed. Where were her companions? She drew her daggers and weighed up her chances. If the others were in there they would be fighting by now, unless they were dead, captured, or, hopefully had left when they saw the Goblins approaching. If that were the case, Ysabell going in to fight the Goblins would be a pointless endeavour. She had managed, with luck, to kill ten back in the forest, but here, where there were reinforcements possibly close, and anywhere from a dozen to twenty Goblins in the building, it would be suicide.

149

She crept along the side of the building, keeping herself in the shadows, moving as silently as she could. Once near the front, she listened for any clue as to what was happening. The Goblins spoke a mix of broken common and some guttural language she remembered having heard from the goblins in the woods.

It was hard to decipher what they were saying, but she could make out some words from the broken chatter. Her friends had been surprised and captured. They were taken to the cells with the dwarves.

They also mentioned something about a vault in their chatter and a glowing weapon. That must have been Guin's mace. Now she had to find out where they held the Dwarves, then where the Vault was to get her friends and their weapons and belongings back. This mission was getting worse and worse.

She headed back to her prisoner. She would have to be the one to question her now. There was no time for subtlety. Despite that, Ysabell didn't think she would be capable of torturing the creature. That was a road she hoped she would never take.

She dragged the goblin into a small house off the alley and tied her to a chair before going to find some water. Dwarves used ingenious arrangements of aqueducts and sluice gates to move water around their cities and towns. In the house she entered was a chain over a basin in the sink, that when pulled released water down into the basin. She filled a bowl and brought it back to the goblin, checking she was still tied securely. Then Ysabell threw the water in the goblin's face, waking her. She spluttered and swore in her own tongue. Ysabell brought over another chair. They were a bit small for humans but they'd do. She reversed it and sat facing the goblin.

"Can you understand me?" she asked. "Can you understand me? You speak my language?"

"Yis, yis. Spik good," the goblin answered, staring at the blades strapped across Ysabell's chest.

"My friends have been taken to where your people keep the dwarves. I need to know where that is, and I need to know where the vault is."

"Yis, I help. I show."

Ysabell didn't much like that idea, it would be much better if she just told her, but would the goblin be able to give good directions? Ysabell didn't have the time to waste with guessing games.

"Ok, you will lead me," she said. "We will stick only to the back alleys and shadows. If we meet a patrol or you lead me to a trap, I will gut you before anything else can happen."

The goblin gulped, then nodded. Ysabell decided an extra measure of fear in the little goblin would help keep her in line. So, as drew her daggers to cut the goblins bonds, she let the shadows crawl across her skin. The little Goblin screamed when the shadows wrapped around her. Ysabell pulled the goblin to her feet and headed to the door. As they stepped out into the street, she turned to the terrified looking Goblin.

"Do not cross me, I'll kill you at the first hint of treachery."

The Heavens Burned

Chapter 29

Athress gazed wearily at the reports in front of him. Less casualties each day, but only because those defenders who were least capable with blades died early on. The more experienced fighters tended to live longer.

Roughly three thousand defenders remained, nowhere near enough, but there was nothing they could do about it. The enemy had also been decimated. The forty thousand strong goblin horde was now only about fifteen thousand. With these attrition rates, it might be possible for the defenders to win, but word had come in from the scouts that the second army of around thirty thousand was only a week away.

Athress considered every option, but the result was always the same. They were all going to die. He had had no word from Vaaldreth in days now. It was safe to assume they were dead. The last contact had been interrupted when mid-discussion he had heard a shout from behind Vaaldreth. He had sent them to their death and now he was leading the whole city to theirs.

It had been a rough few weeks. Six days ago, he watched as the main gates were destroyed. and goblins came hurtling through. Four Mages had stepped out of the first warehouse on the trade road just inside the gates. Each one sent a fireball through the arch, incinerating hundreds of goblins. Then they summoned a wall of flame to block the gates long enough for Dartag Crawhammer and his team to roll a huge stone block, on steel trolleys, out of the warehouse and ram it down into the arch to seal it. Once they did, a group of druids on standby planted and grew several oak trees inside the blockage. In minutes, nothing would force the barricade back. However a second blast of explosives from the goblins knocked a lump of rock loose from above the arch. It tumbled down and crushed Dartag, killing him instantly. He had boosted the morale of all who fought with him for weeks and a falling lump of rock had slain him. It was such a waste of life. The whole battle was.

Athress sighed and put aside the casualty lists. He started looking at the other reports on the walls and how they were holding up. A daMaged section near the Traders district was now weakened significantly from multiple attacks using explosives. Several cracks had appeared in the wall. Much more and it would fall apart. Scores of men had been badly burned trying to shoot down at the goblins placing the explosives, they were still leaning over the wall when it went off. Garaveigh had gone there to help with the healing.

Athress wondered if he should send reinforcements there to hold the wall from further daMage, but looking at the report, it was going to come down no matter what he did. He called his assistant and sent him with orders for battle-ready Mages to head there immediately and recall two units of archers from the east gate. They were to hide in the roof tops in that district with a view of the cracked section of the wall. Five hundred additional soldiers were to be pulled from anywhere that could spare them, to be set up in teams of ten and sent to hide in the buildings in the Traders district, ready for when the wall fell. Then Athress headed to his cell to try to rest. Sleep had not come easy lately. He held the responsibility for so many lives in his hands.

Someone banged on his door in what only seemed like ten minutes later. He glanced at the magical clock on his wall. It was never wound, and never went wrong. It was several hours past midnight. He called for the visitor to come in and Gregor, his assistant, rushed inside excited and breathless.

"It's down, Sir, the wall," he said excitedly. "You were right, they blew through it. The forces you called for were already in place and by all accounts it's a massacre, Sir. The goblins haven't made it past the wall yet, the Mages have been blasting everything they've got at them, Sir."

Athress wasn't so joyful. "It's too soon. There'll be nothing to celebrate when the Mages are worn out from casting, the archers run out of arrows and the soldiers are dead Mister Gregor. They outnumber us five to one without the reinforcements that are coming behind them. The defenders down there will be overrun in a matter of hours."

His assistant looked shocked. In Athress' mind the boy was clearly daft, with no concept of reality and with the delusion that they were somehow going to win this. Athress was a realist, he hated naivety. Unless Ysabell and her team managed to kill the damn Demon, Carraigbán and every one in it were as good as dead. There had been no word from Deep Crag or Glanmyrdwyrr, so he couldn't know if any aid was even coming. He prayed the party were still alive, but even if they succeeded, there was no certainty the death of their king would be enough to make the goblin generals here stop their assault on the city, or even that they would know. But he assumed the Demon was communicating with them somehow, it would be foolishness to leave a horde of goblins off the leash as it were. If not the traitors in the city probably were in contact. Once news spread it would likely get to them... He hoped. But knowing that the second Horde were led by another Demon, that dampened any hope for him that they'd survive much longer without military aid.

Athress scrambled for his robes, dressed fast and hurried from his chambers to the base of the tower where a carriage was waiting. Several runners were on horseback to follow him and carry any messages or orders he had to other units. As they raced to the Trader's District, he wrote hurried orders. If the Goblins had any brains, which was questionable, they would divert all their forces to the collapsed portion of the wall. If they did, he could afford to leave only token forces on the other walls and bring the bulk of the rest down there to defend.

It would be messy fighting, street by street, in the alleys, but the Goblins had no idea what was where. His defenders knew the city. That would give them an advantage. He sent out his orders for the troop redeployment. Then sent an order off to the Mages left in the tower. He wanted them, including acolytes, to firstly get all civilians evacuated from that whole side of the city. Then in rotating teams to join the defence, aid the druids in creating barricades around the Trade District. They needed a second wall of defence, and they needed it now.

The Trade District was in chaos. Garaveigh was struggling to get the units coming in from around the city organised and send them to the fight in a way that made sense. When Athress stepped out of the carriage, he could see the relief on the old Priest's face.

"Over to you, organising troops was never my thing," Garaveigh said.

Athress smiled and patted his shoulder. "Nor mine, old friend. You take over the stretcher bearers and get them running wounded to the new hospital, I had it prepared in trade district, two of the market warehouses have been cleaned for you I know it's awkward to move the wounded that far, but we are setting up a second line of defence around the district, when we abandon the district, and eventually we will, we don't want a hospital full of wounded and healers left to die."

Garaveigh nodded and set off. Athress climbed up on top of the carriage and cast his voice projection spell. "Alright, silence!" he bellowed. "All units get in your formations. Commanders, front and centre. I want all reports from the breach here now. The rest of you, hold formation, await your orders."

He climbed back down and met the runners coming forward with the reports. He pulled out a map of the district and started giving each commander his orders, sending the units to best places to hold the line. The last three units he sent forward to the breach itself along with a contingent of Mages to relieve those who had been casting for over an hour and would be ready to keel over. Magical over exertion was fatal. A mortal body could only contain and control so much energy before the mind literally burnt out, leaving the Mage either dead or mindless at best.

The breach was as Gregor had described it, a bloodbath. Hundreds of burnt, smoking bodies of Goblins filled the gap in the wall, making it harder for the others to climb the rubble. Athress had spent the last few weeks using any spare minute he had to study the grimoire of Marveth and had a surprise for them. Ultimately, he knew nothing could stop them considering their impending reinforcements, but he could buy the defenders time. If they defeated the last fifteen thousand or so of this army fast, they might have time to repair some of the daMage and prepare for the next army. The spell he had planned was frightening, it should never have been created, no one man should hold that much power. But right now, he was glad it had been. The spell would likely leave him dead or mad. Containing that much magic shouldn't be possible in a mortal body, though by all accounts Marveth had done it.

He climbed the wall to the right of the breach and walked along it, his Mage shield up around him diverting arrows and bolts. He needed to remind the enemy of what they faced. He needed to make them seem weak both to themselves and to the defenders. To achieve this without sapping his own strength, he had four Mages tracking him along the inside of the wall, channeling the shield protecting him. When he reached the breach, he began to cast his own spell. Below a further nine Mages stood channeling their strength to his, allowing him to avail of their bodies as well as his own to try and contain the magic he was about to summon.

More arrows rained at him, spears thrown. The Mages shielding him were fast being drained of their powers to keep him safe. Two more ran in to aid them. Garaveigh sprinted down through the rubble next shouting to the Mages, "What the hell is he doing?"

Before he could interrupt the Mages, strong hands pulled him back. One of the Unit commanders spoke to him. "He knows the risks, sir. He knows them more than anyone. But the city will fall within hours if we don't do something fast. We can't beat that many, but maybe we don't have to, if he can break their formations and scare the hell out of them, it might be enough to make them flee. They are Goblins sir, fighting, unified like this is already against their nature."

Garaveigh shook his head in disbelief. Two of the Mages shielding Athress collapsed, one of them dead, the other barely alive. Garaveigh hurried to try to aid him. Garaveigh could do nothing to help the young Mage, his malady was magical, no prayers could help.

Above, Athress' shield failed just as his spell finished. He jerked as the magic was released. The nine Mages linked to him were thrown to the ground, at least two of them didn't look like they would rise again. The sky lit up in a burning orange colour, as if the very heavens had ignited. As they did, a spear lanced through Athress' side and he collapsed on the wall. Garaveigh ran up the steps to the wall, calling on Assaurot to protect him. Racing to Athress, he picked the elderly Mage up, cradled him like a child in his big arms, and carried him back towards the stairs. They descended slowly back behind the safety of the wall. Garaveigh lowered Athress onto a waiting stretcher, the Mages eyes opened as he was laying him there.

"Should have known you'd save me, old friend," Athress said. "Always there when I need you." Garaveigh smiled, but it was strained, blood began to seep from his mouth.

"Not anymore, Athress. I'm sorry, but I must leave you. Assaurot calls me to his side. You can win this, don't doubt it. I have seen it, they are still... alive..." Garaveigh gasped once, then slumped to his knees and collapsed forward against the stretcher, rolled to the ground, dead. Five arrows protruded from his back, they were in deep. He hadn't even flinched when they struck, but instead kept carrying his oldest friend from the line of fire.

Athress broke down at the sight. Gregor ordered the stretcher bearers to place him in his carriage immediately. The soldiers didn't need to see this part. To them, Athress was a god of battle. They couldn't see the human side, the side that felt grief; that wept for his friend who died to save him. The stretcher bearers ran off with Athress, as Gregor turned to follow them a loud explosion made him stop.

Great balls of flame had begun to fall from the burning sky onto the battlefield outside the walls. They rained down on the army gathered below. The ground turned to flame and smoke as if the abyss had been opened here on the plains before Carraigbán. Hundreds were dying, screaming and running for shelter. The Goblin army broke, the horde splintered as those that weren't killed, fled in all directions. It was possible they would re-join the reinforcements coming behind, but unlikely. They had seen the power of Carraigbán and goblins weren't known for their bravery.

Athress heard the Defenders cheer. Some fell on their knees thanking the gods. Some wept over the bodies of fallen loved ones and others just that they might live.

While the city celebrated with music, laughter and celebrations that lit up every street, Athress lay in his sick bed, wondering how long they had. How long before that second horde arrived. He could not cast that spell again. The drain on his body had been incredible, even with the power the others channeled to him. It had killed two of them, and one more was catatonic.

Garaveigh was dead. His oldest friend, someone who had always been there, always calm, clear headed, self-sacrificing. Athress rolled over in his bed to face the wall and he wept. Dragar the dwarf, who he and Nuthionel had adventured with in their youth died in the Mage district leading the militia. He had lost the closest thing he had to son in Nuthionel, and now his closest friend. All dead.

Was there any hope left? His mind strayed to Ysabell and the others. Garaveigh's last words said they were alive. If that was true, was there a chance, however small, that it might have been worth it? It would never be worth it to him, but that was personal. Of course it was worth it if it saved the city and the thousands dwelling there, but the one thing he was sure about was that Carraigbán was no longer a home to him; it was a mausoleum full of dead memories.

The Dungeon, the Vault and the Thief

Chapter 30

Ysabell and Ing'Luk had travelled across most of the dwarven town, leaving darkness in their wake. Each Brazier they emptied, Ysabell broke the lever off, so the chutes couldn't be closed. No one could relight them without repairs and she doubted the Goblins had the skills to fix the Dwarven engineering.

At the far end of the town, Ing'Luk led Ysabell down a corridor which ended in a small, square, metal room. There was a strange metal wheel protruding from one wall and nothing else. No other doors except for the entrance. Ysabell immediately suspected a trap and ordered the goblin girl in ahead of her.

"Why are we here?" Ysabell asked. "This is a dead end, if you've betrayed me–" Ysabell was cut off by the little goblin squealing in terror.

"No, no, no betray! Way down, must go down. Dwarf room move up and down!"

The Goblin, who had named herself as Ing'Luk caught the wheel with both hands and began to turn it. The room lurched slightly and started to move. Ysabell looked in amazement at the way they came in. It looked the floor was rising in front of them to seal them in, then she realised, it wasn't the ground out there moving. The room they were in was dropping slowly down. They were in a shaft, a huge shaft and this room was lowered and raised by some kind of pulley mechanism.

She shook her head at the ingenuity of the dwarves. They were a marvel. It was slow going and Ysabell had to take over winding the mechanism as the goblin was getting too tired. Eventually another opening appeared in front of the open side of the steel box. She continued to lower until the floor inside and outside the moving room were level.

She let her Goblin guide take the lead again down a short passage, until Ing'Luk stopped and pointed at a closed door ahead. "Friends and dwarves, some guards. Guards see me help you, I dead. I wait."

Ysabell understood what she meant, but she couldn't trust that the little goblin was afraid enough to do as she promised. There wasn't much choice. She needed her guide to find the vault after this, so killing her was out of the question. On top of that, the goblin girl had done everything Ysabell asked, she hadn't drawn attention, she helped Ysabell put out the braziers. Even led her to some that they wouldn't have passed by otherwise. Killing her now would be... wrong.

"Very well," she said. "You wait here. Do not go back up in the moving room. do not go anywhere until I get back. Understood?"

Ing'Luk seemed nervous and jittery, Ysabell wondered was there something she hadn't told her. Then she spoke in a quiet voice. "You tie up Ing'Luk? Guards see me wait, I die. If I tied up, no one blame me."

Ysabell couldn't help but smirk. The little goblin wanted an alibi just in case Ysabell didn't survive. If tied up, it would look like Ysabell had captured her and dragged her there against her will. No one would suspect she was helping the 'thieves,' as she thought Ysabell and her friends were. It made sense though, plus it meant she could relax knowing the goblin couldn't run off to get help.

She nodded her agreement to Ing'Luk, took twine that the Goblin offered her, and then bound her, not too tight, with her hands behind her back and ankles tied together. If Ysabell didn't come back, the Goblin would be able to get out of the bonds given time. If anyone else came along she looked well-tied. Ysabell extinguished the torches in the passage and crept in the darkness up to the doorway at the end.

She drew her weapons as she reached it. She didn't need to worry about figuring out how to open the lock, the guards inside had noticed the absence of light from the passage and opened the door to see what was going on. Two of them marched out, carrying flaming torches to get a better a look and to relight the extinguished torches. A few steps in and they saw Ing'Luk, tied up and looking terrified in the torchlight. They rushed to her, but as they did she closed her eyes and turned her face away.

The two Guards looked at each other in surprise at her reaction. Ysabell leapt from the darkness before they could turn around. Both guards fell to the ground, dead, daggers having pierced their temples, straight into their brains. A small puddle formed on the ground under Ing'Luk.

Ysabell turned away and walked back to the door. It was bright inside, well-lit with lanterns, but there didn't appear to be anymore guards. She crept in and began putting out the lanterns. She realised too late, it was trap. Someone must have seen her from behind killing the first two guards. The door swung shut, a goblin, sword in hand standing before it. The door on the opposite wall swung open to reveal more guards.

Ysabell moved her left arm like lightning. Before anyone had reacted, she had one throwing knife already airborne to the Goblin guard by the entry. It buried itself deep in his right shoulder but didn't kill him. As he screamed, a second blade shot across the room through the far door and killed the first of the goblins coming through.

She leapt up on the table, grabbed the main oil lantern from the ceiling, and flung it to the ground in front of the other goblins running in from the door. Oil splashed all over the floor and the first of the Goblins. Then, spinning on her heel, she hurled another throwing knife to silence the injured goblin at the door to the lift passage. He gurgled, clutching the blade in his throat.

Turning back to the corridor in front, Ysabell saw the oil had caught almost immediately and burst into flames. A goblin screamed and threw itself down to try and beat out the flames. Using the distraction, Ysabell leapt clear over him and landed feet first on the chest of the goblin behind, sending him careening back into another. Both Goblins and Ysabell, crashed to the floor.

The narrow corridor suited Ysabell far more. There was no room to swing a larger weapon, but plenty of space to stab a dagger. She drew her black blades and the remaining goblins shouted in terror as she summoned her shadows around her. Before they could compose themselves, the first was dead and the second was scrambling to flee. He made it nearly four steps before Ysabell's dagger caught up with him, burying itself up to the hilt in his lower back. His screams were silenced as Ysabell drew her blade across his throat.

She quickly checked that there were no more surprises, and then proceeded down the corridor to where the dungeons lay. There were cells, but the Goblin's hadn't used them since they weren't enough to hold a whole clan of Dwarves. So instead they had herded them all into the floor where the cells were, and then just locked the door into the passage out and used the whole area as a giant prison.

Ysabell reached the door and looked around for a key hole or release mechanism. To the left of the door was a large lever attached to some kind of mechanical device built into the floor. She drew the lever and the door lifted in front of her. Standing there smiling was Cali.

"Told them when the screaming started that it was you," the Halfling laughed. "Daft buggers didn't believe me; I said no one can make a Goblin afraid of the dark better than Ysabell. Plus, the Mage could track ye with yer stone so we knew you were on the way. Didja have to kill many to get in here?"

Ysabell couldn't believe the overwhelming relief she felt at seeing all her friend's faces sticking out in the crowd of dark, curious dwarves. She grinned and retorted. "Not even ten. Hardly worth the effort. Can't believe you needed me to come save you from ten guards, I was tempted to leave my weapons outside and do it barehanded just to keep it interesting."

"Yeah, yeah, it's a lot easier when a steel door isn't blocking you from reaching them. Our friends here, the Dwarven clan who own this here mine, well they're a wee bit pissed off at the bastards who've moved in upstairs They'd like to help by slaughtering all the Goblins. I've told them not to be greedy; that there's enough to go around for everyone." She appeared delighted to have met some friends who seemed as anxious to kill goblins as she was. Ysabell couldn't help but think that Cali should have been born a Dwarf.

"All your armour and weapons are in a vault," Ysabell said. "Along with the 'wealth' this Demon has stolen from the dwarves here. I have a... I have a guide of sorts." She glanced at the angry and determined-looking dwarves. "Just make sure our new friends don't kill her. She's been most helpful."

With that, Ysabell turned and led the way back out of the dungeons with her companions and the dwarves behind her. There were at least a hundred maybe a hundred and fifty of them, could be many more, but in the dim light it was hard to tell. They reached Ing'Luk quickly, and the goblin looked terrified when she them coming up the corridor. Ysabell untied her and asked her to lead them to the vaults.

"You no come to steal, you come to kill king and make Goblins leave Dwarf city?" she asked Ysabell, though she didn't take her eyes off the dwarves.

Ysabell saw no point in lying to her and answered with a simple "Yes".

Ing'Luk shook her head. "King kills you. He kills all Goblin chieftains. He says follow me or I kill you. All Chieftains say no. Dwarves live here, we no want to come, Dwarves kill us when we go near. King kills all Chieftains and say 'Now I am big Chieftain, I am King, all Goblins obey or I kill'! You kill King, we go home. No more dying in king's war."

Ysabell was shocked. She hadn't expected that the goblins weren't here willingly, well at least not all of them. Maybe a fight with the Goblins wasn't inevitable. If some wanted to flee, that would make the fight against the demon that much easier.

The dwarves were led by a large, old, grey bearded Dwarf, but tough as old boots by the look of him. Barendar was his name and he was the 'king' of this clan until an enormous Goblin army, tens of thousands of them, invaded.

"We've spent the last 5 years trapped in the dungeons, more than 50 of my people are dead down there. We intend to pay back that debt. If there is a demon leading these things," Barendar looked around at his people as if assessing how many could still fight. He looked back at Ysabell. "We'll be more than happy to have your help fighting it. But with or without help, we are going remove that filth from my throne and his vermin from our homes!"

The dwarves opened a hidden door near the moving room, or as the dwarves called it the 'elevator'. King Barendar explained it was for maintenance. If the elevator broke they needed a way to get down to the other levels to fix it, so they had carved passages to walk between the levels too, it led them back up to the City. The Vault wasn't far, the dwarves obviously knew the way, so Ysabell sent Ing'Luk on her way, before she went she gave her the bag of loot the little Goblin had been stealing when Ysabell found her.

"You helped me Ing'Luk," Ysabell said. "In doing so you now have chance to save the lives of many of your people. Make sure you are out of this place as fast as possible, take any of your people willing to flee. Once I am done here, I doubt the Dwarves would let any Goblin live, even one who helped free them. Good luck."

The goblin girl bowed before Ysabell and said a single word before running off into the darkened streets. "Friend."

Ysabell turned back to Barendar. "Best if most of your men head to wherever they can procure weapons. Is there an armoury or similar? Too many of us marching through the streets could alert the Goblins before we have a chance to surprise them and we can't afford this 'king' of theirs to flee. While they do that, you can guide us to the vault."

The old dwarf thought about it for a moment then said, "Very well. I don't trust easy girl, certainly not humans or elves, but I heard those screams down in that dungeon. Something tells me there's more to you than meets the eye. Luckily for us the fools don't seem to know how to relight the braziers. Darkness will make things easier."

"I'm sure they know how, they were all lit when we arrived, but I dumped them and broke the levers so they couldn't be relit. I don't like the light much. Give your men their orders and we'll set off immediately."

Barendar ordered his men to get armed, and then hide by the Vault's front entrance. When they saw the signal, they were to come out in full battle formation, and they would march to the throne together. The Dwarves headed off into the gloom, quietly considering there were well over a hundred of them. Barendar led Ysabell and the companions in a different direction, heading up towards the still lit part of the city. He knew every nook and cranny like the back of his hand.

The vault was built to hold the treasures and wealth of his clan. He had rightly surmised that the Vault would have heavy guard. What the Goblins didn't know was that there was another way in. Dwarves were no fools; they had hidden doors and passages all over the place.

An hour after they had departed, Ysabell, her companions and King Barendar were climbing through a hatch in the floor of the sealed vault. When they climbed up through it, they saw the ingenuity. The hatch looked like every other slab on the floor. If they closed it, they'd have a hard time finding it again.

Who's the King of the Mountain?

Chapter 34

The Vault wasn't quite what Ysabell had imagined. They had pictured gold and silver and precious gems piled to the ceiling. Instead they found suits of armour, old books and manuscripts, masses of them, old weapons and busts of long dead Dwarves.

"The wealth in this room is beyond measure to my clan," Said Barendar. "Here is every record of every battle fought and honor conferred. Of contracts, promises, marriages, deaths, oaths sworn, judgements passed, and sentences given. Here is every weapon of note from our clans' history of two thousand years, the armour of each of our kings in all that time. Our testament, our story, our laws, our very soul. Aye Gold and Gems are fine, we can craft great beauty with them, but they are for cosmetics, appearances, for trading. This." He waved his arm across the room. "This is where our true wealth lies. In knowledge and remembering what came before us."

Ysabell realised she had falsely believed the description of Dwarves as a race who would forsake the world for gold. She made a mental note to try and challenge her own preconception about all these new races she was meeting, she had thought all elves were nature loving and peaceful too. A bit like Ériu, soft and gentle and kind. Nuthionel had been her friend and mentor, but he was also a cold-blooded killer if you were his enemy, he had no mercy in him. Nothing like what she had thought elves would be like.

Guinevere interrupted Ysabell's thoughts, shouting in delight, she stood near the great door of the vault by a huge chest. She was holding her Mace aloft, its inner glow throwing an eerie light around the walls of the vault. The light made Ysabell notice something she hadn't before. The walls were gold, maybe solid gold. She turned to Barendar who was smirking.

"Like I said, gold is nice," he said. "How better to honor our greatest treasures than to encase them in gold?" He chuckled to himself as he headed towards the rear of the vault.

Ysabell shook her head. Her companions were gearing up fast and preparing themselves, checking their gear and Cali of course was caressing her axe blades with an oil stone. Barendar called for Ysabell, he was at the back of the Vault, moving some boxes and armour stands aside. She came up behind him and saw he seemed to be trying to get to a suit of armour at the back. It was ornamental as far as she could see, with a dull goldish colour. A huge, matching two-handed battle hammer lay beside it.

"The founder of our clan was Barendar the First, I am Barendar the Third. He led us to conquer a savage world, and found our first city, our first mines, far from here to the south. Five hundred years ago, that home and most of our clan was destroyed by molten rock. We lived among another clan in the great Dwarf city of Deep Crag, for the next few hundred years, I was born there. But we had no home of our own, so about a century ago, I led my people out here, to found a new home. Where we could carve our own future once again."

He looked at the armour of his ancestor again.

"Nothing lived this far North, as far as anyone knew after the Twin Cities was nothing. Rumours of goblins, seems they were true after all, it seemed perfect. Available mountains, ripe for the delving. Now we come to this, my people slaughtered, their new homeland seized. Their anger is great, but their morale is low, back there is the armour of Barendar the First." He indicated the ornamental armour he was trying to get to.

"He had it made as symbol of hope for his newly formed clan. It's the most important piece of our history. He is greatly revered. Wearing that armour, I will rally my people, I need to build their morale, to strengthen them. But.." He grunted, trying unsuccessfully to lift a giant stone bust of some King or other, "I can't reach the bloody thing with all this crap in front of it. Any chance you could nip over there and get it?"

Ysabell laughed, she couldn't help it. All that, a big history lesson in the middle of a raid on a vault held by the enemy, and all he wanted was a hand in getting some armour? She thought *These are the kind of people who Cali should belong to.*

Ysabell easily leapt over boxes and statues, dropping down next to the armour. She lifted it off the stand expecting it to weigh a ton, but it was light as a feather. She tapped it to be sure it was metal, which it was. She carried it back to Barendar, who thanked her, then she went back in to get the Warhammer. It wasn't nearly as light. She had to drag it back until Barendar could get his hands on the haft. He lifted it with ease and gave it an experimental swing. Ysabell marveled at the strength of the old dwarf.

"This'll do very nicely," he said. "Oh yes! Time to crack some skulls I think." Ysabell had to admit the golden armour looked as though it was made for Barendar. He buckled on the armour and picked up his hammer. Together they joined the others near the door.

"Ha! Ye look like ye belong on a pedestal in a brothel with that gold crap on ye," Cali laughed. "When you die, can I melt that down to make something pretty? Where's yer real armour?"

Ysabell looked at Cali in despair. "Cali," She said "This is the Ceremonial armour of King Barendar the First, who founded this clan. King Barendar the Third is wearing it as a symbol of hope for his people." Ysabell hoped Cali would take the hint and shut up. But that was clearly blind optimism.

"Oh, well, yer a brave man. I could cut that in half with a butter knife, but you go on there, bein' a symbol. At least ye won't tarnish after they cut a hole in ye. Good luck to ye your high Symbolness!" Cali walked off chuckling. Ysabell felt the need to apologise on her behalf, but when she turned around King Barendar was laughing too.

"Aye, she'd be right normally. Gold's as soft as butter, but this isn't just gold, it's been enchanted. You felt how light it is, it's also damned hard to break. Your Halfling friend might just change her mind after we've fought together."

Barendar led the companions to the main doors of the vault. The inside of the door was a complex assembly of cogs, wheels, bars, bolts and pistons, levers and counterweights, impossible to make head or tails of. It looked incredibly complicated and probably unpickable. Luckily, they were on the side where all the moving parts of the lock were. Barendar reached up, turned a small wheel on the left of the door and all the other parts of the lock began to move with it. When they were done, Barendar and Guinevere pushed on the two titanic doors and they swung open. Vaaldreth cast a flash of light to illuminate Barendar.

"For effect, make him look Godly," Vaal said, winking at Cali. "Bit of inspiration for his troops."

<><><>

Hag'Irt and Joc'Kun were on Guard duty at the vault. It was easy duty, no one was stupid enough to try steal from it. The lock couldn't be picked; they knew because they'd tried. So had everyone else. But it was light duty, just standing around for a few hours. A strange creaking noise came from the doors, the two Goblins looked at each other to see if they were hearing things. The noise got louder, it sounded like the bolts were sliding back. They drew their weapons and stood back from the great doors. The doors started to move, slowly pushing open, a blinding white light flashed in the vault, when their vision cleared they saw six heavily armed warriors facing them. Standing at their centre a large dwarf in golden armour wielding a huge Warhammer, they looked at each other again, then turned to run, only to find an army of dwarves behind them. There was nowhere to run to. Hag'Irt briefly thought how his wife had advised him to not to join this new king but go off with her and hide until whatever this was had ended. He wished he'd listened to her. He turned back to the six exiting the Vault, just in time to see the Golden Clad Dwarf's hammer swinging. He saw or knew no more.

<><><>

Silence descended again. The Dwarves gathered below, staring in awe. One of their legends had come to life to lead them to victory. Barendar gave them time to take in what they were seeing, then he raised his Warhammer and in a powerful voice that echoed through the streets he spoke.

"A usurper sits on the throne of our homeland! A demon playing at being a goblin King. He believes we are too weak to hold our homeland. He believes he is unbeatable; that his goblin servants can protect him. Is he right?"

"No!" Came the response from his people.

"IS HE SAFE?"

"NO!"

"Who belongs on that throne?"

"Barendar!"

"WHO BELONGS ON THAT THRONE?"

"BARENDAR, BARENDAR, BARENDAR!" The dwarven army erupted. Weapons clashed together, armoured feet stamped on the ground. In the shadows beyond them Ysabell could see goblins fleeing as fast as they could for any bolt hole. The chant grew louder and more unified. Barendar turned to Ysabell, his eyes burning with a fire Ysabell knew all too well. That was when she knew they would succeed. No demon was going to stop this Dwarf. No number of goblins would be enough. Ysabell hoped some of the dwarves back in Carraigbán were like him. Then maybe the city would still be holding out.

His voice low and rumbling with anger he said "Let's take my throne back." Barendar turned and led the Companions with the entire Dwarf army behind them up the great wide staircase to his throne.

The Final Stand

Chapter 35

Athress and the Arch Druid Haydleth stood at the collapsed section of the wall. Haydleth believed it best to raise a new stone barrier in its place, but Athress wasn't so sure.

"They will attempt to enter here," he said. "It's the logical choice, it's also the easy choice and these are goblins. We should use that to our advantage, if we seal of this whole area, so they cannot get into the rest of the city, they will be caught in narrow alleys and roads surrounded by mostly wooden buildings. If we let them in here, we could torch the whole district, kill a thousand or more in one go. It would be a huge defeat for the general. His first engagement of the battle sees his troops slaughtered. It would also buy us a little extra time and give our troops some hope."

"Athress, the risks to the city are great. There are thirty thousand of them. Killing a thousand or fifteen hundred in one hit would be great, but ultimately it wouldn't give us any advantage. If we rebuild the wall, they will come to a field completely full of the bodies of the previous army, an army bigger than theirs, all dead. Should they then see the walls looking solid and unbroken, that would still give you the same blow to their morale. That forty thousand of their fellows died attempting this and completely failed to even make a crack in the walls. That would put much doubt in their minds."

They had bickered over this for days, but time was slipping away and they needed to decide. Without Garaveigh, Athress was feeling the strain and pressure of leadership a lot more. Haydleth had stepped in to help him, but that relationship wasn't the same. They were friends, but not in the way Garaveigh and Athress had been. Garaveigh knew him inside and out, knew what he was thinking almost before he'd thought it. This war had cost him everyone he cared for, a part of him nearly wanted the walls to wall, so he could join his friends.

Athress sat alone in his chambers, staring into the bone fire he had created weeks ago. Every minute of every day he wasn't out on the walls he was here. Just in case. Though it seemed hopeless by now.

He sighed and moved to his desk to begin sorting and reading the reports from the last few days. The second goblin army had been spotted by scouts, less than a day's march away. A decision on the wall needed to be made fast, but he just couldn't get his mind focused on it. He knew he was procrastinating. He knew why. He was still hoping there would be some word from the North, hoping and praying there was still a reason to fight on. He lay back and listened to the crackling of the fire, then realized that there was no wood in a bone fire. The only time it crackled was...

Athress leapt up and spun around to face the flames. It was changing shape, the iMage of Vaaldreth appeared it. It wasn't clear, but he could make it out.

"Still alive... don't give up... a few more days... Ysabell...Dwarfs, an army ...Griffon back" Athress focused on the fire and fed magical energy into it with all his will, trying to strengthen the signal.

"Vaaldreth? Can you hear me? It's unclear what you are saying." Athress' efforts cleared the communication a little, though he knew he could hold it only for a few minutes.

"Athress, I'm sorry. Trying to make a bone fire with limited materials and no equipment. Been delayed, but still alive. We're almost there, old friend. Hold out!"

Athress' heart leapt. He couldn't believe it. They'd reached the Goblin's settlement, this could be over in a day or two, the City saved, the people saved. He called for Gregor immediately. His assistant came rushing in, looking like he'd been asleep.

"Gregor, get a message to Haydleth immediately. He was right, we rebuild the wall tonight. Then summon the senior Mages. They are to meet me at the fallen section of wall in the trade district as soon as possible. Our companions in the North are alive and well and preparing to kill the Demon King. We must hold. We must give them their chance!"

With a wave, he sent Gregor running with his messages. He threw one last glance back at the bone fire and smiled, his fist clenched around his staff. *Let them come,* he thought, *if I must burn the whole army to ash singlehandedly I will. They will have their time!*

Before he left his chamber, he picked up Marveth's Grimoire. He knew most of it by now. The power was dangerous, the devastation that could come from this book, it was unimaginable. He had studied one last spell from it, a last resort. Men should not have, should never have had that power. He wondered briefly if whatever catastrophe drove people to this world was man made. A misuse of power such as Marveth's. He made his mind up there and then and threw it into the bone fire. It lit immediately, flared in the magical flame and turned to ash.

Crowds gathered. Soldiers lined every surface they could find to watch. There were no civilians as the district was evacuated when the walls had crumbled. But every soldier wanted to see the magic that had made the great city walls. Athress and his Mages stood in a line before the broken wall, leaving room for falling rumble. Their arms raised, staffs above their heads, they began their chants

Tremors could be felt in the ground throughout the district. Slowly rocks started to move, tumbling to the side as a solid stone hill rose from beneath the soil. The dwarves that had worked with Dartag on the original wall were already standing by. There would be no time to carve the inside with parapets, but they would make damn sure the outside was unclimbable before morning.

As the Mages finished, Gregor had two carts brought forward and the weakened Mages were helped into them and carted back to the tower to rest. The spell took incredible amounts of magic, it left them drained. Haydleth stepped forward with two other druids Athress didn't know.

"The dwarves will be hard pressed to make the outside presentable before the enemy arrives. We will use nature's power to ensure that the inside of the wall is also functional." He smiled at Athress. "I don't know where you found your fire, but it's good to see it back."

Athress' lip twisted. "They are alive Haydleth. Vaaldreth made contact. The Demon king will be dead shortly, then they are returning here, communication was broken, but they mentioned Dwarven allies on Griffon back. I don't want to jump to conclusions, but it sounds positive to me. Whatever you and your circle can do to help us hold till they are done, do it."

Haydleth nodded. The two druids who had accompanied him were busy directing vines, massive thick vines to climb the new rocky section of wall. They formed a walkway along the inside just below the top. Giving men shelter, but also a platform to shoot from and repel climbers. Soldiers cheered as the wall was taking shape. Haydleth looked up at the men cheering the two druids on.

"How quickly they forget their hatred of us," he said. "I wonder, when this is over, how quickly will it return?"

Athress considered it for a moment, then said, "I don't think it will. I think people will remember your druids fighting beside them, tending their wounds, defending this city. They will also remember the Nobles who demonised you are nowhere to be seen"

By morning the wall was finished and once again manned by soldiers. Not a moment too soon. On the horizon, a cloud of smoke and flame rose from the trees. A signal fire from one of the scouting parties. The enemy was here.

Orders were shouted in every direction. Messengers ran between walls and districts, troops moved back and forth on the ramparts. No shifts, they needed to give the impression there were more of them than there were, otherwise the enemy would simple spread out and attack all walls at once.

The enemy was coming from the east as before, so the walls to the west of the city had only a token force, the druids also arranged two surprises for the approaching army. The first they were about to march in to. The plain before the walls was still littered with the decaying bodies of the first goblin army. Priests and many of the citizens had wanted to remove them; it could cause disease and was a pretty gruesome sight. Haydleth had advised Athress to let them lie. It would be massively demoralising to the enemy as he figured it was very hard to focus on fighting when your foot keeps landing on a dead comrade's head or gut.

As the goblin army marched closer to the walls, a deep rumbling sound began below their feet. It was loud, very loud. Soldiers stepped back from the walls, wondering what devilment this was. The Goblins stopped in their tracks, their formations losing shape as they looked around panicked, wondering if this was a signal of what had wiped out the first army.

A small jet of water burst from the ground to the south of the army. It spouted high into the air and all eyes turned to look at it. It grew thicker, as more of the ground crumbled away around it. As it did it got lower, but the volume of water kept increasing, rapidly, within minutes it was deluge deeper and more forceful than a river. It flowed downhill away from the city at speed, right through the invading army.

The ground suddenly burst outwards, spraying mud and earth for hundreds of feet. It swept away anything in its path, the goblin forces separated, fleeing to each side of the water, trying to escape getting swept up by it. The bodies of the dead were picked up and tossed into the living who were struck with enough force to knock them over and back into the current to drown.

Those that fled to the city side of the gushing river, a few hundred, were peppered with arrows from the Carraigbán walls. The others, the bulk of the army, gathered on the other side, looking on helplessly as their fellows faced a bloody slaughter.

The water continued to flow for another twenty or thirty minutes before finally easing off and stopping. The goblins set up a camp to wait until dawn to attack, but Athress knew their morale had to be sapped.

"A fine display," Athress congratulated Haydleth. "Demonstrating the futility of any army against nature. So, tell me, what is your second surprise?"

"We can't use the water again, that all but emptied the aquifer below the city. I figured if this battle lasts we'll have starved long before we run out of water anyway." He glanced back at the enemy camp. "Ysabell and her halfling friend, from what I've seen, appear to have the bizarre technique of attacking, always, even against undefeatable odds. So, I thought in tribute to her efforts up north, perhaps we should employ her technique here."

Athress raised an eyebrow, his mouth curved up on one side and regarded Haydleth quizzically. "Attack? They are still nearly thirty thousand strong. We have, even with the new conscripts, maybe three thousand swords and archers. They would slaughter us."

Haydleth grinned. "Oh no, three thousand against an army would be ridiculous. No I propose about one hundred soldiers attack. I think it has a good chance of inflicting a large blow to their morale. There is nowhere near here for them to get enough supplies to feed an army that size for long. If we can set their wagons alight, and burst their water barrels, we could severely limit their capabilities."

"Haydleth, you make good points, but they have a watch patrolling all around their camp. A hundred men marching out of the city would be noticed and killed."

"Not if they travel my way."

Now it was Athress's turn to smile. Of course, the druids could bring the soldiers right into the heart of the enemy camp from the earth. "Speak to the commanders. Find their one hundred best. Do it now and hit them in the next few hours. But keep it quiet, the soldiers don't get told what you pick them for, neither do their commanders. Tell them once you have them in your grove, isolated from everyone else. We still have a traitor here and I want no pre-warning getting to the enemy." As Haydleth started walking away Athress called after him. "Good Luck, Haydleth, you'll need it."

Sending a Message

Chapter 36

As Ysabell, her companions and the dwarven army approached the doors leading into the throne room, six goblins, wearing good-quality dwarven armour and bearing two swords each, stepped out of the guard's post to the side of the door.

Ysabell figured they must be mad. There was an army facing them, yet they seemed to have no fear. Their faces almost appeared bored. They wore metal, jewel embedded torcs, fitted tight to their necks. The gems glinted strangely. There was definitely some magic at play.

"Thrall Torcs," Barendar muttered to Ysabell. "The one wearing the master torc can control them, see through their eyes, hear through their ears, and control their movements. Don't expect them to fight like Goblins. If that demon is any good as a warrior, they will have his skill."

Ysabell nodded. She didn't draw her blades yet, though she could hear the whisper of steel against sheathes behind her as the others drew theirs. She continued walking straight at them, not slowing and not drawing her weapons. Suddenly a blue streak flashed by her and one of the Goblins burst into flames, she swung to see Cali, holding the crossbow, a gleam in her eye. A young dwarf beside her looking impressed!

She faced the goblins. "Well? Are ye daft? Yer friends burning, Cooey! Over here, I shot him, who's next in line?" A second bolt flew, lighting up another goblin. The other four raised their swords and ran forward. Cali chuckled with delight, swinging her crossbow back onto her belt, she drew her axe, and roared, "Kiss me axe, for luck, ye big bastard!" Her hatchet flew from her left hand and buried itself in the Goblin's face. Ysabell looked on in disbelief.

The Goblins reached them fast, too fast. The first swept Ysabell blades to the side with one sweep of his hammer, then followed through with his charge, Ysabell flew across the stone work and slammed into a wall. She looked up in shock as the Goblin came after her, He was fast and moved well, not at all like a Goblin. He had thrown her with ease before she had even had time to react. She scrambled to get on her feet and stumbled back against the wall. She was dizzy from her spill. As the goblin raised his blades to swing, his head exploded sideways, spraying the doors with blood and brains. His decapitated body fell to its knees and Ysabell saw Guinevere standing behind it. Her mace was dripping with the remains of the goblins brains. She reached down and offered Ysabell a hand, pulling her back to her feet.

Barendar was facing the last two goblins alone. Ysabell hurried to help him but then noticed the Dwarves weren't moving. They stood back, weapons at their sides. *It's a test*, she realized. Barendar wore the armour, he had to prove worthy. Dwarves don't follow Kings because of an inherited name. They follow leaders.

Ysabell reached across and stopped Cali from firing her crossbow again. "This is his fight, Cali. No help." She gestured towards the Dwarves all watching in silence. Cali nodded her understanding and moved back to stand next to her dwarven buddy. Vaaldreth was leaning on his staff watching the battle with Ériu.

The Goblin to Barendar's right slashed low with his left blade, holding his right-hand blade back for a strike when Barendar's defences were engaged. The other Goblin on his left was doing the exact opposite, there was no way to defend against both at the same time, so he didn't try. Instead, he attacked both at the same time. He swung his hammer at the right-hand goblin, and let it go, whilst diving head first at the left hand one, smashing him to the ground. He bashed his armoured fists into the creatures face twice, crushing its bones with the force. The second Goblin was busy trying to pry its face guard off. The Warhammer had beaten it into its face, blood seeped from all around it as the goblin desperately clawed at it. Barendar, slowly and taking his time, walked over, picked up his hammer and smashed it through the goblins ribs. The swing lifted the goblin off his feet and sent him tumbling down the stairs. The dwarves stepped aside to let it fall, then closed ranks again.

The king raised his hammer over his head and bellowed, "Barendar!" His people chanted the name with him.

He turned, placed his two hands on the great doors and pushed them inwards, revealing the great hall and throne room. Two to three hundred armed Goblins lined the room. At the back on the Golden throne sat the Demon King. No longer a goblin, he had taken his true form.

He was human-looking, but his skin was black and eyes glowed red, like flames burned within him. He was about eight feet tall, too tall to be a human. Two wicked-looking, curved blades rested against the throne beside him.

Ysabell scanned the room wondering why the goblins were not reacting to his demon form, then saw it. The thrall torcs were on every goblin in the room. *How many can he control at once? All of them?* They wouldn't have a hope.

"If he isn't challenged he can control all these Goblins, but if he must focus on something else, we may have a chance," Vaaldreth said to her. "We need to keep him busy."

Ysabell nodded and told him to tell the others and Barendar. Then she strode forward into the hall, her head held high. Her fear was gone, burned away, for when she saw this demon, she saw his master, Xelazenivein. Today she would be sending a message. She was coming for him and whatever he sent in his stead she would cut through until at last she had him, and her vengeance for Nuthionel.

Her companions and Barendar stepped up to stand beside her. The dwarves filed into the room behind them, weapons drawn, ready for battle. Then Ysabell spoke in a low, menacing tone.

"So, you are what the coward sends in his stead? A mutant half demon? A pathetic servant whose best attempt is an army of the weakest and most spineless creatures in this world? Run away, run back and summon your master if he has the guts to face me."

The demon leapt from the throne. "The master would not bother with such trivial details as you and your rag tag band of dwarves and elves," it hissed at Ysabell, its voice sibilant and angry

A shout came from behind Ysabell. "And halflings ye blind muckraker!"

The demon continued as if he heard nothing. "You are as an ant beneath his feet to be stamped upon and scrapped off. But you will prove an interesting distraction for a few minutes. I shall enjoy watching my thralls cut you into pieces."

The Dwarves' eyes darted from side to side nervously, but Ysabell smirked. "Your armies haven't stepped foot in Carraigbán yet. Xelazenivein must be so pleased with your success so far..."

The demon grabbed his blades and roared at her. "Human Bitch! Your city will fall, but first, you will!" He ran straight at Ysabell while at the same time all three hundred Goblins moved in. They moved with skill, but not like those outside had.

"Give him a lot to think about!" Ysabell shouted.

She had barely spoken the words when the demon seemed to flicker and vanish only to instantly reappear right in front of her. Swinging both his curved swords, Ysabell had no time to react. Something caught her from behind and hurled her out of harm's way. The blades whistled past her instead hitting Ériu. One sliced deep across her face, the other across her ribs. Neither was a fatal wound by the look of it, but the gentle druid flew into a rage.

She swung to face the demon and screamed, the scream deepening to a roar, Ysabell couldn't believe her eyes as the soft-spoken druid changed shape. Her skin darkened as hair sprouted from it, her face became elongated as a snout formed, her hands enlarging into giant claws. It happened in seconds. She had become an enormous bear, easily twelve feet tall when up on her hind legs.

She bared her sharp, vicious teeth and roared in the demon's face. The Demon stabbed forward with his blades to try and gut her, but with one giant paw Ériu swatted him and sent him flying to crash into a pillar. He vanished as he hit it, appearing behind Ériu. A blast of ice smashed into his side from Vaaldreth to knock him off balance. As he turned toward the new threat, a blue, flaming bolt slammed into his back, dousing him in similarly-coloured flames.

He blinked clear of the circle made by his enemies, reappearing at the throne again. Barendar was waiting for him, hammer already swinging. He smashed him from his feet and off the dais. Ysabell looked around and saw that as he was losing concentration. the goblins were losing their skill, being easily dispatched by the dwarves.

"Keep it up, its working!" she called to the others.

The demon blinked again and appeared behind Cali. He caught the Halfling with a blow to the side of her helmet, she flew forwards. Spinning he searched for a new opponent, and as he did Ysabell hurled her throwing knives. One stabbed into his shoulder, the second straight through his left cheek, and the last missed and clattered harmlessly off a wall. As he tried to pull the blade out of his cheek, he was hit hard from below.

Cali had recovered from the blow, used a pillar as a launching point to get height and swung with all her strength, smashing the demon in the side of his head. He stumbled head first into a pillar. He staggered back from it, but before he could vanish, a huge claw ripped across his front, shredded his armour and sliced open the skin. Black blood oozed out from the wounds. He tried to teleport again but only flickered. It had failed. He caught his footing and sprinted towards the doors.

The demon was so focused on staying alive he abandoned his control of the torcs. This left them plodding and useless, easy for the dwarves to slaughter.

A wall of ice formed in front of the doors to seal off the demon's only exit., He swung around, lashing out with his blades and killing the two dwarves closest to him with barely any effort. The companions spread out around him in a semi-circle.

Barendar was the first to step forward to engage the demon. He took a mighty swing but the demon leapt high into the air out of the way. His blades pointed downwards to skewer the king on landing but Cali fired a flame-bolt from her crossbow immediately. The bolt caught the demon in mid-air, instead of splashing him with the contents, it exploded on contact, blasting him clear, to land on his back in front of Ériu. Her great fangs bit deep into his left leg, picked him up and hurled him against the pillar to her left.

The demon dragged himself upright, leaned against the pillar with his left leg now useless. He roared and swung his blades like lightning, but they whistled through nothing but air as the companions took a step back.

His eyes scanned the companions, noticing too late one was missing. Ysabell darted from the shadows behind the pillar and stabbed both her daggers into his chest. He dropped his swords and fell to his knees, looking up he tried to speak. Her blades pierced his lungs before he could. Ysabell stared into his eyes, full of hate, and then with her second set of blades, Nuthionel's blades, she severed his head from his shoulders, it fell and rolled to Barendar's feet.

Assassins on the Streets

Chapter 37

The raid that had been so successful was a distant memory now. The Goblins fought with fury and desperation, with at least half of their supplies destroyed, most of their water barrels destroyed. They had procured some more from local abandoned farms, but not enough. It was a fight for survival for both armies now. Unless they took the city, the goblins would be starving within days or would have to cease their attacks while they found more supplies.

The defenders were dwindling in number, but as their numbers reduced, those left became toughened and harder. Surviving in battle becomes a matter of habit. These were those with the most skill, and that skill tempered with every hour they survived. They fought as if possessed, and again and again the Goblin forces gained the walls only to be thrown back down. There was no comparison in losses, the Goblin army was closer to 22,000 strong, still insurmountable. But a long way from the thirty thousand plus who had marched to Carraigbán only weeks before.

The druids were relentless. Since the army had arrived they had infested the goblin camp every night, with insects, vermin, fast growing vines, and rain summoned to soak them when they had no shelter. The Mages were relentless in calling down fire, ice and bolts of shadow on the goblin forces all day and night in shifts. But it wasn't enough. Athress knew they were running out of time. He had promised to give Ysabell as much as he could, but as much as they had inflicted massively disproportionate losses on the goblin army, they were decimated themselves. Their dead had filled every morgue in the city. Churches and warehouses had to be used instead, with student Mages taking shifts using ice spells to keep them cool so the bodies wouldn't begin to decay.

<><><>

Athress had one last trick up his sleeve. He had studied Marveth's spell book long and hard looking for anything that might help before he had burnt it, and he had discovered a spell that could. But there was no way he had the strength to survive it. It was his last resort. Channeling the power of other Mages to try and control it was no longer an option with many of the most powerful of his tower dead. Those that were still alive would be needed to rebuild the order when this was over. If there was another sacrifice to make, it would be his.

He was leaving the tower to head back to the walls when a messenger found him.

"Sir, its Haydleth sir," the man said. "He's injured. He's asking for you urgently, please this way!"

Athress hurried after the messenger towards the Druid circle.

<><><>

Haydleth arrived at the tower some ten minutes later seeking Athress. The Mage at the Tower door seemed confused at seeing him. Something was wrong.

"A messenger just summoned Lord Athress, said you were injured, he hurried off with the messenger, the southern gate sir, towards the druid circle!" Haydleth's face lit up in fury. *The traitorous scum! Humans in this city betraying their own people, without Athress the people would lose hope fast and holding the wall would become impossible.* He turned and ran, even at 351 the elf was strong and fit, as he picked up speed he dived forwards onto his hands, before they touched the ground they had become paws. His body changed mid-air, from the Elven High Druid to a large cat, much larger than any cat in the wild, as his paws hit the grass he bounded forward. Picking up speed he disappeared through the trees.

<><><>

Athress should have paid more attention, he cursed himself as tried to pull the crossbow bolt from his back, with no success. He watched warily from behind the low garden wall he had dived over after being hit. The messenger had ducked down an alley and ran as soon as they reached the middle of this street, before Athress could react, a bolt had smashed into his lower back. He was bleeding heavily, and needed help fast, he had no idea how many were out there, or what kind of weapons they, at least one, with a cross bow, was it poisoned? He heard a stone crunch on the road, someone was moving, maybe they thought him dead. Good. That would make then complacent. He crawled quietly to his left, further down the wall, so the bow man would be aiming at the wrong section of wall when he rose. As he did, the ground shook with a great, deep vibration and booming sound. He had no idea what it was, but it didn't sound good. Athress waited until the creeping footsteps were about 10 feet from him, then standing up he thrust out his staff muttering words from Marveth's grimoire, a blast of blue and black shadows burst from the staff, Athress dropped again from sight. The Bowman's flesh was torn away from his bone. It happened so fast, his body hadn't even fallen yet when there were just ragged strips of flesh, muscle sinew and internal organs hanging from the remains of what was once a human. It crumpled to the ground.

A shout went up from across the street. "Rush him!"

Footsteps hammered on the road. Some eight or nine men armed with swords and clubs rushed at him. Movement from the direction he had come in to the alley caught his eye. His strength was failing him. He couldn't muster enough energy to fight all these and more. His vision started to swim, but not before he thought he saw a huge cat sprinting into view.

"Bloody Hellfire!" One of the would-be assassins shouted, pointing at the giant cat running straight for them. The mercenaries turned to face it, but they were too slow to react. The cat bowled straight into them, its vicious claws killing two as it knocked them over. As it did, its fur changed, getting darker. It's body also seemed to get bigger, and the giant cat became an even bigger bear. It tore through them in seconds, with only minor scratches to show for it.

As the last one fell, the bear lumbered over to the wall Athress had collapsed against. It transformed into Haydleth while walking, a few shallow cuts on his torso. Athress was struggling, a pool of blood had gathered beneath him.

"The bolt pierced your kidney," Haydleth said after studying the wound. Athress was too injured to respond. The druid laid his hands on Athress and began to channel nature's magic. The bolt pushed itself out and with Haydleth's magic feeding it, the skin began to knit back together. It wouldn't give Athress back his lost blood, but he would lose no more. Haydleth sat back, exhaled.

The old Mage groaned and sat up. "You saved me," he said. "Not for the first time either. Do we know who they worked for?"

Haydleth was staring off into the distance. "Yes, one of them was one of the survivors from the raid in the circle a few years back. A minor noble here I believe. I would guess his family are the traitors. The rest all have the look of cheap mercenaries. But we have more pressing matters. I sent two scouts out to look at the gates on the western walls. They are too obvious a target. I refuse to believe the Demon General here wouldn't be smart enough to target them, they are the weakest points, two experienced scouts, neither has returned. Something's going on Athress, I can feel it."

"Okay, get me up, and find me a messenger, I'll pull 250 from the trade district to cover the western wall if the gates go. The rest can be there in thirty minutes. The Goblins would have to go around the walls, so it would take their main force longer to reach them, if we have the time we'll get a secondary line of barricades up inside the gates."

Haydleth helped him up and they headed for the Druid circle nearby. As they reached the grove, Gregor was there, looking panicked, "Lord Athress, we couldn't find you, to give you the message-" His eyes strayed to the blood on Athress' robes. "You're hurt! What happened? I.." Athress cut him off.

"I'm fine! You were here flustered with a message, what is it? Spit it out boy!" Gregor stepped back, tried to calm down and regain his composure.

"The Gate, Sir, the Western Gate. The Goblins mined under it and planted their explosives. It's... it's gone sir."

Athress grasped Haydleth. "You must send a message for me, fast as the wind. I need all but 250 of the troops to the gate now. I need another messenger sent to inform the Mages tower that I want it emptied. Every man and woman is to gather at that Gate. If they pass the wall, we're finished. There is no second line of defence here!"

Haydleth nodded. He selected two druids to deliver the messages. They changed form to large cats and dashed off into the streets. Haydleth sat Athress down to take a better look at the wound. Something felt wrong in it. He placed his hands on Athress' back and probed with his mind. Corruption. Unnatural energy moved under the skin. He removed his hands and sighed.

"A poison, demonic, I cannot heal this, I would send for a priest, but I think we both know that would be pointless, you are going to die, I can delay the poison only. Maybe for a few hours at best. I am sorry old friend."

Athress pursed his lips and narrowed his eyes. "To be honest, I didn't expect to survive this battle anyway." He looked up and off towards the West. "Go Haydleth, do what you can to reinforce the gate. I will join you there."

He nodded slowly, rose and walked away, then breaking into a run he leapt into the air arms outstretched, they kept stretching and formed into giant wings, a fanned tail spread out behind him. In seconds, he was a huge falcon shooting over the city.

"Well, well." Athress exclaimed to himself. "That was impressive."

One Last Service

Chapter 38

The gates were in chaos. A handful of soldiers had battled to hold back the twenty or so Goblins that had come up through the ground while gates themselves lay in pieces. A tangled heap of twisted metal and wood, half buried in the rubble that was the gate arch. More soldiers began arriving by the minute.

Athress moved through the crowd, walking slowly, the poison was working fast. Haydleth approached him.

"Haydleth, there is one last service I can give this City, and gladly. See that they treat Ysabell and her followers as the hero's they are, give them the respect they are due, and tell them I am sorry, but I couldn't be here to see them return. Now if you'll excuse me, I have a spell to prepare. My last spell. It needs to be spectacular, and it will be Haydleth, it will be."

He smiled at the Arch Druid. Slowly he walked up past the defenders, leaning heavily on his staff. Soldiers stacked fences, carts, pretty much anything moveable together, to make a presentable barrier in a U shape around the inside of the collapsed gate. The goblins would be caught in this killing arena, assaulted by arrows, spells and swords from all sides. The sounds of the Horde approaching were heard from outside the walls, just as the fastest of the groups from the other walls arrived. They needed time to assign posts and orders and get their defenders into position.

Haydleth watched as Athress painted a lonely silhouette against the setting sun, the wind making his torn and blood soaked robes flap around him as he stood alone on the rubble outside where the Gate had stood. Arrows started to whistle in the sky, just one or two over optimistic archers from the Goblin forces. They were well out of range still. Athress' chest as he took a deep breath.

His eyes scanned the horizon, slowly. Haydleth wondered what the Mage was thinking of in his last moments. He seemed so calm and accepting of what was to come.

At last Athress turned his attention to the Goblins running towards him. Steadied his feet, and lifted his arms, his staff with them. He began to chant, though the words were lost amid the sounds of the approaching horde. As he spoke, Haydleth saw the wind starting to picked up, dust and small branches being swept past the old Mage towards the goblins. It got stronger as he cast, his staff glowing the colours of burning embers.

It looked as though it was burning in his hands. But he showed no pain. Arrows screamed towards him, but the wind was like a hurricane now and robbed them of their direction and their speed. The horde had stopped, some trying to fight forward still, others just trying to get a foothold or purchase to not be blown back. Trees were uprooted and hurtled into the amassed army. They ploughed through the goblins killing all in their paths.

Athress' head turned to look at Haydleth and smiled, then finished the spell. The burning embers of his staff spread out into the air and the wind took on a hue of burning smoke. The Goblins were in full retreat. The defenders stood and watched, in awe. Not a hint of a breeze even reached inside the city walls, but outside the raging torrent of burning wind swept forth from Athress.

His robes ignited, but still he stood, not faltering. He continued channeling his spell as his hair burst into flame, a human torch unmoving in the eye of the firestorm. It incinerated Goblins in scores, hundreds burned as they tried to flee and even those who were furthest away still received burns or were struck by flying debris as the landscape was stripped bare. Flaming trees flew through the air into the Goblin horde, even the river boiled and steamed, killing more who got too close. Then, as suddenly as it began, it faded to nothing more than a warm breeze.

Where Athress had stood was a pile of ash that quickly blew away on the wind, like it had reached out and picked up his spirit to carry off with it. The Arch Mage was dead. Some three or four hundred goblins were incinerated as many again burned too badly to fight. Tears streamed from the eyes of many in the ranks of the defenders. Their leader, their inspiration, a godlike figure they had believed all but immortal. Dead. He had given his life to save theirs.

Over a thousand Goblins were removed from the battle with his last spell. Haydleth knew in years to come, Athress wouldn't be a human at all, but remembered as a God come to help the world against the forces of the Abyss. That's how stories worked, and future generations would never believe any human could have created such magic. He knew Athress had burnt the grimoire and was grateful to him. Such power would have seen this world torn asunder.

They had a few hours to prepare their defences before the Goblin horde was back on the march. But it had been a crucial few hours. Haydleth didn't even want to consider what would have happened had Athress died in the alley or had he not cast that spell. His sacrifice had bought them time. Time to erect the barricades and given the druid's time to reinforce them by bringing the wood of the carts, fences and everything else they could pile together, back to life. Deep roots now supported the barricades, thick branches intertwined and wove through each other, it would not be easy to break.

But the Goblins tried. Again, and again they assaulted the barricades; the killing ground was filling with bodies. There was still over twenty thousand Goblins attacking through the gap and trying to scale the walls still standing on either side. The defenders were fighting like never before. The new High Priest of the City had gathered all the remaining civilians in the Palace Grounds where they prayed. He had, unknown to anyone, had great barrels of Dwarven explosives placed around the entire area. If the Goblins made it this far, he would ignite them. These people would not be hacked to death, tortured, these children would not know the horror the Goblin horde would bring with them.

Haydleth was like a man possessed, sprinting across the battlements above, changing form as he did, tackling any goblin that made it to the wall. Despite the defenders, there were more and more of them making it. To the defenders it was as if they had lost one God of war in Athress and another had appeared. The Druid was unstoppable. He switched from elf to bird to cat in seconds to make it across the gap in the walls and tear the throat out of a huge Goblin that had reached the top. He hurled two of the attackers over into the hordes below. Then as more Goblins reached the walls, he changed again into a great bear and drove them back. But it wasn't enough; the barricades were buckling under the strain.

Defenders were being attacked from behind as Goblins reached the walls and leapt down behind those on the barricade around the collapsed gate. A huge eruption of flame tore through the barricades, explosives had made it through, the explosion killed some thirty defenders and seventy or eighty goblins in one go. Blowing many more clear, leaving them maimed and bloody amongst the carnage. The way was open...Haydleth swung to see, dismay hit him like a ton of rubble, they couldn't plug that hole, it was over. They had failed, it was all for nothing. As despair took him, he screamed, changing back into human form, a barbed spear protruded from his stomach. He tried to catch his breath, but it was so hard. He staggered and fell from the wall to land amongst the rubble and bodies strewn below, as his head rolled to the side he saw corpses everywhere. To his left was one of the shattered carts that had been part of the barricade, there was a boy, no more than thirteen, lying under the cart, his chest crushed, and scorch marks across his bloodied head. His eyes open in shock. But there was no life in them. Haydleth's last thoughts were confused he thought he heard a great horn, he wondered was it the Gods calling him to the afterlife. His eyes closed as he slipped into darkness.

The Demon General stood on a hillock watching over the battle. Millennia old he had fought and led battles through the ages in the Abyss. He had fought celestial creatures, demons, abyssal creatures and more, he had never been defeated. Goblins were less than ideal, but sheer numbers should guarantee him victory.

Hearing the same noise as Haydleth, he turned, that was a Dwarven horn, he grabbed the spyglass from his lieutenant, and looked to the North, sure enough, on the horizon there was movement. A flickering golden reflection. As it came closer he saw it was a Griffon, astride its back was a Dwarf in Golden armour, a giant Warhammer held over his head. Trailing out behind him were some forty or fifty more Griffons, all carrying armed figures on their backs. As he swore inwardly a second Horn echoed over the battlefield, the General spun to look, to the west.

A lone dwarf stood at the edge of the trees, a horn in one hand and a banner in the other. The Goblins had ceased all attack on the city now, wondering what was happening and if they needed to protect their flank. The defenders were looking at over the walls to see what had come now, was this salvation or doom. The solitary dwarf marched forward holding his banner high, it was the banner of Deep Crag, a roar went up from the defenders as the word spread. Through the lines and down into the city the news spread like wildfire, Deep Crag had sent aid, and the Heroes of Carraigbán had returned from the north! From the trees behind the Horn Blower marched the armies of Deep Crag, the largest of Dwarf Cities within a thousand leagues. More than 8,000 Dwarfs marched across the plain, their feet stamping, their weapons clashing as they sang a battle song. Goblins began back peddling as fast they could, trying to set up a defence. To the North, an airborne Dwarven force, to the East the City walls and to the west a huge Dwarven army, to the south their own General screaming at them to reform into battle formations.

A battle within a battle

Chapter 39

f this army had been led by a Goblin, it would have broken. But Xertu was an old Demon, ancient, he had led many armies through the ages on many planes. He had left his underling to see to ruling over the Dwarven city his Goblins had captured. Seeing the Dwarves and companions he assumed now that city was lost and his protégé dead, consigned back to the Abyss. He did not panic and while he stood, the Goblins stood, more afraid of him than of the Dwarves or humans.

He watched as the defenders of the city, with Athress' skinny young assistant Gregor in their midst, brandishing a sword he had picked up from a fallen soldier, left their city and charged into the Goblin forces. The Dwarven contingents moved in, the Deep Crag army splitting to close off any escape to the south and reinforce the north. The battle was far from over. The goblin horde still stood at over twenty thousand, with the dwarves added to the defender's numbers, they were still outnumbered at almost two to one.

The armies met on the field in the shadows of Carraigbán's walls. The sounds of weapons clashing, screams and war cries filled the air once more. Xertu watched with his personal guard and using Thrall torcs organised his units in the fight to devastating effect on the open field.

<><><>

Ysabell, with her companions and Barendar's forces, cut a bloody swathe through the Goblins, the griffons tearing through them, limbs and bodies flew through the air. As the Dwarves and the Companions dismounted to join the fight, the Griffons continued to tear into the Goblins. Some shredded on the ground, other grabbed and lifted to be dropped on the battlefield from a hundred feet up. Ahead of her Ysabell could see a tall and powerful Goblin fighting with a war hammer, killing with skill and speed, all who came in his reach were being cut down. His skill was far beyond that of any goblin. Knowing what to look for this time she quickly spotted the glinting gems of the thrall torc.

"Vaal'" She roared above the battle. "His neck!" She indicated towards the goblin ahead. Vaaldreth saw what she had and nodded back to her in understanding. The Demon General was here somewhere, and he was controlling some of these goblins. Possibly the squad captains. He must be distracted and killed to give the armies any chance. Guinevere quickly summoned a prayer to locate the demon. She sensed him immediately, swung towards the city and identified the general of the enemy forces. But the prayer also singled her out to him. As Ysabell and the companions turned to face him, from across the battlefield Xertu also turned towards them.

"Careful." Guinevere warned the group. "He is far more powerful than the one we faced beneath the mountains. This is the true leader of the Xelazenivein's forces here."

Ysabell saw Cali's eyes burn and a smile began to spread across her face. From his magical mutterings, she guessed Vaaldreth was preparing his protection spells. Each of the group prepared in their own way as they moved towards the demon and he towards them. Ysabell was pretty sure he knew who they were and was preparing as much they were. The demon's guard cleared a path before him as he approached. When he came within fifty yards of them he raised a hand and waved it across the battlefield, bodies were thrown in all directions. Both goblins and the cities forces flew from a large clearing he made in the field. As fighters rose to their feet, they knew this was a fight for the companions.

"Barendar" Ysabell's voice called to the dwarf. "Your people need your leadership, this one is not your fight."

The dwarf snorted back at her. "You killed the one who claimed my home, you freed myself and my people, and you think this is not my fight?" He tightened his grip on his battle hammer. "I owe you, but I also owe him. He's the one who controlled the hordes that took my home and killed so many of my people."

Ysabell nodded. There was no point is saying anything else. The others were all in this to the end. The companions spread out to face the demon. The battle raged around them, screams, sprays of blood, the clash of weapons all faded away as they focused on the fight at hand. Guinevere drew a blessing upon them all, as Vaaldreth cast a shield upon himself. Ysabell's shadows began to twist and wind around her, slowly she faded into them.

Barendar raised his Warhammer and broke the stand-off with a blood curdling battle cry. He sprinted at Xertu, as he did Cali let fly with flaming blue bolts one after another, running towards the demon from the other side. The demon drew a huge broadsword from his back and swung it at Barendar; black lightning crackled down its blade and shot out from the tip smashing the dwarven king from his feet. A burst of blue whiskey fueled flame erupted from the back of demon's head, with a wave of his hand it leapt from him, formed into a ball and shot back towards Cali, she was blasted into the air, alight in flames. Guinevere extinguished them with flash of Holy light even as Cali crashed to the ground. The halfling and dwarf rose slowly. The companions circled more cautiously now. This Demon had use of magic, how powerful, they didn't know.

Ysabell made a feign forward, as Xertu turned to face her, his sword coming around to blast her, she leapt to the side and rolled, his blast missing her, but his attention diverted long enough for Vaaldreth to cast. He unleashed an orb of glowing energy, it seemed to grow and transform as it flew. Flames, smoke, lightning and ice all crackled and blazed across its surface. It slammed into Xertu knocking him to his knees, Cali's throwing axe smashed into his armour at his left thigh. Using the distraction Barendar ran in close enough to engage, whilst Guin summoned a tower of Holy light to blast down onto the demon. He shrugged off the blow from Cali, with a sudden leap, he rose, parried Barendar's hammer and backhanded the Dwarf clear. The Holy flames still crackled across his armour, he turned to retaliate against Vaaldreth, but froze and spun, suddenly realising Ysabell was gone from sight.

Her attack from behind was too slow, one dagger slashed deep at his ribs, but his knee rose and smashed her from her feet. In one movement, he swung an armoured gauntlet and picked her up by her throat. But Ysabell had been here before, this time she was ready for it and embedded both her enchanted daggers in his wrist and twisted. She dropped to the ground as the demon reeled back screaming. His hand dropped beside her, burning up as it fell. He rose his sword in rage to finish Ysabell, but as it fell it was blocked by a blazing white mace wreathed in holy flames. As her mace touched his corrupted blade, Guinevere's whole body lit up in Holy Light. This mace was created by Asetha with one purpose, to destroy Demons. It recognised the evil and reacted by activating its enchantments. A shimmering armour of golden light assembled itself around Guinevere. The demon's strength was great, but so was Guinevere's and it was aided by the strength her Goddess had placed in this weapon.

They were evenly matched, Ériu wasted no time in capitalising, she ran forward, growing as she did. Xertu was hurled to the ground as a bear of gigantic proportions slammed into him from the side. Barendar's hammer crashed into his ribs as he fell and a bolt of lightning flew into his back from Vaaldreth's fingertips. With a scream the Demon unleashed a wave of energy in a sphere all around him, blasting the companions back from him. All but Vaaldreth, whose magic shields protected him. Xertu rose and swung his blade, magic shields were no match for the weapon, it cut through them and barely even slowed as Vaaldreth's left leg was severed at the upper thigh. He followed through with a mailed fist into Vaaldreth's chest. The Mage flew like a rag doll and crashed into the ground screaming as blood spurted from the stump of his leg. Ériu changed form and abandoned the fight to run to his aid.

To buy her time Ysabell ran in and leapt, using Cali's shorter form as she had before, to launch her. Her blades ripped the demons helm apart. Cutting deep gashes into his face and across the side of his head. The helm crashed to the ground in mangled heap. Ysabell hit the ground on her shoulder and rolled back to her feet still intent on attacking. Guinevere's mace crashed into the demons back spinning him around and splitting his armour, that crack was all Ysabell needed, she sliced across it with her enchanted blades and rolled clear in time for Cali to send an explosive bolt into the open wound. It blasted a hole in the demons lower back. Enraged he dropped his sword and hurled a fireball from his hand, Guinevere threw herself to the side just in time. It flew past her straight towards the injured Vaaldreth and Ériu.

Ériu had little time to react; she rolled Vaaldreth clear and took the full force of the blast to the right side of her head. She erupted like a torch, her hair alight, the skin on that side of her face blackening and burning away along with her eye. His bleeding stopped by the druid, Vaaldreth raised a hand a doused the flames and burning with ice. But Ériu was out of the fight, as was the Mage. Ysabell feared neither of them would survive, but there was no time to help them now. Her rage grew inside her. The thought of more dead friends fanned the inferno.

Seeing the demon unarmed, Barendar took his advantage. "Parry this ye bastard!" He roared as he swung his hammer two handed at Xertu's knees. The hammer crushed the armour and whatever was underneath of the demon's right knee. It stumbled only to meet the holy mace of Asetha coming at its face. Xertu was lifted off his feet and hurled into the air, crashing heavily to the ground. He opened his eyes to look up, above him stood Cali, her eyes burned as she swung her battle axe at his neck. Rolling fast, sacrificing his already maimed arm to shield himself, Xertu escaped the killing blow. He rolled unsteadily to his feet, reaching out he spoke a word of Magic and his sword flew from the ground back into his hand. He lashed it out blasting Cali clear with the black lightning that flew from it. Barendar engaged him again, parrying the broadsword and smashing an armoured fist into the demon's midsection. Ysabell watched and waited for this moment, as Xertu buckled forward she leapt from the shadows, ran up his back and plunged her blades over his head into his two eyes.

Xertu's head lashed back as he screamed, throwing Ysabell from his back. The demon lashed out blindly striking Barendar and knocking him back a good ten feet. Though blind, Xertu could still see something through the pain and agony. A figure of light stood before him. He realised too late it was Guinevere bathed in holy light. He needed no eyes to see that cursed flame. The mace of Asetha swung two handed, with all her considerable strength, she used her massive seven-foot frame as a counter weight adding to the force of the blow. The demons head exploded in holy light. Guin grasped his shoulder as the headless demon fell to his knees, then flipping her grip on the mace's haft she plunged its head down his neck. It burned through his insides. Beams of light began to burst from the cracks in his armour, growing brighter until they joined together, and with a final word of Prayer to her Goddess. Guinevere unleashed a great shaft of holy light down the length of the mace. The demon exploded. The remaining companions were hurled clear and Xertu was no more.

The explosion was seen across the battlefield. The remaining Goblin forces lost any hope of winning and tried to flee. Not many survived to do so, neither the dwarves nor the militia of Carraigbán were in any mood to be merciful. The Goblins were cut down in their thousands as they tried to retreat. The battle was won, but at a huge cost. The plain was littered with thousands upon thousands of bodies of dwarves, humans, elves and goblins alike.

He's Still Out There (Epilogue)

Chapter 40

Vaaldreth and Ériu were carried to what was left of the druids' grove to attempt to save them, Ysabell, Guin and Cali travelled with them, unwilling to leave their sides. There they sought news of Athress, Garaveigh and Haydleth. Learning that all three had died shocked them deeply, Athress' last stand was becoming a legend already, though it was only hours before. Haydleth's body was interred under the great Oak in the city grove as per his own instructions should he die. The city was still standing, it had survived, but it was bereft of leadership. This battle was won, but Xelazenivein was still out there. Somewhere in the abyss, plotting. This was far from over in Ysabell and her companion's eyes.

Weeks past, slowly the city began to recover. King Barendar agreed to take over running the city until the remaining council traitor or traitors had been rounded up and a new election take place. Walls were rebuilt, refugees were cared for and a new trade road to the Northern Mountains began construction, to open trade routes between Deep Crag and Mount Barendar with Carraigbán in the middle. All three would benefit greatly.

Under the Druids care Vaaldreth and Ériu recovered, physically at least. Ysabell spent her days by Ériu's side, caring for elf as the gentle druid had once cared for her. She surprised herself by how much she had come to care for this soft spoken, gentle, yet ferocious when angered, Elf. She surprised herself with the depth of fear she had felt at the thought of losing Ériu. Something had changed in their relationship when Ériu had been hurt, Ysabell couldn't explain in, couldn't articulate it. But as they spent each day together, Ysabell caring for the small elf, they both felt it, there was no need to try put words on it. A small part of Ysabell, and it grew as each day passed, knew that this couldn't last. Soon she would have to continue her search and find a way to put a stop to their enemy once and for all.

Vaaldreth's injuries were the most severe, but with the care of both their druids and Guinevere's healing prayers, he began to recover, the druids shaped a leg from an oaken branch to strap to his stump. Stoically Vaaldreth accepted his disability with barely a grumble. In a matter of weeks, he was walking, albeit slowly, with a limp and a staff for support, once again.

Far to the North, buried beneath Mount Barendar, The Watcher felt the world changing. He knew the time was fast approaching. He was being awakened. The time of the prophecy was near. For ten thousand years, he had slept in his crystal tomb. The world had fallen twice due to the arrogance of his people. His task, his reason for living until the extinction of his people was forgotten by all, was to ensure their legacy did not topple the world a third and final time.

The End

Printed in Great Britain
by Amazon